THE STORY OF
THE DAMASCUS DRUM

Christopher Ryan

The Story of the Damascus Drum

Christopher Ryan

HAKAWATI PRESS
HAWICK

Published by Hakawati Press, Hawick, Scotland

First published 2011
Copyright © Christopher Ryan 2011

Designed and produced by Ged Lennox – gedlennox@me.com
Set in 10/13 Minion
Cover illustration: Jethro Buck – www.jethrobuck.blogspot.com
Map: Aliya Ryan
Engravings by Edward Whymper
(Picturesque Palestine, edited by Charles Wilson 1881)
Additional illustrations, Ewan Macdonald

Printed the United Kingdom by Severnprint, Gloucester

ISBN 978-0-9569552-0-3

For further information: contact author at damascusdrum@gmail.com

To Mary Anna, Aliya and Azima

ACKNOWLEDGEMENTS

Thank you to Ros Diamond and David Ish-Horowicz,
Peter and Alison Yiangou, Sheila and Michael Buck,
and Charles and Denzil Verey, whose lovely homes provided
the perfect retreat in which much of this book was written.
Also to the staff and students of the Beshara School at
Chisholme House, and above all Bulent Rauf (*merhum*), for
immeasurable inspiration and abundant nourishment of every
kind; to the readers, for their generous comments and
judicious use of red ink: Dr David Clark, Ruth Morozzo,
Ewan Macdonald, Hakima Elliot, Jill Wright, and my family
for their encouragement, most especially the ever-patient
and highly critical Francisca; to Sama, for her love of Ibn 'Arabi
and true Syrian hospitality at home and in the best restaurants
of Damascus; to Riyad Atlagh, thoroughly modern dervish and
essential guide to the mysteries of Old Damascus and Salihiye;
to the noble shipowners of Tartus who eased my journey and
opened the way to Arwad and Krak. And lastly to my editor,
Zimmy Ryan, for not allowing natural filial regard deflect the
editorial blade. Respect.

PROLOGUE

This is the story of a drum. It began its life in the hills above the ancient and venerable city of Damascus.

'Ha!' someone says, 'a drum cannot have a life. It is inanimate. It cannot move of its own volition, nor can it breathe or speak. It does not resound with the 'I am' of being and self-identity. So, it can hardly be predicated of something that is barely half a step evolved beyond the state of a stone, motionless upon the face of Mt Kassioun which looks down in protective benevolence upon the once-green city of Dimasq-i-Sham (as the locals call Damascus), that such an object as a drum can have a life, let alone a story.'

Well then, so be it. If that is the extent of your vision, stop reading immediately. Go! Go on! Away and be useful elsewhere, but leave us alone. This story would only be a burden to you.

But if you feel some irritation of the mind, an unfamiliar stirring among the mysterious sea of cells within the shore of your cranium, then stay. Perhaps you will find some thread which will lead to... who knows?

To hear the story of the drum, we need to listen with the stillness of stone itself.

ONE

Daud finds himself at a loss

AUD the Arwadi awakened to himself crouching, naked and shivering behind a bush as dawn broke upon the mountains. He recalled the events of the previous night. He had risen to answer a call of nature. Then they had attacked. That was hours ago and now he found he was still clutching his shrunken member. In the excitement he had lost the urge to pee. With the coming of the sun he realised he had lost a lot more besides.

Daud was not the same man he had been just three weeks earlier when he had crossed the short sea passage from Arwad to the mainland. In Tartous he had loaded his camels with bales of cloths and spices, precious ores and other riches, and begun what should have been a brief overland trek south to Damascus. At the point of departure he still had the light of plenty in his eyes, that light which comes from the comfortable self-satisfaction of having achieved success in the world: material, marital and political success, in that order.

Arwad is a tiny island which lies about a mile off the coast of Syria in the furthest east of the Mediterranean Sea. It is a small island of strange people. Clever, resourceful people, but more often it was 'us against the world and the world against us'. Without a doubt Daud was resourceful, and independent, but his natural curiosity and appetite for life kept him free of the usual insular xenophobia.

They said Daud had had extreme good luck early in his career. Luck? Well, yes, maybe he was lucky, but perhaps that was just another way of saying he was gifted, and awake enough to use those gifts. First of all he had the 'eye': that is, he was capable of seeing the advantage in things. What things? Anything really, he wasn't particularly bothered as long as the thing in question had an end which suited his purpose. Maybe also it was a kind of clairvoyance, although Daud would have scoffed at any suggestion that he had mystical leanings. Yet he had this ability to see clearly the full potential of some thing or situation that appeared at the outset rough and undeveloped, unattractive even. Broken things and cast-offs he had a way of turning around so their beauty shone again. Daud had a boldness which comes from seeing forwards, not backwards. Wisdom? No. Not yet at any rate, though it might come later. Canny he was, however, and possessed of just the right spirit of competitiveness to propel him into seizing the main chance when it arose.

Daud had forsaken the usual trade of shipbuilding, which most Arwadites have entered as a matter of course at their fathers' sides since times biblical (and we know that the Arwadites were there at the Genesis, or at least shortly after the seventh day... well, after the Flood, at any rate, along with the Zemarites and the Hamathites and the Jebusites and the Amorites, and all the other generations of Noah and Shem and Ham and Japheth). Turning his back on the adze and awl and a life of lumber, from a young age he embarked upon a career as a merchant. Daud realised early on that the people who built ships had a hard life for limited reward and little adventure. And those who sailed them upon the high seas, while somewhat better off in the short term, more often than not suffered the ultimate consequences of their pelagic wanderings. They would eventually disappear off the map, either through storm or piracy, or just simply getting lost. Daud was definitely of the type who believe that worse things happen at sea.

But trading was different. The work was not laborious, and the risks rarely mortal. It demanded a different style of throat-cutting from that meted out on the high seas. In addition to business acumen, a successful merchant trading in the Levant requires determination, patience and a high level of 'people skills'.

Daud had honed his innate ability to turn a dirham by trading among his playmates. Even as a child he had recognised that the real skill in selling lay in marketing, showing his product in the best light. It was simply a matter of making the deal appear so attractive to the customer, that closing a sale was never an issue, but merely a matter of how many or how much. Daud was no common hawker or haggling street peddler. Rather, he would appear as the magnanimous dispenser of gifts, giving favourable discounts on the supposed price of an item whose value was undeniable. 'Because of our special relationship' he would confide, seducing his client to a secret collusion. Above all, Daud wanted his client to enjoy the seduction as much as he did. Business had to be fun. Fun in the risk, fun in the reward, or why bother.

Daud first entered the world of commerce when he was eleven years old. He sailed at his father's side to Tartous, the fortress town on the mainland a couple of miles across the water. They went to buy timber for his father's shipyard. Oh, the romance of that first trip! While his father consorted with the timber merchant, Daud made friends with the son of the oxen driver who had led the ox-train loaded high with the cedars of Lebanon, oak and pine, up from the mountains in the south. The ox-train boy had a trick which so impressed Daud – he could swing his father's huge leather whip over his head and make it crack like lightning. Daud was spellbound. Crack, crack, crack! time and again he did it. He let Daud try, and by the end of the day the young Arwadi too could make it snap the air. What made the explosive sound was a tiny little bit of frayed string tied to the end of the leather, which the lad from Lebanon replaced from time to time as it slowly disintegrated into smoky fluff. For Daud it was a revelation, how something so simple as a piece of string could make such an impressive sound.

Back on the island, Daud hatched his plan. Digging around in the shoreline flotsam he found a length of rope, a short stick, and a piece of string, from which he fashioned a homemade whip. Then out on the rocks where he swung away, cracking for all his worth. He quickly learnt to produce the desired effect at will and within a day or two he had all the boys on the island queuing up to have a go. At a price. A small price,

admittedly, and the craze soon passed once all his young friends had had a turn and the secret of the string was discovered. Then everyone began to make their own whips. But he had made enough pennies so that next time he was abroad with his father he was able to buy some coloured dyes in the bazaar. The lad had seen through the coloured bird sellers' scam straightaway: sparrows dyed yellow with saffron to imitate canaries, and other species in stranger pigments of the bird sellers' imaginations. Daud decided to try it with seagulls. After all, the bigger the bird, the better the price, surely. The recipe was simplicity itself. First catch your seagull, preferably a very white one. It was a messy affair, certainly, and not without some danger to clothes, eyes and skin, but minor inconveniences could not dampen Daud's energetic enthusiasm for this project.

Arwad is a small island barely half a mile long and a quarter of a mile wide, its narrow, twisting lanes curl in a tangle around the remains of the central castle built by Frankish knights, forming a web whose strands always lead down to the sea. Every square foot of earth is built upon with each house adjoining its neighbour in an endless chain of habitation, and every yard of shoreline north and south beyond the little east-facing natural harbour is a shipbuilder's yard, a chandler's or an engine repair shop. Only in the south east where the low tide reveals a wide stretch of flat rock beneath the defensive walls is there, so to speak, enough room to swing a cat. At evening time Daud would stand out on the furthest rocks, casting with his whip as if fly-fishing. He had extended his original whip with a length of twine and a metal hook at the end with a piece of fish attached. The seagulls would wheel around excitedly and one would always take the bait. Once hooked, Daud would haul in his makeshift line and roll up the exasperating bird in a scrap of torn fishing net. Then tying the beak and legs, he would clip the long feathers of the wings so the bird couldn't fly, and bring it home to be dyed in the privacy of his own rooftop.

His first attempts at bird makeovers were hurried affairs. He daubed the dyes haphazardly by moonlight on fear-crazed birds. If their wings had not been sufficiently clipped, they would take off in erratic flight to wash away the outrageous assault on their plumage in the warm waters of the East Mediterranean. Some, in shock and awe at this violent treatment inadvertently jumped to their death off the edge of the roof. But gradually Daud learnt to take better care of his merchandise, feeding them up well before applying the dyes, and his artistry developed subtlety as well as panache. Soon he had a consignment of twelve birds, all plump in calm submission, and embellished in the bright hues of a tropical paradise. He constructed a makeshift cage from bits of fishing net and driftwood and took the birds over to Tartous. It was the time of the spring festival, and the biggest market of the year, when all the hill tribes came bringing flocks of new lambs and kid goats to sell to the townsfolk and fishermen of the coast. Daud's gulls were a sensation. He traded his first bird for half a dozen sheep from one of the big tribal leaders. Daud's birds of paradise became instant status symbols, and soon the chiefs were ripping the gold bangles from their wives wrists and vying with each other to obtain one of his fabulous seagulls. Daud was in business. He sold his dozen within the day, and was back in Arwad that evening preparing a second batch which he sold as quickly a few days later.

Daud knew that, like the lightning whips, the fashion for rainbow gulls would short-lived. When the spring festival was over he decided to invest his considerable earnings in something with a more stable future. He set up as a trader of timber, and went scouring the hills of the Levant to find suppliers. He often bought directly from the forest owners, picking out suitable trees after having first ascertained the specific requirements of the shipbuilders on Arwad. Or if buying from another trader, he knew how to choose the best-shaped pieces of wood: curved for the ships' ribs, tight grained and straight for planking the hulls. Then he would arrange transportation door to door, hiring local oxen and drivers to bring the cargo to Tartous from where he shipped it to Arwad. His father was his first customer and paid Daud in advance, thus providing the necessary capital to pay the Lebanese timber merchants. His business thrived because his knowledge of shipbuilding enabled him to give his clients exactly what they wanted. Daud offered personal service, as well as attention to detail. From supplying timber he progressed to trading in all manner of ship-builders' materials, ropes and sails, bitumen for caulking, iron nails, as well as ships stores. It was so exciting, the way one thing led to another, always expanding.

Soon Daud began to think about entering the import-export market, where the real money was to be made. He was well placed to hear of the best deals; he shared in the gossip of the ship captains who regularly dined with his father in Arwad, and his contacts in Aleppo kept him informed of cargoes coming from the east. He had a real coup early on. A ship, en route for Tyre with a cargo of wool had been driven by storms into the safe haven of Arwad. At the same time a large caravan of silk from Cathay had just passed through Aleppo on its way to Tartous. He brokered a deal between the captain and the leader of the caravan in which they exchanged goods, and he took ten per cent of each cargo as commission. Both ship and caravan were able to turn around smartly on their respective return journeys without having to spend costly time in port finding buyers for their wares.

By the time he was twenty five, by luck and a keen sense of how to turn someone else's apparent misfortune to his advantage, he was a rich man. He never lost his flair for being able to make his apples look the shiniest in the market, even if they were identical to his competitor's on the next barrow. He courted the ladies in like manner: with charm and wit, quietly flattering them with earnest ardour and generous compliment. He married well, for both himself and his family, a beautiful daughter of Arwad's richest ship owner. He always treated her as the princess she had been brought up to believe she was, and in return she was happy to produce for him an endless succession of heirs and daughters. This success, however, did not circumscribe his other amatory endeavours, which he continued to pursue energetically on the regular visits to his trading offices in every port in the Eastern Mediterranean, from Alexandria to Smyrna.

Daud did not consider these adventures in the field of love as infidelities; rather, he saw them as his way of keeping in training. He would have felt himself unfaithful to his own nature, not to mention his sense of justice, beauty and the chase, had he disavowed his inclinations. However, he was as discreet as he was irrepressible, and with the passing years his passion, while not waning, did soften, like a flame of a lantern that is turned down for optimum brightness while paying heed to economy of fuel and wick. In Sidon, in Akko and in Haifa, he maintained certain ladies whose attractions, through the providence of birth as well as their own careful attentions, had stood the test of time, and who now ably ministered to the needs of his encroaching middle age.

As well as offering him the comforts of a home away from home, Daud's regular periods of absence allowed these paramours to preserve a lively tension in their relationships. Regular intervals of freedom and independence were balanced by times of romantic fondness and solicitude in which nagging had no place. They were intelligent women, and he welcomed their advice on his business matters, reflective and intuitive as it was, provided in the cool arbour of the feminine embrace. His own sense of the daring and the bold had stood him in good stead in earlier years as he built the capital foundation of his fortune. But now the main part of his business progressed upon a fairly steady course, governed by seasonal opportunities of harvests. Expansion continued, but it was a more subtle affair. He was no longer looking simply for quick profits, just as he sought no more the quick conquests of his youth. Instead he opted for capital security and long term growth with modest but reliable dividends. And as he generously maintained these fair ladies over the years, in like manner they returned his favour with undemanding faithfulness and agreeable acquiescence to his time-mellowed ardour.

And so it was that at the age of forty-one, Daud found himself on the road to Damascus. He was travelling with an enormous caravan: 200 camels loaded with goods that he had collected in his entrepots on the coast. This convoy of riches was timed to coincide with the pilgrimage season, when hundreds of thousands of people would pass through Damascus on the way to, and returning from, Mecca. Mecca, the Holy City of Arabia, where first Abraham had established that men and women worship according to unity; Mecca, where he set the imprint of his feet in the wondrous Black Stone fallen from heaven and which became the orientation and lodestone in this world for the travellers in the spirit of the next.

The caravan journeyed safely along the coast road south from Tartous, turning inland just before the great mountain range of the Jebel Lubnan. As the land rose to green, fertile hill country, Daud spied in the distance the beautiful and forbidding white stone fortress of Krak de Chevaliers. Even Saladin had decided to bypass this virtually impregnable redoubt in the interests of economy and effective warfare. The now-abandoned hilltop castle commanded both the coast and the entrance to the Bekaa and the fertile valleys of Lebanon. It also guarded the mountain passage known as the Homs Gap which led to Damascus and the desert routes further east, to Baghdad and Arabia. Daud mused that this would have made a splendid entrepot.

At Homs the caravan turned south again. As the travellers broke camp one morning on the outskirts of this city, a lone heron appeared from the direction of Damascus, circled the dusty baggage train and flew

on. And Daud, while he did not consider himself to be unduly supersti-
tious, nevertheless always welcomed a good omen, and a white heron
gracing his view above the mists of the early morning was surely such a
portent. After all, he thought, was it not due to his wit and his effort that
he had reached such heights of worldly success? And was it not one of
the just desserts of this success that he could now muse upon the potential
of further financial gain that he was sure to make in the coming weeks in
the great metropolis? In Damascus he would meet with traders from
Samarkand and Constantinople, Cairo and Isfahan, all on pilgrimage, to
be sure, but trading during pilgrimage was sanctified by holy tradition.
The big deal makers would have brought their factors and their secretar-
ies – Jewish, Greek, Armenian, no matter, all were welcome in Damascus
– to finalise the clauses and dot the iotas, while their masters continued
into the shriving wastes of the desert. Returning from their *hajj*, with
contracts arranged, the goods would flow in abundance like the waters of
the Tigris and the Euphrates, long and sure through the coming year. The
Damascus pilgrimage trade was certainly one of the highlights of Daud's
business calendar, and he was looking forward to it with all the excitement of a little boy before his birthday.

It was early spring. As the caravan headed south, the road climbed
again, leaving the greening pasture of the river plains. Although warm in
the day, old winter snow still lay in scattered drifts in the deeper folds of the
hillsides and at night the drivers huddled in groups around campfires to
keep warm. They were not so far now from their goal, but still, these were
wild places on the edge of the sown. The desert stretched away forever on
one side, and desolate rocky mountains rose on the other, mountain paths
that must traversed before arriving at the destined oasis of Damascus. One
night, as the noble camel drivers curled by the fireside under the mountain
sky, and the flames of the earthen hearths sank and only glowing embers
remained, black shapes gathered unseen in the shadows of evening. The
dark raiders of the Banu Merg fell upon the camp in silence. The forty
souls, already surrendered to death's gentler cousin, sleep, were dispatched
as peacefully as the sacrificial lambs of the *Id al Fitr*.

Daud, who had drunk too much tea that night, had woken to answer
an urgent call of nature at what transpired to be a supremely opportune
moment. As the assailants were conferring before the final murderous act,
the trader of Arwad had risen quietly to perform his toilet. Consequently,

of the forty-one wayfarers, he alone survived the massacre. From his vantage point, crouching under a bush in a cleft in the rocks a few yards away, naked under a thin camelhair wrap (for unlike the rest of the crew, he had an abhorrence of sleeping in his clothes), he watched as the event unfolded. A hundred or so black-cloaked demons crept noiselessly into the camp and lay gently down over the sleeping caravaneers, as if to cover each in an extra blanket. A sound like the frothy gurgling of a ruminating camel, came from each doubled form as short blades of Damascus steel gently unseamed their victim's throats. Forty breaths escaped their prisons of flesh and bones and joined the soft night air. The slaughter performed, the baggage camels were gathered and reloaded. Then, still in silence, the fully dressed corpses of the caravaneers were loaded on their own riding camels, and the camel train moved off in the direction of the desert, lit by the newly risen waning moon.

Daud, who in the shock of the aforesaid drama had forgotten to pee, now emptied his bladder over the purple-dark stones of the mountain and stood up. With the dawn came the realisation that he had lost everything. The main purpose of this journey had been to transfer the bulk of his assets to the more secure stronghold of Damascus. His caravan had carried gold in considerable quantity, hidden in the bales of cloth and carpets which comprised the manifest cargo. Now all that remained of his fortune was a piece of camelhair cloth.

TWO

Taqla and the Angel

HE wind from the Syrian Desert entered the hearts of the sleepers in the tents, in the villages, of those still blessedly alive and snoring by their flocks in the hills and valleys. It entered too beyond the veils of fatigue of the sleepers in the towns and cities, through keyholes, open windows, and doors left ajar. It blew from the south, from beyond Arabia, and its perfume was a gentle but insistent breath which carried with it scents of love and death, departure and longing. In the soul of every sleeper it shaped images, according to whatever state dominated the mind's eye at the moment prior to waking – sweet dreams where it found happiness, and grave and disturbing images where anxiety reigned.

Taqla was blessed with sweet dreams as befitted a young woman whose simple life of constant but undemanding labour brought her little pain and much happy recompense for her efforts. Taqla had dreamt of an angel, a tall and beautiful angel with shining golden hair. Really, it was such a handsome young man who came to her in her sleep, offering her a loaf of bread, still warm and smelling of life itself. She woke with a wonderful feeling of lightness and well-being, as well as a craving for breakfast.

Taqla donned a pair of thick woollen socks over her stockinged feet, and then strapped up her tough leather sandals. It was a cold morning and she would be walking far today. Under her heavy, dark wool skirt she still wore the warm cotton shift in which she had been sleeping. She added a blouse and a woollen cardigan, and then a thick, blue shawl which she wrapped around her shoulders and over her head. Taqla did not wear the dark balaclava-like headdress which the nuns wore. She did not cut her hair either, although that was hidden, tied up in a white scarf, the corners of which were adorned in lacework of dusty blue forget-me-nots. If Taqla had possessed a mirror, she would have beheld a smiling face with huge eyes, full lips and very rosy cheeks. But Taqla did not have a mirror, and the only clue she had to her appearance lay in the response it elicited in those whom she encountered in the course of her day. 'O Taqla, your lips are so red, your eyes so big, your cheeks so rosy,' and other words with which her novice friends would greet her, giggling and smiling. The older nuns never made such comments, but even they smiled when they saw Taqla, so that she felt herself inhabiting a climate in which few clouds ever passed to obscure the sun of her happy disposition.

Taqla was going home today. She went home every year at this time, just after Easter, to spend a week or two with her mama and papa, who lived a long day's walk over the hills to the north. Taqla was not a nun, and so far she had no intention of becoming one. She had been promised to the Convent of Seydnaya as a servant by her parents, in return for the grace which had saved her papa during an illness, grace which had been granted in answer to her mama's prayers. It was the normal way of things.

Her mama needed her papa, and so had offered to give up the thing she loved most in all the world, to save the thing she most needed. Taqla had acquiesced willingly, for she loved her parents, and working in the convent was no harder than her life in the village. She had missed her girlfriends at first, but later some of them had joined the convent and were now training to be nuns, so life continued much as before.

At breakfast she was finally able to satisfy her craving for fresh bread which the sweet scent of her reverie had provoked. After eating heartily, she packed her bag with a loaf, some cheese, olives and some dates for her journey. Then, filling a water skin from the kitchen, she walked down to the little door at the back of the convent and let herself out. She felt the sun soft and pure upon her eyelids as she closed them in enjoyment of its warm embrace. The early morning really is the best time of the day, she thought, before it becomes weighed down by too much heat. Looking north over the broken rocky hillside, beyond which lay her family's village, she saw the length of the day extending ahead, its untrodden path simply waiting for her own steps to fill. The earth did not look so dry in this early light. Long shadows still stretched down from the steep walls of the Convent, perched high above her like a castle. The sandy scrub and rocks of the landscape were clearly outlined against the deep blue above the horizon. The cypress by the back door stood tall and green, in sharp contrast to the earth and sky. Its dark foliage seemed to shiver as she passed.

Taqla began to walk, steadily, slowly, without stopping. Lightly downhill at first and then winding up over the first hill until soon her convent was out of sight and she was alone among the pale rocks. Alone that is but for the occasional bird, a buzzard perhaps, flying high in the blue, some crows passing, black wings across the rock face, or sparrows flitting and fluttering near at hand. Small lizards slithered in the undergrowth as her skirt swished the dry grasses. Insects creaked and croaked as they too awoke under the sun's warmth. The breeze still carried cooling scents from the south, and Taqla began to enjoy the delicious freedom of having the whole day to herself.

She walked all morning in this way, without tiring, pausing at one point to drink a few sips from her water skin at the highest point of a pass. She stood and let her eyes go far across the desert below to the distant horizon. Remaining there for what seemed like ages, full of wonderment at the plasticity of space, she was amazed that there could be such distance, such vastness, and that her eye could travel in it so effortlessly. That it could go on almost forever, she thought, and that it must keep on going all the way to the ends of the world.

As she set off on the downward track into the narrow confines of the valley, this thought stayed with her. Not in a troubling way. At first it was more of a novelty. Then, as she gave it space, a change occurred. It was as if something in her was expanding too. It wasn't physical. It was barely even mental. Rather, it showed itself more as a deepening sense of connection with her surroundings.

Taqla was blessed with the humility natural in those who keep close to the earth, the easy and unselfconscious humility such as a child might possess. But Taqla was no longer a child, certainly not physically so, and although not literate in a conventional sense, she did exhibit a pleasingly mature and discriminating intelligence. She was able to view the world, and its apparent subsequences and consequences, with a mind uncluttered by conditions of self-attachment and historical convention, so that she saw things just as they appeared to be. So, this new intimacy with her environment did not seem something foreign. It came simply as an extension of the relationship she had always experienced with the rocks and the trees and birds, the sky and all manner of natural appearances, that inner sanction in which she felt completely at home. And this sense of her self, of an ever mysterious yet now awakening identity, was more real to her than simply the tangible evidence of her senses.

But as Takla descended the dusty path of the valley, in the heat of the late morning, she began to experience a need. It was like a thirst, or a hunger, an extreme longing for something to complete a lack. But for what? It was a perplexing state, in which the defining boundaries of her existence became blurred. Her personal identity had vanished and at the same time she felt connected to everything. There was no obvious focus, no single object of vision, within or without, with which she could identify.

At midday, as the rocks bleached shadowless in the sun before her widening eyes, and the snowdrifts in the northern faces of the mountains shrank imperceptibly, she turned from the path to a place where she was accustomed to stop and rest. Passing under a few bushes lodged in a steep crevice, she found herself within a grove of trees, which masked the entrance to a small cave at the base of a cliff. A tiny spring of water issued from the cave, a rivulet which formed a pool from which it then flowed underground, re-appearing somewhere much further down the slope. Neither pool nor cave could be seen from the path, or from the surrounding land, the rocky crevice blending into the general effect of the cliff face.

In the cool shade of the trees Taqla sat down. There before her, also sitting in the shade, was a man. In a flash, it was done. Not a blinding flash, not the inadvertent catching of the sun in a mirror, but a flash of recognition as they exchanged glances, the known taking the place of the unknown. The flash was in the eyes, but the recognition between souls was of the deepest intimacy. Taqla had recognised in the person opposite something very familiar. It was like looking in a mirror. Her heart opened and her bewilderment changed to ease. And then something lovely happened, he smiled at her and said 'Hello'. All the rigours of her earlier expansion vanished. She smiled back at him. 'Hello' she said. Then voluntarily, yet irresistibly, they drew close to each other, so that first their hands joined, and as their breaths mingled their lips met. Then, as water meets water, they flowed in each other in the greatest closeness that is possible between bodies.

Taqla's union was the most natural and delightful event that this young woman had ever experienced. She felt refreshed throughout every atom of her body. Her mind, now no longer bewildered, was as calm and reflective as the pool in which she now bathed. She took time to look closely at the form of the man lying asleep in the shade a few feet away. He was naked but for an old camel hair blanket wrapped around him. She smiled. He looked so peaceful, like a sleeping boy. He was handsome, she knew that instinctively. A well-proportioned face lay beneath the dark stubble of a week's growth of beard, muscles well-formed but not over-developed sat on wide shoulders, and a certain generousness of girth, albeit a little depleted by recent privations, spoke of wealth and ease, and gave balance to the overall composition. Of course, she did not think all this right away, but in later times, she always felt nourished by this memory.

For the moment Taqla knew only the pleasure of beholding him, the same pleasure which she had felt when their eyes had met, and the world around her had dissolved. Its subsequent reconstitution, (which could have taken place within the blinking of an eye, or after an eternity) took nothing away from the experience. To say that what she felt was profound love would not be true, for she did not yet know what it was. But it was love indeed which had taken her like a wave, pulling her from the shore of her innocent unknowing into the depth of its original impulse, and bringing her all inside out and back again on its return. She was certainly in love, but did not yet love, and somewhere in this surge she had travelled to the still core of life itself and glimpsed the beauty of its perfection. From this core she now emerged, glistening and glowing anew, with the order of the original metal itself. This being, this state of perfection – this she would learn to yearn for and to love.

Taqla dressed, not waking the man who carried on sleeping peacefully in the shade. She left beside him her blue woollen shawl and the loaf of bread, and continued on her way. Her journey took her far into the night, but in the darkness she walked with a deepened sense of belonging, for in being brought so close to herself, she now felt close to everything. Even the stars no longer seemed distant. Their bright glances reflected familiar presences collected in her own heart, a heart which now she felt could embrace the whole universe. In her mind's eye she knew she could travel to these heavenly bodies as easily as she had walked to her own village.

THREE

Goats do roam

SA'ID bin Adam herded his flock of twenty-seven goats on the steep slopes and summit of Mt Kassioun, in the days before the army took over this vantage point, planted barbed wire among the bushes and erected radar masts upon a peak best left to the surveillance of eagles and angels. Sa'id bin Adam loved his goats, just as he loved his wife Maryam. He loved the life they led together, away from the smoky city below. He loved the way the sun rose each morning on the desert's distant edge, and the way it vanished each evening over the hills behind him. He loved the moon and the stars which appeared each night, and he recognised their different patterns as they moved across the sky.

Sa'id bin Adam was not a simple man, even if the appearances of his life were reduced to the simple requirements of eating and sleeping, shelter and companionship, and a useful occupation which did not interfere with the natural cycles of existence. On the contrary, he found deep satisfaction in life's intricate complexities as they revealed themselves in the mirror of his uncluttered heart.

Somehow Sa'id bin Adam had never felt within the urge to discover whether or not, in fact, the grass really was greener over the hills beyond. He had simply relied on the reports from those who passed by from time to time, that yes, some of it was, and no, some of it wasn't. His own meadows took colour with the seasons, and waxed and waned according to the pattern of his grazing flock. He concluded that any advantage or disadvantage to his roaming further afield than the generous providence which the Merciful God bestowed upon him would in all likelihood have been equal. His response to his situation was one of gratitude, and an unwillingness to alter of his own accord the benevolent arrangement of his life as it unfolded.

Sa'id bin Adam had a billy goat. He was the leader of the herd. A big-shouldered shaggy horned thing, with a straggly tuft of a beard. He was golden in colour and Sa'id bin Adam had named him Shams, the Sun, on account of the glorious colour of his fleece, and for the punctuality of his setting out and retiring with the dawn and closing of the day. The unerring regularity with which he led the procession of the herd's grazing across the face of the mountain side, cyclic yet never quite repeating the previous day's pasture, was as dependable a clock for Sa'id as the sun itself.

The steadfastness of Shams was equal to the placid wisdom of his master, and the goat looked after his flock with the same quality of faithfulness to duty and sense of service as Sa'id bin Adam himself. And all the she-goats and the little baby goats followed this order with the delight and ease of water in the stream bed, jumping over rocks, rummaging in the nooks and crannies, and proceeding calmly and unhurried as they spread across the mountain.

But Shams the Goat was getting on in years, and the pride and thrill he used to feel as leader of the flock, when he too jumped on the highest boulders and stood sentinel on the sharpest ridge, had settled into a calm and steady nature. His youthful feelings, and the exploits that ensued from them were merely memories, and no longer attributes necessary for life. It was a case of distillation, from the froth of youth, through the passions of manhood, to the essential spirit. He was getting old, and he felt it every day, in his bones and in his teeth.

Then one morning Shams the Goat woke up and things were different. It was not something he thought about at the time, or could have explained had he so wished. He just knew things were different. That morning he no longer felt stiff in his legs, although he still moved carefully out of respect for the aged carcass which had done him such good service over the years. And when he grazed, he no longer struggled to loosen the clumps of forage. His teeth always alighted upon tender shoots which gave to the mildest tug and shake of his jaw. He felt a lightness he hadn't enjoyed for ages as he led his flock out in the sunlight, seeing them all munching away behind him as he turned on the upward morning climb.

On the mountain top, at midday, Sa'id bin Adam sat down in one of his usual places in the shade of the trees and contemplated the distant desert. The heat of the day was suffused into sweet aromas of cypress and pine, and a balmy scent rose from sage and thyme crushed under foot and hoof. Not even Sa'id bin Adam, in his gifted and almost universal awareness of his little world, had noticed that the leather strap holding the bell around the neck of his lead goat had become torn some weeks earlier. The friction of the brass ring connecting the bell had hastened the strap's deterioration. Shams the Goat, who was entertaining the possibility of nibbling the heads off a clump of saffron crocuses, shook his head to dislodge a fly that seemed intent on taking up lodgings in his left nostril. The fly flew off, and so did the bell, which fell with a clink and a thud to the grass below.

Shams suddenly felt unaccustomedly light-headed. The bodily ease which he had been feeling all day now culminated in a real sense of rebirth. A hitherto unknown urge entered him, as if a guiding light now overtook his whole being. He no longer saw the tasty posy of crocuses, he no longer felt attached to his faithful harem of she-goats and the offspring of their combined loins. The sweet memory of their fruitful couplings was erased in that instant, and all sense of need for the salient order of his days and nights upon Mt Kassioun dissolved. It was as if some desert wind had blown away every trace of desire for family and for familiar ties. What remained for Shams as identity was a blank white page, a boundless sky, and a featherlight feeling of wonder.

With this sense of wonder came an urge, like a beckoning door in the depth of the sky, or the need to turn the page. It was the sense of the other side of the hill, and the beginning of an irresistible and compelling curiosity. There awoke in him an intense desire to move beyond his flock, grazing contentedly among the rocks, even to part company with Sa'id bin Adam, who was travelling in the restful meadows of his own meditation. Shams drifted away to the borders of his usual pasture. Reaching the rambling dry stone wall at the very top of the mountain, invigorated and enlightened by the remarkable state in which he now found himself, he leapt. And in leaping, he departed his homeland in a singular act of abandonment. Like some space voyager of old, he cast off the liens of his earth's gravity and began a journey into the unknown.

Reclining in the shade of an old acacia tree, Sa'id bin Adam became aware of a disturbance in the equilibrium of his inward flight. That single chime of freedom released Shams from his erstwhile occupation as leader of Sa'id's herd. This was followed, only seconds later, by the distant soft hoof scuffle on rock, and a brief but insubstantial shimmer in the air above the wall.

Sa'id took it all in with the accustomed equanimity of one who looks first, and comprehending all possible aspects, allows the scene itself to enlighten him. In this case, Shams was gone, evidently. So the old goat-herd led his flock slowly back home where Maryam his wife had just put the kettle on for a cup of tea.

FOUR

Shams to the rescue

AUD was not the man he had been a week ago. In a million years he could never have dreamed the events of the past seven days. Now Daud woke up from a deep sleep to find himself being licked all over by the largest, hoariest, old billy goat he had ever seen. He had been dreaming he was bathing in the delicious waters of his homeland, the indigo seas around the island of Arwad. He was being washed by dolphins, who rolled him gently over and over in the foaming sand and surf. Then supporting him under his arms, they rushed him through the waves to rinse him. But now as he rubbed his eyes what he saw was no sleek dolphin, but a hairy old goat scraping him with his tongue, a tongue ribbed like the rasp his father's men used to rub down the rough timbers of a boat frame.

Daud felt a little like a boat frame himself, all ribs and keel, with nothing much to keep the water out. He was so completely skeletal in his being, so much in need of reconstruction that he submitted without protest to the scouring ablution of the goat's tongue in the belief that this treatment would somehow restore him to himself, in spite of the discomfort.

'Well I suppose that will do for now.'

Daud was surprised, simply because he had not heard any voices in the past week of lonely wandering. His ears were attuned only to the unintelligible sounds of nature: the wind over rock and through the trees, the whispering leaves, the song and chatter of different birds, the murmur and tinkle of the snowmelt as it ran down the hillsides, the creaking and groaning of insects – even at times the subtle movements of the earth itself. He was not at all surprised to find that it was a goat doing the talking.

In fact the goat hadn't spoken at all, at least, not in the way one might generally term speech. No, Shams the Goat had expressed his satisfaction regarding his work in progress in what can only be described as a 'sentiment of being' – that is, a relationship of names and qualities shadowing forth an original meaning from the universe of pure light to these lower worlds of subtle forms and gross appearances. But Daud did not know that then. He thought he had heard a voice.

And so, Daud replied with a sentiment of being of his own, vocalised with a long sigh, which stated simply his gratitude regarding the termination, finally, of his scrub.

'Aaaaaah…'

He sat up. Nearby he saw a dark blue woollen shawl, and half a loaf of bread. Scattered crumbs lay about which a lone sparrow was hoovering up, unconcerned by the presences of goat and man. And before these two images, one of shelter, the other of sustenance, had begun to divide Daud's attention, he was rejoined in a memory of such sweetness that for a moment he forgot his hunger and discomfort.

It was a confusing memory. It began a week before, when, crouching naked and bereft, Daud had watched the haematic dawn rise over the life-enriched dust of the Damascus road. Daud was not one to shock easily, and gradually, as an uneasy dream loses its sway in the traffic of day, the dark happenings of that murderous night dissolved under the brightness of morning. He took stock philosophically. His personal losses, though considerable, did not weigh heavily upon him. The fortune he had just lost, could be made and lost again if providence so wished. What fascinated him now was the thought that he no longer had ties with anyone, or anything, and rather than feeling lost or helpless, he felt quite the opposite. Perhaps his response was the result of shock. His present situation had little to offer, yet nonetheless he enjoyed a certain euphoria at finding himself alive.

This is not to say that Daud had failed to recognise the danger of his predicament. Before departing the crime scene, the dark assassins from the desert had removed all traces of their deed and carefully raked dust over the ground where the bloody murders had taken place. Anyone pondering the non-arrival of the caravan in Damascus would quickly assume that, as on previous occasions, following the usual fruitless forensic discussions, the merchant and cargo either had changed destination post-embarkation, or, as was known to happen, had just disappeared. The bandits would not be so *laissez-faire*. After a careful assessment of their booty, they would by now be aware that the owner of a certain riding camel, complete with personal luggage, was unaccounted for. And for Daud to be unaccounted for in such an audit would mean that he had become a liability encumbered with an unsustainable level of risk for this company of thieves, a risk which if ignored, may render their entire venture insolvent.

Taking all this into consideration, Daud headed for the hills in time-honoured fashion. He walked away from the road, away from the desert, until evening came. His wandering was not so much aimless as trackless. When night came he lay down out of the wind, and fell asleep beneath the stars, curled up in his camelhair blanket.

After three days journeying in the rocky mountain wastes, with nary a morsel to eat and only melted snow to slake his thirst, Daud became considerably light-headed. The boundaries between his waking conscious-ness and the subtle states of his inner imaginings, began to blur. Something different was happening in the way his surroundings appeared to him. The rocks, the trees and birds, all of nature began to exhibit what he could only describe as their 'selfness' – a kind of identity, not human, but conscious nonetheless, and each thing expressed this uniquely. Rocks were – well, rocky – yet alive and present in their rockiness, solid, dependable, and so very, very quiet. They moved, but their movements were imperceptible, in a time stilled to the movement of the earth; what geologists call 'deep time'. Likewise the trees and birds displayed unique qualities, qualities which poets mistake as human-like, whereas Daud saw that their actions displayed purely what is synthesised in man. The trees were covering, compassionate and protective; great repositories of wisdoms, bending and stretching, speaking wisdom-speech from every leaf and bough, pronouncing their tree-words upon the wind. And the birds were simply the forms by which angels delivered their orders over the face of the earth, thread-needles sewing the patchwork of each day's destiny; and when not messaging, they were the praise singers of the skies.

On the fourth day Daud's perception had become so refined that he was able to see forms that were not solid like the trees and the animals, but subtle, vaporous relations of coloured light and energy. These shapes occupied space and walked on the same tracks as he did, but paid him no heed. At times they even appeared to pass right through him, as if they couldn't see him. 'Perhaps to them I am just another form of nature, part of the landscape,' he thought. 'They might just see me as I see the rocks and plants. Maybe they don't realise I am conscious too.' And then, stranger still: 'Or maybe I am seeing into another universe, parallel, strangely co-spatial, contemporary even, and they are not even aware of my existence.' It was as if he was being ignored and suddenly he felt very lonely. He then decided to address these shapes directly. He said 'excuse me' when he passed one coming straight towards him. There was a quivering, like ripples in water after a splash, in the body of this light form, as if shocked by Daud's words. It stopped abruptly on the track. Then it responded with a silent movement acknowledging Daud's presence, and moved obligingly to Daud's left rather than continuing, as it might have, straight through him. Following this encounter, Daud only had gently to extend himself in thought with the intention of a respectful greeting, which the approaching shapes acknowledged with a gracious shimmer of their light bodies as they passed by his side.

On the fifth day Daud heard a voice, apparently dispossessed of form, but a voice nonetheless. He was unable to tell whether the voice came from inside himself, or whether what he heard was a kind of collective voice for the world outside. And although he couldn't make out in words what this elusive voice was saying, yet somehow the meaning it conveyed was intelligible to him. He understood that it was offering its services as a guide. By now Daud was in such a state of heightened sensitivity, the normal reaction of fear, self-preservation or disbelief did not interrupt his desire to find out more. And in his acquiescence he began a journey of discovery in himself, which revealed things of which he had no prior knowledge: the sounds which appeared from nowhere he felt as sensations in different parts of his body, heat in his chest, light in the space behind his eyes, a flowing like a trickle of cool water within the confines of his throat, a delicate movement of energy like butterflies dancing in the air above his head and a wave of heat arising from his abdomen. The result of these discoveries was a growing sense of connection to all manner of beings that comprised his now expanded world. That day he spent a long time lying face down, breathing with the earth. And that night he walked among the stars.

On the sixth day Daud began to ask questions directly of the voice, questions which became turned around in the asking, uncloaking themselves to reveal their own answers.

He asked himself 'Where am I going?' and the voice seemed to reply, by showing him that all he saw outside of himself only reflected what was inside him, in his thoughts, his feelings, his needs. And as the week progressed, what initially he had thought and felt and needed, about his survival, his personal life, his future and so on, he now found to be of little importance. He began to feel that what he was, what he really was, was not what he had ever thought. His old world was disappearing fast. His new life lay before him like an uncharted ocean, vast and indistinct. He had regained the pure instincts of his animal soul. He slept like an animal, not feeling discomfort or cold on the hard ground, but connecting to the warm, energising breast of this mother earth. He drank water because it refreshed his spirit in the morning. He eventually stopped sleeping in the accustomed sense of falling into a state of unconsciousness. When he lay down at night, he simply closed his eyes and relaxed, while a part of his awareness remained like a hovering bird of prey alert to its surroundings, even as his body rested.

On the seventh day he was empty. So insubstantial had he now become, so tenuous was gravity's hold, that if a strong wind had blown he might have been swept away to India. His inner sense of guidance brought him to the steep rocky crevice and compelled him to enter beneath the bushes which masked the hidden grove. He sat by the pool, gazing neither inwards nor outwards, and the thought came to him that he was dying. At this point he felt a tinge of sadness, a faint and seeping pigment in the now-featureless horizon of his soul. Ah, what pale melancholy he felt. He had seen through the illusion, he was on the brink, cleansed, purged, emptied of all his sins and all his good deeds. Nothing remaining but a shred moved by an imperceptible breeze, and a nostalgia for something... but for what he just couldn't fathom. Not for the past – that had died already, as if it had never been, a story of no consequence told of someone else. No, this was a memory of something so deep down inside him that he had never noticed it until this moment. Through all the years of frantic living, business dealings and adventuring it had remained unseen. Now, like a hidden treasure, untouched and perfect in all its originality, the time had come for it to be discovered.

At that moment he looked up and what he saw took his breath away. Sitting opposite was a woman of such pure and luminescent beauty that his body might have fainted on the spot, had not his soul, full of the desire for union, compelled him to move towards her. Daud entered that beautiful presence as an image emerging from a mirror and seeing its original, might desire to join with the form it reflects. A returning to itself.

salt into water
dark into light
fire in air
rain upon the sea
o what a state of affairs
does a comet falling within the aura of the sun
shine less brightly in its extinction?

Daud gazed at the blue woollen shawl and the half loaf of bread as if admiring a work of art. He contemplated the arrangement, the casual way in which the two objects appeared together on the ground. Had someone been sitting and got up momentarily, intending to return? An interrupted thought, a meal half eaten, a piece of clothing shed in the act of sitting. Then the near ground of the pool, the hidden cave, the grove of trees and scent of sweet herbs, the atmosphere of the scene seemed to hold an after-glow which set his heart beating. That someone had recently departed was clear. The imprint lingered in the air like the imperceptible stirring of water after a vanishing fish.

Then Daud began to remember, and in remembering began his pain. Not immediately, of course. First he remembered the meeting, and then her face; her eyes, breath, lips. Then this explosion as energy rushed up from his toes, opening into the space of his heart, not just the pump of his blood, but ribs, lungs and all. At the same time a sweet and expanding liquor of light descended, flooding his brain, filling his chest and dissolving the boundaries between his skin and hers. It seemed his seeing became spherical like the sky. The words they shared were unspoken. Their language was the silent breathing of their hearts.

Her face. So real, now so insubstantial. The memory was confusing. Daud ate the bread and drank from the spring. Eating brought back some of his strength. But when he remembered the sweetness of their union, a gnawing began in the pit of his stomach, and he began to hunger for that beautiful face. And with that hunger came a yearning through his whole body as if every cell nurtured its own memory. The concerns Daud had felt with regard to the events of a week ago were now erased. He cared little for his material losses, but still he felt something was missing, something so essential to his existence that he would have given his fortune a thousand times to regain that wholeness. His sense of loss was assuaged only partially by the memory of her face. But memory was poor nourishment if the image did not join him wholly with the person it represented. For the first time in his life he felt abandoned by the world, a world he had always grasped with both hands in a huge, joyful, greedy embrace. Now all he felt was tired disdain. The one thing he really wanted might just as well have been on another planet.

The old goat snuffling in the bushes nearby raised his head and gave Daud a long look of haughty condescension, 'Oh diddums, diddums!' he seemed to say, 'come on, little Bo Peep, you're alive, and you've got me haven't you?' Then the goat began to walk back through the trees to the road, where he turned right and set off in the direction of Seydnaya.

This strange communication from the goat only added to Daud's collapsed sense of dignity. Nevertheless it woke him out of the well of his self-pity just sufficiently to allow him to stand up. As he picked up the blue woollen shawl the sparrow jumped away from the remaining breadcrumbs. Daud wound the cloth around his head in a rough turban, and set off after Shams, all the while wondering to himself, 'What use is an old goat?'

Shams didn't answer of course, but in the past few hours something had come back to him. Shams too had felt a kind of longing, but his memory was of she-goats. Not for his own flock back at Kassioun. He now felt an inclination for new and untilled pastures. Daud, following, noticed a shiver run through the old goat as the seeds of a new spring began to rise in the fertile earth of his old but intact loins.

FIVE

A bargain is struck

HAMS too had woken that day with a scent in his nostrils, the scent other than which no goat loves more, that of a flock of she-goats. Milky white and pale brown ones, golden brown and black, black all over or pure white, russet red and pinky roan, whatever colour they come in, is the pleasure of an old billy goat's eye. Since witnessing the meeting of the two humans, a meeting he had been privy to from unassailable heights above the hidden grove, and the subsequent departure of the female of the couple, the scent had grown even stronger. What mysterious force inclined him to descend and perform that rite of ablution on Daud, a rite which Shams had known she-goats to minister to their newly born, the old billy goat did not know, but then his life had been very different since he had jumped the wall at Kassioun and begun his new career as goat-errant.

Now Shams' spirit was buoyed up by anticipation which the scent, born on a breeze from the south, had awakened. And his old carcass was strengthened by the consumption of half a loaf of sweet bread. Why half a loaf? Surely the appetite of the goat is unrestrained? Under normal circumstances, it may safely be assumed this would be the case. But Shams was in a new life, and it must allowed, even for a goat, that when destiny takes a hand, the rules may change. It is possible, even, that

29

Shams' anticipation for the she-goats was not born solely of the memory of past engagements, but of his eagerness to follow the imperative of his nascent destiny.

That evening, as the sun fled Syria's dusty rocks and desert wastes, and slipped seaward beyond the western flank of the Jebel Lubnan, Shams broached the hill overlooking the valley of the convent of Seydnaya. There he found his heart's desire. Below the ramparts of the convent, congregating for the evening milking were ninety-nine she-goats, and he recognised instinctively that there was not a single male goat to protect and provide for them. At the same time, into the weary mind of Daud, who had been following his four-footed guide without protest for many hours, came a thought, as instinctive for a business deal as that of Shams for paternity, that perhaps he could offer the services of this well-hung billy to the convent. It was a true meeting of minds.

Mother Superior was standing on the flat rooftop of the convent, contemplating the evening air, when she saw the great billy-goat approaching, followed by the wild man. She descended the labyrinth of staircases and passages to the front gates to greet them. Now, why on earth should the Superior of one of the most important places of pilgrimage in the Holy Land condescend to welcome in person this barely-clothed vagabond, barefoot, unshaven and tousled hair tied up in a blue scarf, and his equally hoary old goat? Perhaps it was the icon of St. John the Baptist she had been contemplating that afternoon which had stirred in her an appreciation of wild men of spirit. Or maybe it was because her flock had not yet been serviced that year, and she was quick to see an opportunity when it presented itself. More likely, though, was that she had been blessed by the same spirit of hospitality that inspired Abraham to feed the angels in a valley not so very far from here.

When Mother Superior apprehended the poor and distraught lover Daud, she was moved to compassion, for she was well-experienced in the ways of the heart and recognised the signs. Here was one who had been waylaid by love, and left floundering in the stormy waters of heart's emotion. She was not aware that he had been mugged thoroughly of all his earthly possessions into the bargain.

Daud and Shams climbed up to the convent entrance. Standing before Mother Superior, Daud attempted to speak, but nothing came from his mouth. So he just pointed, first at the goat, and then at the flock in the valley below. Mother Superior smiled.

'Don't worry. If your goat performs, and looking at him I don't doubt he will, you'll get paid well enough!' she said, and motioned to a young nun who had followed her down the steps to take Shams to the she-goats. Shams needed little prompting and was away at a lively trot to make their acquaintance. Daud was invited inside by his hostess who led him up through a maze of walkways and courts and stairways to the refectory where he was given a meal of rice, spinach and yoghurt. Afterwards he shown where to wash and given a room in which to sleep.

Shams, meanwhile, was in goat heaven. Or at least soon would be at the rate at which he was performing the contract undertaken on his behalf by Daud and Mother Superior. He took the dear ladies one at a time, gently at first, then strongly, then surging wavelike upon them in a crescendo of loving desire. For their part the dainty-hoofed maidens submitted to him as one body, with the ease of an ocean receiving a well-travelled river. The old goat paused between each coupling for just as long as good form required: a fond farewell to one, followed by a most charming greeting to the next. Shams, far from becoming exhausted, felt a growing lightness as his night of love progressed. It was the same lightness that had preceded his leap across the wall on Mount Kassioun, a lightness which had been his familiar companion ever since.

As the dawn rays rose upon the flock, lying peacefully asleep in the valley, Shams collected in his shaggy embrace the ninety-ninth she-goat, the most patient of them all, and performed his final service. In that climactic moment he achieved the ultimate lightness to which he now gave up his goatly ghost.

The nun who looked after the herd was watching nearby as Shams expired his last breath. In that very instant, so as not to offend against the prohibition of eating carrion, she performed the ritual slitting of the throat of the goat with the appropriate prayer of dedication to God. And so, the life force of Old Shams, its work finally done, flowed back into the earth. The skin was cleaned and given to Daud, along with a payment for Shams' noble service, and a promise of one tenth of all the goats born, to be collected in a year's time.

Before leaving, Daud had visited the room which housed the convent's sacred icon, a painting of Mary, the sainted mother of Christ, by the disciple Luke. It is said that the satan cannot assume the form of Mary, because she is the perfect servant, and pride cannot stoop to imitating such complete humility. Daud was not a religious man, but he was grateful to providence for the generosity he had been shown, and did not begrudge people their forms of worship when it came out with such kindness. He entered through two low, barrel-vaulted antechambers into a small semi-circular chapel in the centre of which was a marble stand where lighted candles were set. From the ceiling, a cobalt dome struck with golden stars, hung fifty brass oil lamps suspended on thin wires. Low in the centre of the curved wall was set a shrine, darkened with candle smoke, which held the sacred icon, obscured by small tokens of beaten gold, left by devoted supplicants.

Daud knelt a while and wept a prayer of longing to be reunited with that source of joy and pain. For a moment it was as if a breath from that original beauty entered his soul and his heart became light. Then, as he left, his eyes now adjusted to the gloom, his sight fell upon an icon of the Annunciation high on the back wall: a handsome youth, upright, martial, with a spear in hand and full of life; Mary, her eyes averted, showing the troubled look of a girl discovered; and above the white rays of the spirit descending from a dove's wing.

A single bell rang for one o'clock, shattering for an instant the mood of the past hour, announcing the next. Outside in one of the many courtyards Daud sat a while in the shade by the twisted trunk of an old pine, a moving contrast to the bleached face of the stonework of the fortress building, with all its angles of steps and parallel lines of railing and corridors. The convent has a spirit of its own and a more mysterious will, enacted in the continual rising and falling, so many levels, arches, pillars, passageways… stairways ascending… descending… 'Pathways of the heart again,' thought Daud as he rose. A few more turns found him stepping outside through a small door at the back of the convent. From here the desert mountain fell away sharply before rising again in a rude rocky skyline that seemed to stretch on forever, drenched in midday Syrian sunshine.

Daud took his leave of Seydnaya the same day. He had been well-provisioned by the Mother Superior for the journey to Damascus and carried the old goat's skin rolled up under his arm. As he tramped along, without any particular intentions as to his future, he thought how much at home he had felt during the night he spent at the convent. It wasn't just the kindness of the Mother Superior. There had been something else, something soothing and restorative about the place, something as intimate and familiar as skin. He just couldn't put his finger on it.

'What am I without this intimacy?' he found himself complaining to his soul. 'Nothing but an empty shell. I feel like a hole which needs filling.'

He left off thinking, and just let his mind roll on. A new landscape opened up in him, of feelings and intimations, of closeness and love, beauty and truth, taking him to a place beyond his usual self, beyond the ordinary view, like climbing a mountain – these things which required energy and resolve always seemed to widen his vision. With such ponderings circling within like butterflies, Daud continued on his way to Damascus.

The carcass of the noble billy goat Shams was stewed and eaten by the nuns for dinner. The dreams enjoyed by the nuns that night, and their subsequent behaviour, reflected the degree to which each had met and dealt with her own passions, natural and spiritual. At least two young novices fled back to the lovers they had abandoned in their villages. And the greetings and embraces between the nuns themselves, the chanting and prayerful ejaculations in chapel, the tears and depth of longing in the singing of hymns, all expressions of love and devotion, emotional and spiritual, took on a heightened fervour. Gradually the heat of their ardent desire subsided, and just as the convent returned to normal, Taqla arrived back from her parents' home and settled into her routine once again.

SIX

A drum is born

OW, it may be reasonably assumed that with the pouring out, first of the seed, then the blood and then the breath of old Shams, and with the subsequent dismemberment of his form, that our friend was done for – on all counts a dead goat.

Yet it is not so, for Shams' seed spread, potentially at least, to the four corners of the world through the good offices of his co-respondents of that one great night of love; his blood sacrificed so willingly had fed the earth; his breath conspired at last in the greater spirit that blows as a quickening wind through all creation; and then his flesh, that tabernacle of passions high and low, consumed by the lovely sisters of the convent, transmuted in the cooking, translated in the eating, and sublimated in the digestion into a whole universe of tastes, feelings and actions, possibly, but not necessarily, ad infinitum.

Daud still had the goatskin and a little money. Furthermore, thanks to the generosity of the nuns, he now appeared less the ragged ascetic from the desert and more the simple peasant. Thus refinanced and freshly attired, though still wearing the blue shawl around his head, he made his way towards Damascus. It was the obvious choice for now. He had given up the idea of returning to his former career. He could have stayed at the convent, but this didn't seem appropriate. At the very least, by journeying to the great merchant city he would be fulfilling his original intention, however diminished the result. Daud was on the road again and it felt good, an open road with no fixed expectations of what the future might bring.

He walked steadily in the gentle warmth of the afternoon, and at nightfall took shelter in a *finduq*, a small inn, on the outskirts of the great city, where the road from Seydnaya met the main route to the Bekaa and the coast at Beirut. In the morning, as the wood smoke from the finduq's kitchen curled up in the still cold air, and mist lay like goose down over the sleeping valley, Daud ate a little bread and curds and made his way down into Damascus. As he skirted Mount Kassioun on his left, the goat-skin roll under his arm seemed to expand and become warm. For an instant he felt a gentle pulsating at his side, as if he had developed a nervous twitch, but the sensation soon passed as he became distracted by the sights and sounds of the approaching city.

Damascus; mere words do not do justice to this city of cities known locally as Dimasq-i-Sham: time's creation and timeless witness to the gathering of peoples, sacred city of prophets, their heirs and descendants. A tree of life more ancient than the cedars of Lebanon, Damascus within whose pounded earth and battered walls are hid the forgotten roots and weathered rings of ten millennia of mankind's settled history. Daud gazed down upon the venerable sprawl and beheld a treasure chest of white, red, brown and black, a filigree of roofs and domes and delicate minarets, strewn extravagantly with the piercing emerald green of cypress trees, silver-threaded with the spring torrent of the Barada river growling under the energy of its snowmelt, all tipped out before a velvet sea of orchards and fading into distant lakes of pearl and mysterious desert.

Daud decided to look up his old friend Touma. Touma was a trader of cardamoms and other spices. He ran his business from a khan off the Souk al Tawil. This is the *Via Regula* of the Romans – the Street Called Straight – where that famous Isawiyyan, the blinded Paul, found fire in his eyes and began to preach sweet songs of the singular spirit of love. Until, that is, his Yahudi employers took old testament umbrage and he had to make an abrupt exit, over the city wall, let down in a basket like Quair Bungle Rye. Touma was a good man who owed Daud a lot. Daud once had an opportunity to put one over Touma in a way that would have beggared him and made Daud immensely rich. In a deal concerning a large shipment of cardamoms, Daud had taken a different tack, and had neither gained nor lost anything, allowing Touma to benefit hugely. When Touma realised that Daud had acted so unselfishly, he went personally to Arwad to thank him. They drank wine like brothers, and an unbreakable trust was established between them.

Along the Barada River down roads lined with trees alive in spring leaf, Daud passed into the centre of the city. By the great walls of the Citadel he found himself caught up in the vortex of the crowds and swept through high portals into the shady avenue of the Souk Hamidiyeh, the main market place of Old Damascus. Then down past Moawiyya Street with its garment sellers, and the lanes where beckoned dark-skinned girls from Arabia and the sandy wastes beyond – fierce ladies dressed in dark colours, their hair tied in black and turquoise scarves, each a kohl-eyed Queen of Sheba. They sat on the ground, their wares spread before them: moody velvets of sapphire blue embroidered in gold, strange cosmetics and scents of musk and ambergris, bejewelled slippers, glassware, porcelain for serving coffee, all the accoutrements of the desert boudoir. Daud let his eyes wander, delighting in the exchange of glances, but not fooled by their obvious deceit. In the Street called Straight, among the shops selling striped smocks and *kuffiyehs* – cotton head scarves patterned in red or black on white – he saw smart black cloaks woven in thick silk and wool, some lined with creamy lambskins. His thoughts turned momentarily to the hide of old Shams beneath his arm, but realised it would probably be too tough and heavy for the finely dressed Damascene about town.

Strong, dry aromas of cardamom and dark coffee filled Daud's nostrils, impinging as mild narcosis, and erasing with pungent acerbity the voluptuous after-images of the desert women. He followed the scent into the old khan. The old stone structure had originally supported two large domes, but these had not been rebuilt since the last earthquake. Arches and squinches remained uncapped, like snapped branches setting the broken eggshells of the domes. A rectangle of walls inset with arches formed the outer colonnade of a cloister from which led off numerous storerooms and offices. A second floor, reached by staircases on either end, repeated the effect. The enclosed courtyard was strewn with wooden cases, bales and containers at various stages of being unpacked. A couple of camels drank noisily from a stone trough in the centre. Daud found Touma in his office on the second floor.

Touma jumped up and raced to embrace his old friend. A tall man, and somewhat portly, the merchant was nonetheless agile and energetic. His manner was urbane and educated, and he enjoyed discourse and argument as Daud might food and drink. He had the appearance of a Greek, and had given Daud to believe that he was descended from the Christian families who had stayed on in Damascus after the great general of the Umayyads, Khalid ibn al Walid, had taken the city. But he wore his religion lightly like Daud, and numbered Jews, Shiites and Druzes among his friends. He hugged Daud joyfully, and only afterwards did he notice his friend's rustic attire. He made no comment, preferring to allow his friend to disclose or not as he wished, the circumstance of his unusual get-up. Daud was still in a somewhat detached state, and by default allowed mystery to have the upper hand over revelation.

'This meeting has never taken place,' Daud said in a low voice, as if by way of revelation. Touma, who loved a mystery, nodded sagely, although he had no idea at all what Daud was on about. But no matter. His friend was involved in a mystery, and by the collusion of this amity, so too was Touma. To be involved in a mystery allowed Touma's speculative intellect to have a field day, limited only by the fact that he was sworn to secrecy about a meeting which didn't take place, subsequent to events to which Daud did not elude.

'No problem, my friend. No explanation needed. But what on earth is that bundle under your arm?'

Daud remembered Shams and sighed. 'Oh… yes. It's an old friend who helped me in a time of need. I thought it might make a nice rug,' and so saying he unrolled the skin on the floor.

'More likely a nice drum,' said Touma, as he looked closely at the smelly fleece. 'I know just the chap who could make you up a fine one – Abu Kerim – and he brews a great cup of coffee.'

'What on earth would I be wanting a drum for?' stuttered Daud, surprised at his friend's sudden interest in Shams' remains.

'Well, I suppose it depends on the drum.' Now it was Touma's turn to become mysterious. 'Would you be wanting to sell it, now?'

At that point a sound akin to a small cry or a bleat was heard. Both Daud and Touma looked around to find its source, except there was nothing in the room except piles of empty sacks and sheaves of documents. They went onto the balcony and looked down. The camels had gone. A dog

was asleep on a pile of sacks. Pigeons cooed on the broken edges of the
dome. But there was nothing in sight that could cry or bleat.

As they returned to the room, Daud looked down at the goat skin, and
remembered something about a girl and a mountain cave. His stomach
tightened and he began to feel faint and helpless. He picked up the skin and
rolled it up again. It may have seemed just a skin, but the sum of all Shams'
life experience was contained in the memory of its cells. Once it had held
blood and breath, and the fire of life had animated it in the form of a goat.
Even now its presence for Daud was comfortingly familiar. He clutched it
tightly under his arm, and as he did so, he felt easy again.

'No, I don't think I want to sell it, but a drum… that's an interesting
idea.'

'OK, then let's go and see Abu Kerim, and have some coffee.'

Down to the end of the Street Called Straight, then through Bab
as-Sharki – the Eastern Gate – they went. Along the outside of the city wall
where the heads of camels hang on hooks, their mouths stuffed with
parsley, and the butchers stand at their blocks, slicing great maroon clots of
camel liver, there in a yard behind the abattoir, beneath an ancient
mulberry tree radiant in new leaf, the two traders fetched up at the shop of
Abu Kerim the Drum Maker.

Abu Kerim sat cross-legged at a low worktable amid his tools. He was
a small man with a full white beard and pronounced eyebrows above kind
eyes. He looked to be fifty or so, but in fact was much older. Although Abu
Kerim was really a musician, drum-making was part of his trade as a
purveyor of skins and furs. From the barrel-vaulted ceiling and walls of his
little shop hung pelts of wolves, foxes and wild cats, as well as drums, large
and small. On a shelf at the back, empty timber hoops were stacked,
waiting to be covered, and rough wooden frames held stretched skins in
the process of being cured. In one corner a small clay hearth smoked with
charcoal. Abu Kerim took one look at the golden fleece of Shams and
exclaimed, 'My God, what a beauty!' He held it, examining it more closely.
'Its perfect, such weight, such evenness.' He looked at Daud, imploringly,
'Please, would you let me make a drum out of it. I'll do it for just the cost of
the wooden frame. Please!'

Abu Kerim was one of those rare people who took a measured
approach life, always considering the situation carefully, from all possible
angles, before making a response. He was a modest man, so this dramatic

display of importuning Daud to work the skin was somewhat out of character. Under normal circumstances, Abu Kerim would never put himself forward unless he was dragged. On this occasion, however, something had compelled him to speak passionately. At first Daud was taken aback by Abu Kerim's show of enthusiasm, but ever since Touma had proposed the idea of a drum, the knot in his stomach had disappeared, and now the feeling of hopelessness which had dogged Daud since his meeting by the cave evaporated entirely. Daud, whose previous life had meant constant dealing with crooks and scoundrels, found Abu Kerim's openness quite refreshing. And as he really knew nothing about drums, drum making or even drumming, he happily agreed to Abu Kerim's request, on the condition that he could watch the process of making the drum.

They started right away. First the golden locks which Shams had worn so proudly were shaved off to reveal the bare hide. The goat hair was purchased by a carpet maker friend of Abu Kerim who took it away to spin into twine. Then Abu Kerim moistened the skin with just a little water, and placed it in a large wooden mortar. Next, he pounded it, gently but firmly, to soften it. There was a certain amount of resistance at first, and the skin squeaked and gurgled beneath the pestle, but under Abu Kerim's light but persistent hand, the skin quickly reached the desired pliancy. Then he rolled up the skin in a muddy solution of water and wood ash and left it in a bucket to soak overnight.

Daud's drum was to be a large circular frame drum, a flat drum of the kind played either with the hand or beaten with a bent stick, as are used in that part of the world to accompany dancing and singing. A number of long flat strips of cedar, each a few millimetres thick were slowly heated in steam over a kettle until they were pliable. Then quickly, before they cooled, Abu Kerim bent the strips and fixed them, one over the other, round a circular form about a metre in diameter, to make a strong laminated ring to take the heavy goat skin.

It was late morning by the time Abu Kerim had finished this first stage in the transformation of Shams' horny hide. He sat down and washed his hands and face, pouring water from a brass ewer into a bowl, and dried himself carefully. Taking a handful of dark green Ethiopian coffee beans from a small sack, the musician-cum-drum-maker heated them slowly in a small metal pan over the fire. Then from a wooden box he took ten or twelve green cardamom pods which he added to the coffee beans. As the beans and the cardamoms began to change colour and give off a honey dark aroma, he continued to shake the pan gently. When they had darkened sufficiently, he put the freshly roasted coffee beans, and the cardamom pods, into a small stone mortar which he held in his lap and quickly pulverised the mix. The powdered coffee was carefully measured, one heaped spoon per cup, with sugar and water, into an old beaten pot. It was a copper pot, tinned on the inside, wide at the bottom, narrowing to a neck and then widening a little again. It had a long curved pouring spout in the shape of a bird's beak, and a wooden handle fixed into the side. A hinged lid shaped like an onion dome closed the top. Abu Kerim whisked the mixture and put it on the flame to cook.

Throughout this procedure Abu Kerim related his feelings about the skin. He said he'd sensed there was something unusual about it the moment he had seen it.

'Sometimes drum skins are like that. It depends on the animal. Not all animals are dumb, you know. The skin of an animal can speak things you couldn't imagine. We had a gazelle skin once, from such a beautiful animal, a young female, which had fallen and broken her neck trying to escape the hunter. So we made a small drum and it sang so sweetly. But every time the hunter played on it he became overcome with grief, until finally he stopped hunting and took up painting instead. Now he works as an illustrator. Give him a love scene from Layla and Majnun, and he's as happy as a felucca on the Nile. But he won't paint the hunting scenes.

'Of course, there are ordinary drums too, usually from sheep or cow skins, that just make a sound. They can be turned into perfectly decent drums if the drum maker and the drummer are skilled, but often they just don't do much else but make a noise. And then camel skins, they're very tough, and they need a lot of working in, naturally. That's how it is, I guess. So, there's no telling what a drum like this will do,' Abu Kerim laughed and looked over at the bucket which was gurgling quietly nearby.

'Ah, but the coffee! we mustn't forget the coffee!' He opened the lid. The coffee had begun to rise and Abu Kerim just caught it before the frothy head began to boil. He took the little pot from the flame, let the froth subside a little and tapped it three times on a brick at the edge of the stove. He returned it to the heat, let the froth rise again, and tapped it down once more. He repeated this process a third time, and the coffee was ready.

Skin, that holy interface of the internal and external worlds, the

birthday balloon of the inflation of spirit. Skin, the surface which both accepts and rejects, absorbing and repelling, permeable and impermeable. Skin, with its blotches and blemishes, like the pits of meteors on the surface of the desert, hairy like the scrubby edges of a dry watercourse, immaculate, undulate as a sand dune and soft to itself. Skin, the smooth surface, the flat of the belly, the curve of the thigh, the angled symmetry of the shoulders, the scrawn and scrunch of neck and crutch. All the old goat's topography folded and squashed, bubbling and gurgling in a bucket of ash mud. Shams groaned, and a wet rumble and hiss like the sound of a lava flow, followed by the loudest and most indelicate of fart sounds, issued from the bucket.

Abu Kerim simultaneously squeaked and jumped, Touma gasped 'Wow! what the …!', and Daud, who was developing an affinity with the idiosyncratic presence of Shams and his noisome sentiments, just murmured quietly 'Ah!'

Abu Kerim's hands were still trembling as he poured the coffee, first sharing out a little of the creamy froth into tiny white china cups before filling them brimful. His eyes were wide and excited as if something rather important had just dawned on him. Touma looked over to his old friend Daud, thinking, 'there's a lot more to this chap than I ever imagined.'

Daud, for whom the excitement of the past week had been almost too much to bear at times, was decidedly nonplussed. He sat quietly sipping his coffee. Afterwards he returned with Touma to his store in the caravanserai. Touma ordered food to be brought up, freshly baked little pastries filled with mincemeat or goat's cheese and mint. After they had eaten, Daud began to speak.

'I suppose you deserve an explanation, but unfortunately there's not much I can say.' He paused, looking at Touma apologetically. 'You see, its such a long story. I was lost, and then there was this billy goat, and I followed it, and it brought me to safety. Then it screwed all the she-goats at Seydnaya and dropped dead. I got paid, and was left with the skin. And here we are.' Daud found it difficult to explain anything even to himself. He wanted to mention the girl too, but whenever he thought about that episode, he became all tied up inside.

'Don't worry about it, old friend,' said Touma, 'When you're ready. Look, I can see you're in a bit of a state. I could give you lots of advice, which you probably wouldn't thank me for, so I won't interfere. But you know you can stay here in the store as long as you like. No need to worry about food, money, anything. I can make up a story to cover your being here. No one is going to recognise you in that get-up anyway. You can come and go as you please. When you're ready, if you want, we can talk, and if I can help at all, you know you can rely on me.'

Daud looked relieved and accepted his friend's offer with thanks. 'But don't say anything about this to Abu Kerim.' He paused. 'I think the skin gave him a bit of a shock. It was rather strange, don't you think, the way it made that noise? But it was probably just air escaping or something.'

Touma gave Daud a sceptical look, 'Just air, eh? Mmmm... Yes, probably. Anyway, I'm off now. You make yourself at home and I'll see you in the morning.'

The next day Touma and Daud went back to Abu Kerim's shop. They pulled the goatskin out of the bucket and rinsed it thoroughly. It didn't make a sound. Then Abu Kerim scraped away the remaining hair with a piece of flat metal, rinsed it again, and laid it out in the sun. As the skin slopped onto the hot ground it seemed that it emitted a faint, pleasurable sigh, like a bather sinking onto the warm sand after a long swim. The three men looked at each other, and then back at the skin, but said nothing.

'It should dry well in this sun', said Abu Kerim, as he poured coffee a little later. 'Come back in the late afternoon, and we can finish it.'

When Daud returned, Abu Kerim was moistening the dry skin with a little water to bring back its flexibility. It squeaked occasionally as he massaged it gently, but for the most part it just lay dormant across the old drum maker's lap. Then he took the cedar frame and laid the skin over it, tacking first one edge to the wood, pulling it tight against this and tacking the other side. Not a sound. Then he began to pull the edges of the skin right over the wood and back inside. He got Daud and Touma to help him stretch it as tight as possible, and then using an awl, he sewed a fine leather thong through skin and wood around the whole circumference of the cedar hoop. With a sharp knife he trimmed off the excess skin. As a final touch he attached a few short pieces of light metal chain on the inside edge of the rim, which sounded shrilly when the drum was shaken.

'Well, here you are. Its finished, or at least my part in it. For you its just beginning. Don't expect it to sound much at first, drums need playing in. Warming, you know, like a good bed.' Abu Kerim rubbed down the finished drum, still wet, with a cloth, and handed it to Daud.

Then with a thoughtful look at Daud he said, 'Take your time. Sometimes the drummer needs playing in just as much as the drum.'

Daud thanked him, and paid him for the cost of the wood. He tried to give the old man something for the time he had spent, but Abu Kerim just laughed and refused, saying he would have done the drum for nothing.

'Just let me know from time to time how you two are getting on,' he said, as they parted.

Daud stood there, and stroked the drum a little. It responded immediately with a strange wobbling sound as the skin fluctuated gently beneath his palm. He almost dropped it in surprise. Abu Kerim gave a knowing shrug, as if to say, 'I said you may need playing in,' adding aloud, 'In time… in time…'

SEVEN

Taymir al-Bad the bad begins to lose the plot…

IKE every soul awaiting its turn upon the boundary of eternity, Taymir al-Bad had chosen his destiny beforehand, pledging his fealty to the Lord of Existence who then blew the clement breath of being upon his eternal essence, delineating this unique possibility and sending it hurtling down through aeons and universes of light and darkness until its innate desire for expression inspired the joining of egg and seed in the womb of this world.

Yet, even as the barely-formed hull of his fleshly form launched itself upon the slipway of his mother's uterus, Taymir al-Bad was already displaying those characteristics of objection and rebellion which would colour his day upon earth from this awkward dawn to the eventual setting of his shadowed light. The little clot-grown seed, the pink and pudgy blood-fed babe-in-waiting, perhaps intuiting the future difficulties which his hidden potential would demand in order to arrive at the strangeness of his particular completion, began to kick, and kick and kick. In so doing so he rotated himself 180 degrees through the vertical plane so as to be better placed for his retreat back to the womb. The more he resisted the inexorable slide into the sea of forms, the more his mother determined to expel her burden. Eventually the midwife, frustrated at this precocious display of ingratitude for life, when a tiny foot was seen poking reluctantly through the rose-petalled portals of birth, she grabbed hold and pulled firmly. Unfortunately for the crawler, his other leg was at that moment at the furthest stretch of an upward step in his attempts to regain the warm seclusion of his amniotic abode, and although birth was effected without much further ado, he forever bore the consequences of his natal recalcitrance. His stance, once established, was biased and bowlegged, with his firstborn leg stretched an inch longer than its twin, this latter inclined upwards and onwards, so that in his way of walking he always appeared to go against the natural flow.

In time, things did not improve. Never for an instant did he turn from the lesser *jihad* of externalised conflict, to the greater contentions within his own soul. Consequently, his life was one of contrariness and objection. His satisfaction came in deviating from the norm, a mode of behaviour which took him further and further down the road to his inevitable and inherently longed-for destruction.

Take the matter of his bandy-legged limp. Without this attention-seeking strategy (for there can be no doubt that his intra-uterine manoeuvres were the result of some unconscious inspiration) Taymir might never have acquired so early in life the self-justifying qualificatives of victim of loathing and object of ridicule, so that subsequently he could develop the double-barrelled defence of anger and deceit to such a pitch of self-righteous rage and guiltless detachment. Life takes all sorts, and his life developed according to inclinations typical of those born to serve under the squeezing sway of their own pride.

Taymir's anger found its outlet in violent confrontation. He fought his way out of kindergarten and primary school at an early age. His parents – whom he had chosen way back at the edge of eternity as most suitable launch pad for his adventures in relativity – served their purpose well by divorcing when the lad was approaching puberty.

His father, Abu Taymir, was an imam He had coveted the young wife of a street sweeper in Homs. The pair had been caught *in flagrante delicto*, Taymir's father having lured the young lady up to the top balcony of his mosque's minaret on the pretext of conducting an astronomy lesson. It was an unfortunate choice for a clandestine tryst, licit or illicit, as the acoustics of the elevated site were designed for maximum broadcast. There were few in the neighbourhood who did not hear that night the avid grunts of the protagonist's advance and the squeals of reluctance subsiding into acquiescence by the victim, and the subsequent urgent groans, the ecstatic and climactic cries and then post-coital languid sighs. When the imam became aware of his congregation gathered below the balcony, he quickly stood up, tousled, flushed and panting, and informed them that he had been engaged in mortal combat with a jinn, which he had defeated. This novel explanation held their attention long enough for the street sweeper's wife, hidden by the stone parapet of the balcony, to escape unnoticed down into the mosque below.

Taymir's mother, 'Umm Taymir, on the other hand, when she confronted her husband back home, was not fooled by this imaginative excuse. For a start, jinn, like angels, abhor the odour of garlic, and whatever had taken her husband in close quarter combat had fairly reeked of the stuff. The acrid smell of the street sweeper's wife's lentil and garlic supper clung heartily to the garments of the randy imam. 'Umm Taymir then unleashed such a tirade of bitter recrimination upon her husband that he had no choice but to agree to her demands. She compelled him to liquidate their joint assets and return her dowry with interest. Together they moved to Aleppo where the imam's wife quickly dispensed with her husband altogether. She eventually became a rich and successful brothel keeper.

The imam, to his small credit, rescued the street-sweeper's wife from the tempest of suspicion gathering in her neighbourhood in Homs, suspicion which inevitably would have fallen in a hard rain of stones had she remained. He brought her to Aleppo where they set up a small shop together.

Taymir took advantage of his parent's break-up to further his own career. Living on the streets he developed a reputation as a tough and fearless fighter. Mugging, breaking and entering, and eventually extortion brought him to the attention of the real sharks of the Aleppo underworld. He became the number one hit man. Although brimful of anger, Taymir was not without a certain deviant intelligence, which he now honed to a fine edge of deceit and resourcefulness. He was ugly, defiant, ruthless, and prone to outbursts of rage, yet from this toxic ground he now cultivated a centre of power, and as his power grew, so also did his ambition to wealth.

Taymir's rise through the sewers of Aleppo's underworld soon came to the notice of one Omo Sharleen. Omo Sharleen was a pillar of the East Mediterranean banking community, descended from a long line of money changers, lenders and launderers. The family business had its base in Beirut and for centuries had handled accounts for various members of the ruling houses of Milan, Florence, Rome and Constantinople, and in more recent times for the British Government. (Their future clientele would number customers from the New World, in particular from certain states bordering the Caribbean Sea, who required their money to be 'refreshed', as one might a pair of socks that had begun to smell.) As we said, Omo Sharleen was a pillar of society and one of the most corrupt and evil men of his time, although, as befits the appearance of a pillar, his exterior shone white as alabaster. Omo had only one aim in life, the continued flow of his income stream and the steady growth of his already broad lake of wealth. The means to this end were irrelevant. In Taymir, he saw an opportunity to further his ends.

The Sharleen organisation's myriad enterprises included the caravan-robbing business. A special agent arranged the transfer of the loot from Taymir's band, to various other bodies responsible for distribution through distant ports to far-off lands where its provenance would be unremarkable and untraceable. Omo never had direct contact with Taymir. To maintain the perception of his immaculate appearance, Omo never dealt personally with any of the fry of the sea of crime. His henchmen took care of that, the pilot fish who maintained themselves by nibbling the leftovers from the table, and running errands for the Big Fish. But, as the Egyptians say (and who would know better than Egyptians, who number putrefied fish in their cuisine), the fish starts stinking from the head. The big ideas were always initiated by Omo.

Taymir's attachment to Omo's organisation came about through a series of set-ups involving the local secret police, the Mukhaberat. The Mukhaberat were technically in the service of the Sultan, but the tentacles of Omo's organisation were long and had a retentive hold on certain high-ranking officers of this feared constabulary. An arrest on charges of drug peddling and fornication, a confession signed under threat of torture and execution, an 'escape' stage-managed by Omo's agents, and soon Taymir was firmly in Omo's bag. Then there was no way out. Financed from untraceable sources within Omo's organisation, and fed with sound information from Omo's network of spies, Taymir assembled a gang of cutthroats in a secret mountain hideaway. There he kept his men in check with drugs, sex and the lash of his unpredictable tongue. Omo's agents provided details of all the big caravans, cargo transfers and movements of money, goods and valuables throughout the country. Taymir plotted the ambushes which his gang duly executed. In these operations, untraceability was of absolute importance. Any breach in security meant all evidence linking the perpetrator with the source of the crime would be instantly dissolved. Which was why Taymir was now in such a fret.

Taymir was perplexed. He was sitting by the huge fireplace in the great hall of his draughty castle, which now resembled both a morgue and a collection depot for a jumble sale. Before him lay forty bodies, by now bloated and beginning to decompose. Each corpse was surrounded by a heap of clothes, shoes, chequered head scarves, purses, rings, saddles and blankets. He ordered his captain to count again.

'It still comes out as forty-one of everything, except things in pairs, which ever way we do it. But only forty bodies,' said the captain, having for the umpteenth time moved each pile, item by item, from point A on one side of the room to point B on the other, and back again.

'Then spread each thing out separately in rows, next to the bodies. We've got to be certain.' Taymir was in a confused state now. If there were 41 cloaks, 41 sets of robes and undergarments, 82 shoes, 41 purses etc, why were there only 40 bodies? He knew there had been 41 people in the caravan. He had counted them himself from his secret vantage point as they passed near Krak, and again outside of Homs. His lieutenants had kept the caravan in sight continually and no one had been seen to join or depart. Now, with everything carefully laid out again on the floor of the hall, Taymir walked up and down counting for himself. His confusion turned to irritation as he came to the inevitable conclusion.

'Someone has escaped. There's no question of it.' And then his worst fear began to dawn – it had been the merchant himself, the Arwadi, who had slipped their net. It had to be. The clothes and blanket that had no companion body were of a finer cut of cloth – silk garments and a cashmere cloak lined with lambskins, not at all like the rough attire of the cameleers. And it had been such a carefully laid trap, that was the pity of it, everything worked out to the minutest detail. Nothing had been forgotten, so what went wrong? Taymir didn't really give a damn any more what it was that had gone wrong, only that it had. One little untied

thread threatened to unravel an otherwise perfect piece of work, and its unravelling would certainly mean his downfall.

'We've got to find him,' he thought, 'before he reaches the authorities and raises the alarm.'

'All you worthless scum of motherless spawn of donkeys,' he

now addressed the assembled band of cutthroats, thieves and bowelless bribe-takers, 'get back out there and don't return without him. Dead or alive... Preferably dead!'

For the next two weeks, Taymir continued to fret. He drank wine to forget, but became even more irritable and unhappy. He smoked hashish, liberally dosed with opium, and retreated into sleep. Alone in the darkness of the castle his paranoid dreams only invited the ghosts of his past deeds. Relief came, albeit short-lived, when one of the gang returned after a few days with a corpse slung over his horse.

'He was hiding out in the mountains near the ambush,' said the brigand, as he unloaded a dark sack from which arose the sour stench of putrefaction. Even Taymir, whose way of life was malodour incarnate, rolled his eyes and pulled his kuffiyeh across his face as the body was tipped from the sack. A dozen or so maggots spilled from a green swollen wound in the corpse's neck.

'That's curious,' thought Taymir, observing that the fellow was fully dressed and shod. 'And how, may I ask, do you know this is the missing caravaneer?' he asked the brigand.

'Oh, that's easy, *sayyid*. I invited him to eat with me and got him drunk on arak. He told me the whole story – it was quite fantastic really – he said that he was a sleepwalker and must have wandered off just before we attacked, because when he woke up in the morning, everyone had vanished.'

Taymir wanted to believe him. And for the relief it afforded he let himself be taken in for a while. The next day, however, a second thug returned with another body. Taymir repeated the question regarding the verity of the its identity and how he had escaped the initial slaughter. Apparently, this one couldn't sleep because of a toothache and had gone off for a walk. Taymir was almost convinced. A third candidate auditioned the following day had avoided the ambush by spending the night drunk in the arms of a wandering shepherdess.

The bodycount increased, and the accompanying stories became ever more fantastical. Taymir's anger, which he had contained in the hope that someone might actually find the real Daud, finally exploded. Like some malevolent volcano he poured forth a searing flow of obscenities upon the assembled vagabondage. Then he stormed off, screaming that they were all fired.

EIGHT

Takla's Christmas present

 AKLA spent only a short time with her parents that year, yet she returned to Seydnaya too late to partake of the amorous feast which Shams, in his comprehensive striving to satisfy all, had provided. She did notice the mood of reflective pleasure and relaxation, the '*rahah*', which pervaded the convent like a sweet breath, but put this down to the ending of the lenten fast, the Paschal celebrations and the coming of spring. Takla too was enjoying a certain reflective pleasure following her encounter in the mountains. She did not, however, connect her own romantic interlude with the story of the goat feast, news of which filtered down to her bit by bit during the subsequent weeks. And she certainly made no connection between the goatherd of that episode and her own wild man. Of her mysterious lover she remembered little in the way of distinct physical features. If you had asked her what he had actually looked like, she would undoubtedly have described an angel.

In the meantime Takla had her own concerns. As her initial euphoria faded, she was left with a feeling of wholeness, of a lack having been filled. This state was so profound and liberating that for a while she barely felt the need of the usual diversions of life such as meals or chatting with the novices. Then as the weeks passed she was visited by a somewhat different and more down to earth state. Inexplicably she began to have fainting fits. In the mornings she felt nauseous and unable to keep her breakfast down. Takla was not so naïve as to remain long in ignorance of the cause of these symptoms. She missed one period. When she missed a second, she was confirmed in her growing intimations; she knew she was pregnant.

Takla, for all her perambulations in spheres of transcendence, was an eminently practical girl. While she had no doubt as to the goodness of what now grew within, she knew her condition must remain secret. But how? First she prepared a solution of tomato paste for monthly application in order that no suspicion would arise from the continually unstained state of her laundry. Then she accustomed her companions to what would become her new fuller figure. She took to wearing loose-fitting clothes to remove the definitions of her slim young form until nature replaced them with her own fecund curves. By complaining of being hungry between meals, she led her companions to think she was becoming a bit of a foodie.

The months passed, and Takla began to expand. The change in her appearance went unremarked as her body took up the slack which her physical and psychological deceptions had created in her associates' minds. The convent had other matters to deal with that year. Each of the ninety-nine she-goats who had submitted so willingly to the enthusiastic seed of Shams the Goat, had duly produced twins. There was not a barren one among them. Throughout the summer the hillsides of Seydnaya resounded with the hungry cries of the one hundred and ninety-eight newborn kids, bleating day and night.

September came, and with it the feast of the Virgin's Nativity. The young cook of the Seydnaya Monastery was sitting down in the kitchen having just put another batch of buns to bake. Pilgrims were arriving from Antioch and Jerusalem, Alexandria and Constantinople – even from far away Rome. Takla was hot, and the sweat combined with the thin film of flour on her arms, face and hair giving her the appearance of a pantomime ghost. Beneath this mask she was bonny and comfortable in her hidden state of motherhood. Gone were the days of vomiting and fainting and she was gaining strength as the child grew within her.

The previous night Takla had dreamt again of the angel, the same beautiful being of light disguised as a handsome youth who had visited from time to time ever since that fateful spring morning. The angel had offered her gold coins, a book and a loaf of sweet bread, signalling that she should choose. She had chosen the sweet bread, at which the angel had smiled – and the smile became like a bird. A very small bird, really just the shape of wings, the quivering imprint of small but purposeful flight, which moved from the angel's lips as a kiss blown on the breath and into Takla. She had woken before the dawn with all the sweetness of this nocturnal visit pervading her soul. Later, as she was preparing the dough for the day's first baking, Mother Superior appeared in the kitchen.

'My dear Takla, how are you on this lovely morning?' the elderly nun greeted the cook.

'Wonderful, just wonderful!' she beamed,

'As usual, busy and full of bounce! Really, Takla, where do you get your energy from?

'Oh Mother Superior, if you only knew how much I love being here!'

'My, aren't you the top of the morning today! If only some of the others would look to your cheery example and not take themselves so seriously. Really, a nun's life is simple indeed, but what goes on in their minds is sometimes quite childish.' She was about to divulge to Takla the confessions of one young novice who had developed unhealthy father-figure fantasies about the goatherd who had visited months before, believing him to be an apparition of St Jerome. But Mother Superior caught herself just in time, and instead she said 'Look, I thought it would be nice to have sweet buns today, in honour of the Nativity of the Virgin, but I see you have already started the dough.'

'No problem, I'll add some honey,' and without so much as a glottal stop of hesitation Takla hopped up and from a large earthenware pot she doled out a couple of large spoonfuls into the mix.

As Takla plunged her hands back into the dough on the big wooden board and continued to knead, Mother Superior spoke of the birth of Mary: how the elderly Joachim, who was a wealthy man, was being slighted by his peers because he had not produced any heir to maintain his remembrance of God. Even Abraham and Sara, at the end of their days, had been given Isaac. So Joachim took himself off into the desert where he fasted and prayed forty days and nights. His wife Anna, who was being similarly tested, thinking now that she had become both childless and a widow, put on her bridal clothes, went and sat beneath a bay laurel and prayed to be given a son. In the event, both prayers reached their goal and were accepted. Joachim sacrificed ten lambs, twelve calves and a hundred kid goats, and Anna promised that, son or daughter, the child would be a gift to God, a servant of the temple.

'It is written that when the baby Mary was three she was taken and dedicated to the temple, and she danced upon her feet. She remained in the temple, like a dove, and was fed by an angel.'

Mother Superior looked at the young girl busily kneading the ballooning mass of glutinous dough. The nun sighed, and the thought occurred to her: 'she's just so perfect…I wonder if…' but she didn't allow the thought to continue. Instead she made a satisfied 'Mmmm,' and said, 'the sisters will enjoy that, and all the visitors.' She then smiled at Takla, turned and continued on her rounds.

As winter approached, enacting the ruse became easier. The days were shorter, the cloisters darker and as everyone in the convent went about wrapped in bundles of thick, woollen cloth against the cold, Takla's inner bundle was able to grow undetected. In late December, on Christmas eve as destiny would choose, when snow covered the slopes of the Jebel Lubnan and blanketed the rooftops of Syria from Aleppo to Damascus, shortly after the midnight mass had been celebrated, Takla took herself to her room. There she was delivered of a bright baby boy which slipped into this world with the ease of a body ocean-borne carried to shore on the incoming tide. Takla pulled the little creature to her and breathed into his ear the Name of God and words of Divine Perfection as the first sounds he should hear, so that he be inspired with life according to his origin beyond the stars. Then he let out a little cry which faded to a soft murmur of happiness as he began to suckle at his mother's aching breast. He had a strong appetite and drank his fill. Mother and child lay together through the deep of the night.

Takla had planned for this occasion. At the darkest hour, when all in the convent were asleep, she swaddled her son from top to toe in old but clean rags, then further rolled him up in some warm woollen cloth and an old sheepskin. She tied sacking on her shoes to imitate larger, booted feet, and quickly and quietly, her bundle beneath her cloak, she slipped out of the front gate of the convent, down the steps and up on to the main street of Seydnaya. In the trampled snow her footprints mingled with those of the congregation who had departed a few hours earlier. Above the full moon neared the end of its course across the deep of the star-filled night. After a short way, she turned off the road and made her way around to the back door of the convent, where she left the babe on the step, fast asleep and still warm as toast. Then she scurried back to her room the way she had come, tidied away all evidence of parturition, and was back in bed before the nuns rose for morning prayers. Takla was not completely without a mother's anxiety, and she prayed her little tot would be safe in the coming hours. But she knew he was well-fed, well-wrapped, and well-placed for discovery by someone other than herself.

That someone made his discovery whilst Takla was clearing away the nuns' breakfast. A cry came from outside the back door. It was the local wood cutter, come for his traditional Christmas gift of a bottle of wine. As the nuns gathered, the old man stood there with his donkey, a startled look on his face, holding a bundle of sheepskin and rags from which a little pink face stared out. The little face looked a bit blank, as it had just woken up.

'It was just a bundle on the doorstep. I thought it was my bottle of wine. I'd no idea. I just unwrapped it and look what I found inside!' the old man blurted out. Mother Superior took in the situation immediately.

'A foundling. On Christmas Day. Typical. Well, the good Lord gives and the good Lord takes away, and today He gives, just like He sent His Spirit and His Word. Perhaps this is a good omen for our convent, like the day the old goat came. Takla!' she called inside. 'Takla, you'll have to deal with this.'

Takla was doing her best to remain calm in the background. She came forward nervously.

'Yes Mother?' she glanced at the nun, and then at her tiny son, cradled in the wood cutter's arms.

'You see what we have here, don't you? God made Man in His Own Image, and now He's just reminded us by popping one of these little images down here right on our doorstep. Well, I suppose we'll have to look after it the best we can until we find it a suitable home. We'll look for a wetnurse in the village, but in the meantime you can feed it on fresh goats milk.' Takla, surprised but undeniably happy, received her baby back into her arms and hurried into the warmth of the kitchen. She returned in a moment having fetched a somewhat better bottle of wine than usual for the wood cutter, who departed cheerfully with his donkey now that the status quo had been restored.

Christmas was always a jolly time in the convent, and never more so than the day the foundling appeared. After all the nuns had made a suitable fuss over the newborn babe, Takla took him to her room with a bowl of fresh goat's milk. She drank the milk herself and fed her child again from her own breasts. Then after tucking him up well, she joined in the preparations for the Christmas feast, disappearing every now and then to her room to check on the baby, to give him a feed and a cuddle, before returning to the kitchen.

At the feast that day, when giving thanks to God for His goodness and generosity throughout the year, Mother Superior also made mention of the community's new addition, expressing gratitude that they had been able to offer safe haven to the needy in this case.

'So, what is the child, a girl or a boy? I presume you've discovered by now,' she asked Takla

'Yes Mother Superior. A boy. But we haven't found a name for him yet.' Takla spoke up from her place at the bottom of the table.

'Well, what do you think his name is?'

'I thought… well… because it's Christmas you know… we could call him Isa, or Gabriel or something like that. But then I thought, Yahya would be nice too, as he is really like a gift of life.'

In fact, since well before the arrival of her baby, Takla had been thinking a lot of the wild man who now inhabited a place deep in her heart. Since that strange encounter nine months earlier, she maintained an awareness of him as one might mind a hermit hidden in a mountain cave, who one knows is there but remains unseen; or a desert wanderer whose distant vision fades into watery mirage upon approach. Sometimes, passing the icon in the chapel, that one of the hairy John the Baptist, then the child within her would kick and leap, and it was as if the hermit woke from his meditation and wandered a while in the undefined tract of her heart. At such times a presence would flood her being with tender feelings of love, yearnings which would swell up and subside, in concert with the child moving inside her.

'Then Yahya it is,' confirmed Mother Superior, 'After the Baptist I presume, not the Divine?'

Takla felt a wave of shock flush through her. 'What does she know?' she wondered, as she glanced over at her Mother Superior. But the smile on the old nun's face betrayed nothing, just the accustomed, kindly matter-of-factness she wore as naturally as her habit.

Throughout the Christmas season, the community of Seydnaya were busy providing hospitality for the many visitors who came to venerate the sacred icon of the Virgin. Takla worked in the kitchen from morning 'til night, and the nuns were equally taken up with attending religious services. Still, Takla found sufficient opportunities to tend to her baby's needs. Yahya obliged by sleeping profoundly most of the time, awakening only when he was hungry, and crying little. The nuns, for their part, were too absorbed to notice that no wetnurse had appeared. As the celebrations acquiesced into fallow January, it became evident that no one was minded to disturb the peace and happiness of the infant growing so contentedly in the environs of the convent kitchen. Although he became everyone's babe for moments each day, and so fulfilled in essence the maternal needs of this community of celibates, Takla carefully contained her own affections for him while in public, safe in the knowledge that each would have the other's undivided attention when in the privacy of her room.

NINE

The Drum plays

INCE arriving in Damascus, Daud had felt at times on the verge of complete dissolution. Not the dissolution he had experienced at the pool by the hidden cave before that vision of incomparable beauty and subsequent union with the maid Takla – that had been delightful and the purest of pleasures. A chasm of unknown now separated him from that earlier bliss. What remained he found dull and empty indeed, and poor company for a man alone.

Daud lived for the most part in Touma's store. He gave his friend a hand occasionally when needed, but for the most part he kept to himself. The Drum (in Daud's mind the reconstructed goatskin had now acquired the status of a proper noun) had lain untouched for two weeks since he had received it from Abu Kerim. This was not from neglect. He was always aware of it and looked at it often, lying there across from his bunk. Daud would have been the first to admit that he was actually quite afraid to take up the Drum.

With hesitancy came desperation; and desperation was followed by decision. Late one afternoon, having lain on his bed most of the day gazing at the ceiling, Daud had the sudden realization that it was better to be something than nothing, better to be alive than dead. And even if life appeared to him at that moment as a deep void, a complete unknown, still, it needed to be entered into and traversed, whatever the end.

With enormous effort, Daud pulled himself up and went over to the Drum. His hand touched the cedar wood rim. He felt the skin of the drumhead. He moved the flat of his hand across it, tapped it, and the skin became taut under his finger tip. He stroked it again. It responded in a friendly way, as if welcoming the warmth from his palm. He tapped slowly, finding a regular beat. His breathing began to slow. Now it was the Drum setting the rhythm, and Daud was the one responding. As he played, tentatively, sensitively, the turgid state which had enveloped him loosened its hold and he regained some sense of that connectedness by which all life moves. He played the simplest of rhythms, *daa-da, daa-da, daa-da*, until his heart and his hand and the Drum joined in a single beat. When he stopped drumming, he clasped the Drum to his chest, and for a while a silent rhythm played on between the drum and his heart. He was ready to move again.

Taking the Drum, Daud slipped out of the store and headed north. He soon found himself in a street market selling all manner of birds and animals: canaries, finches, ducks, chickens and rabbits. In a wicker cage on a wall he saw a poor old Great Gull, the kind that used to haunt the outer rocks off Arwad. Its feathers, which showed the faded evidence of coloured dyes, were soiled and damaged, and its eyes were sunk in its sockets as if, lost here in this inland city, it had given up looking out for the sea. Daud shuddered as he remembered his island home and the great gulls wheeling above the breakers on the southern shore. He gripped the Drum tightly, causing it to swing against his leg and hit the side of his knee. The Drum let out a dull boom, a groaning sound which floated up and became lost in the wind. The gull flapped its wings in alarm, shaking the cage violently. Bird and cage toppled into the street.

'Hey, you, what the hell do you think you're doing, frightening my birds.' The fusty face of the stall owner emerged from behind the wall rubbing sleep from his eyes. 'You'll have to buy it if it's damaged, you know…'

'Gladly. I think this should cover it,' said Daud, and placed a few coins in the wall.

The coins and the face disappeared below the parapet from where a mutter arose: 'Bloody musicians… think the world owes them a living.'

Daud placed the cage upright on the ground and the door sprang open. The gull was awake now. It steadied itself and then, head up, eyes staring straight ahead, it slowly emerged from its prison cell, taking each step with an air of consummate grace and poise, as if remembering its original greatness. It stood there in the street, spread out its wings and flapped. Uncertainly at first, for its joints were stiff, and the missing feathers made its efforts awkward and painful to watch; then from nowhere came a gust of wind which lifted the gull from the ground. The big old bird, tattered but proud, rose high above the street and slowly disappeared into the darkening sky, flying eastwards in the direction of the mountains and the sea. All the little birds in their cages shrilled an enthusiastic chorus of farewell, and wild sparrows darted about among the houses, chirping and chittering, carrying the news of the great escape far and wide.

Daud smiled as he witnessed this. He looked at the Drum hanging by his side. A tide of memories rose up in him, memories of Arwad, the sea, the wind and its wide horizons. He looked around, taking in the sights with the open eye of a traveller. Wisps of cloud laced the sky, marbling in gold and white the deep indigo of the encroaching night. He crossed the glistening court of the Umayyad Mosque. Swallows were diving from nests in the crannies between the buff stones of the high walls. Pigeons and doves wheeled and whirled in the air around the tall minarets. His route led him up past the Citadel, where sellers of old coins and broken antiques had spread their cloths in the dust of the evening and were calling out their meagre wares. He returned their good evenings with an ease he hadn't felt in a long time. He engaged in pleasantries with the fruit seller behind his colourful cart, bantered with the wooden spoon sellers and the bakers carrying trays of warm, crusty bread. On over the Barada River, beneath crumbling stone archways, past creaking wooden housefronts with carved panel doors and lattice-screened windows, where behind sat ladies seeing but unseen.

In time, Daud's stroll took him beyond the old city and up towards the Salihiye Quarter on the lower slopes of Mount Kassioun. It was not aimless wandering, although if asked he would not have been able to say where he was going. He wasn't consciously exploring, or even just nosing along out of amusement or curiosity. Something very definite was guiding his steps, and he was simply following.

After crossing the Tora River Daud found himself in Sheikh Muhyiddin Street, where the road turns left and heads uphill to the tomb and mosque of the Great Sheikh himself. The slopes of Salihiye have been settled by immigrants ever since Saladin's predecessor, Nur-al-Din, son of Zengi the Turk, first gave the area over to refugees driven out from Jerusalem by the Crusaders. Night was falling over the ancient city as Daud entered the unlit lanes and alleys of the northern suburb. The lights of a tea house beckoned. He entered and sat quietly in a corner. It was a small place, just the tea-maker with his charcoal stove, his teapots, a few metal trays and shelves of clean glasses. Sitting cross-legged in another corner was a young man drinking tea. He was slight, with fine features which were neither dark nor light. His wide forehead and small slender face tapered to a well-shaped chin from which sprouted a few straggly hairs of a youthful beard, complementing the dusty fluff on his upper lip. He dressed in the desert style, in simple but finely woven brown cloth, edged in black embroidery. Next to him on the divan was a small instrument case.

'Probably a violin… Must be a musician…' Daud mused. 'He's quite beautiful…'

The young man looked over, and seeing the Drum, he smiled.

'Are you coming to the session?' he asked.

'No, I mean, I don't know…' Daud's words stumbled out. He had spoken so little lately, he found the sound of his own voice strange. 'What session?'

'Just round the corner. Why don't you come along, if you've nothing else to do?' said the young man.

'That's very kind…' Daud paused as it dawned on him that it was the Drum which had brought about the invitation. He was being invited to play. Daud took fright. '…But I can't really play. I've just got the Drum, you know, it's new.'

'Oh never mind that, come along anyway and see what happens. I'm Refik, by the way. From Tunis. You don't look '*Shami*' either. Where are you from?'

'Oh, up north a bit. You know… in the mountains.' Daud wasn't lying, but he wanted to avoid giving away too much about himself. While he was enjoying the newfound freedom of travelling incognito, he hadn't forgotten that he might be on someone's wanted list.

'I'm called Qays.' Daud added. This wasn't entirely untrue. Touma had told Daud that he was 'mad, like Qays'. Daud had understood its implications. It was a lover's name, and suited his present condition well.

They finished their tea. Outside, Refik pointed up the hill and began walking. Daud could just make out a stone tower topped with a strange wooden construction. As they got closer he saw that up the side of the tower ran a pole which connected to a wooden cog and sprocket, and the whole affair was covered with a canopy of sheet iron. They arrived at a small door at the base of the tower. A young boy opened the door and called to someone inside. He seemed to recognise Refik. A moment later a buxom lady dressed in brilliant turquoise satin with a black silk scarf around her head appeared.

'Welcome, Refik, come in, come in!' she said, smiling. 'I see you've brought the drummer, good!'

'Yes, this is Qays,' Refik introduced Daud.

'Welcome. They call me 'Umm Harun. The others haven't arrived yet. Why don't you show Qays the tower while we get some tea ready?' The turquoise lady ushered them in.

Refik led the way through to a small room where Daud immediately became aware of the sound of flowing water, and the creak of wood turning on wood or metal. Refik pointed out a shaft which reached from a hole in the ceiling and down through the floor to what must have been a cellar. Daud peered down and could just make out a channel of water feeding into an ancient wood and iron waterwheel. The wheel rotated slowly. They then climbed up the winding staircase of the tower to a height of about three stories and emerged beneath the metal canopy Daud had seen from outside. In the cool night air Refik explained the mystery of the building:

'Listen to the water – where it comes from, and where it is going. A stream of the Barada River flows under this area. It turns the wheel below, and a system of buckets on a chain raises the water up the side of the tower and into that aqueduct.'

Refik pointed just below the ledge near the top of the tower. Daud could just make out the buckets, winding their way up before tipping their water into a stone channel. Refik continued:

'The aqueduct carries the water to the wall of that mosque over there, above the tomb of the Great Sheikh Muhyiddin Ibn 'Arabi. Then it's piped down to work the fountain in the courtyard. Afterwards it returns to the stream from where it came. It's very simple really, and quite beautiful. After all, the water could have just flowed on down the stream, and we'd have been none the wiser. It's like music, like life. It's there to be played, or not, it's our choice. But if we do, ah! It can be so beautiful, don't you think?' He looked at Daud gently, his eyes reflecting the light from the little lantern he carried. Daud looked back at Refik unselfconsciously. Something had fallen from him in the last hour, imperceptibly, shrugged off like an old musty coat. Now he felt a freshness in his chest as he breathed deeply the evening air. He thought about Refik's words. It was so simple, how the water made its detour for no reason other than so a fountain could play in a courtyard. An intelligent arrangement of wood, stone and metal, nothing more, and the water did the rest. A single stream divided. One part turned the wheel to allow another part to rise and fill the fountain for a moment of beauty, before all were rejoined again in the stream.

'Come on,' said Refik, 'I think the others have arrived.'

The tower house had by now filled up with a small group of men sitting and talking quietly. 'Umm Harun was pouring glasses of tea which the little boy (who was named Harun al-Rashid, after the great Sultan) served to the assembly.

The music began almost incidentally: the ney player, a Turk with a fine moustache and deep black hair, blowing gently across the polished horn mouthpiece of the thin reed flute. The chatter subsided and the tinkling of tea glasses ceased with the soft thrill of air vibrated in wood, sighing as wind in a reedbed. Daud felt a shiver of excitement. The notes from the ney gathered strength, not so much from the efforts of the musician as from the arrangement of the notes and the defining passage of breath – the stopping, the moving on, stopping, moving, the sustain fading into pause, then silence, and moving still in the silence. The music sang from beneath the belly and up into the chest, collected itself a while before rising again to the throat and the crown of the head, and then in a wave spread throughout the body of the room.

Refik quietly opened the black case and took out his violin. A beautiful old piece, the wood of its body drank in the light of the room, the varnish glowing like autumn beech leaves. He placed it momentarily on his knee then closed his eyes and slowly raised the instrument to his shoulder, listening, ear to the wood, waiting for the moment to enter the music. He met the ney player somewhere high up on the E-string, and swooped and stepped his music like a bird which soars the high atmosphere almost beyond sight to meet another hovering in wait. The bow danced lightly in the cadenza, with definite steps upon the unfretted strings, and the freed notes flew higher. Daud gazed in amazement. Refik sat so calm, yet the music cried out in a passion that made Daud's blood surge and his heart race. The music seemed to get louder and louder, until he realised that his hand had begun to tap the Drum. Before he knew it he was standing in the centre of the gathering, beating out a steady, rolling rhythm and turning in a circle, his right foot propelling him upon the pivot of his left, round and round. He found he was watching himself, fascinated but unafraid, careful only to beat the Drum in time. In time to what, he wondered. He didn't know. But somehow he knew the right beat, the right time. It was the same as the beating of his heart. But his heart was racing. He no longer just heard the music, but felt it as a wave of energy turning his whole being. Nor could he see the forms of the people sitting around, for they had blurred into rings of light, moons orbiting a spinning planet. He calmed the beat with his breath. His heartbeat followed, and he turned more slowly. Then suddenly came a new awakening. While still moving, he had become the still point for everything around him. He became aware of every detail of the room and the people in it revolving upon his own axis as if contained within the aura of his being. And then nothing.

Afterwards Daud realised he had closed his eyes, but at the time it seemed he and the world had vanished. He became aware of an endless depth of black, yet it was not darkness – rather, the matter of light itself, before the shining forth, before the addition or differentiation of colours, before the division of source and object. It was a kind of dying accompanied by a profound stillness.

And in the stillness Daud felt something completely new, something which in retrospect he could only describe as a feeling of complete security, a happiness that came from somewhere deep in his heart. If he could have spoken at this moment, he would only have gasped, 'Aaaaaaaaaaaaah!!' And that would have been enough. He had been touched in the depth of his being, where words fail, and cries and sighs convey better such news. For the present, it was the stillness which took him to itself, the stillness that comes when the two ends of self are joined. He opened his eyes and stopped turning. Other musicians had begun to play. He looked down and saw that the Drum, hanging in his left hand, was swinging of its own accord against the fingertips of his right hand. Daud realised then that the Drum had set the rhythm of the music, to which he had responded, much as an instrument responds to the player.

Gradually the music subsided. 'Umm Harun made more tea, and plates of sweet pastries came round. Daud didn't know quite what to think. Here he was, suddenly among a group of people whom he had never met before, with a Drum which seemed – no, not seemed – actually *had* a life of its own. And Refik, the beautiful violin player sitting opposite just looking at him kindly as if he could see right into his soul, as if he had known all along what would happen to Daud, and wasn't surprised that he could play the Drum... but Daud felt too happy to worry about such imponderables. He was alive again. And even if it wasn't quite the life he had known before, it wasn't so different either.

After a while the session broke up and Daud and Refik were standing

outside the tower house again, in the cool night air.

'Do you fancy going for something to eat?' suggested Refik.

'Something to drink, more like…' Daud began. 'Oh dear, sorry, I hope I haven't shocked you.' Daud had been so at ease with his new friend that it had never occurred that Refik might be religious.

'No, that's fine by me. We could go over to the Christian quarter,' said Refik, cheering to the idea.

'My thoughts entirely!' And arm in arm like brothers they walked off down the street.

From beneath Daud's other arm, the arm which cradled the Drum, came a soft, long, drawn out sound, akin to air escaping from skin or tube. Daud noticed the Drum's skin slacken, but only heard what he thought was the sound of a pigeon flap by, close to his head.

'Aaaaaaaaaaaaaaaaaaaaaaah. At last,' Shams exhaled to himself. He had been feeling bored fit to burst these last few weeks. Initially, he had not minded, as he had been quite preoccupied since his departure from earthly pastures at Seydnaya. To begin with, in the process of being re-absorbed into the Light, certain very goatish qualities, such as his need to eat, drink and evacuate, and the desire to procreate enthusiastically and often, had been cut away. Then, just as his horny old hide had been scraped and stretched and pounded in ash, so too the soul of the goat underwent a transformation. It was washed and polished in the light of its capricornian essence, then buffed up until it shone with its original quality of guidance, the same quality which during Shams' time on earth had manifested in the form of head goat leading the herd.

Now Shams had re-emerged, a spiritual presence embodied in a drum, and had made himself heard, albeit tentatively. He had been sorely tempted to make Daud trip up in the middle of his whirling drum performance. That would have livened things up. But no, he wasn't yet ready for such treatment. The poor chap was so earnest it made Shams droop at the thought. So he had contented himself with leading Daud just a little out of the dark cell of his sorry self and onto the threshold of a wider picture.

'At least he's going to have a drink now, and we'll make sure he gets good and plastered. It won't do for him to dwell on tonight's events. Oh, but it would have been such fun to see him land in the arms of 'Umm Harun. She'd have laughed as much as I would've.' The mere consideration of this untoward possibility provoked a chuckle in this shaman-skin, which manifested in strange undulations and the emission of a sound that can only be described as 'whooooaallopullop'. But Daud and Refik were deep in conversation, and heard only the fart of a passing donkey. It was early days.

TEN

The deadly tentacles of Omo Sharleen

HE cool, moist breezes of the Eastern Mediterranean met the warm, desert winds of Arabia over the Shouf Mountains behind Beirut, where, mingling, their combining excitement caused the air to rise and thunderous clouds to gather, presaging rain. Two gryphon vultures circled high upon these voluptuous currents, while below in the cleft of a pine-clad valley, dark forces gathered within the portals of a rich man's palace.

Omo Sharleen stood with his back to the room. He flicked a hair from the shoulder of his dark cashmere jacket. It was a white hair and the jacket had been made by his Jewish tailor, the pattern copied from an English naval officer's uniform. He mused momentarily on the need to have his roots darkened again, then his attention was deflected by the softness of cloth and the beauty of the jacket's cut. Contemplating his image reflected in the Louis XIV ormolu-framed mirror behind his desk, he enjoyed a private moment of self-admiration, pausing briefly from the incessant telling of the fat yellow beads of his amber *tesbih*. Then remembering the business in hand, Omo Sharleen turned back to the room and addressed the four figures standing before him:

'As you are aware, we were involved recently in a take-over bid of a certain asset-rich company on the Homs-Damascus Road. Unfortunately, although four weeks have passed, the transaction has not yet been completed. While all those with power of attorney were unanimous in their agreement to surrender the company's interests in total, the major shareholder – that is, the sole shareholder – is unable, or unwilling to be contacted. Now, this may be of little consequence in the grand scheme of things, but it is untidy, and I do so hate untidiness. You understand?'

The four listened and nodded in silence.

'So it is of the utmost urgency that we contact our dear shareholder that the surrender of the company may be made absolute. Have I made myself clear?'

The four nodded again.

'We shall divide the country thus: 'Abdul Qabid, ' Omo Sharleen spoke directly to a thin man with one eye and a pinched-looking face. 'I want you to take the north coast, up around Tartous and Arwad. I believe you have some good contacts in that area. Perhaps his family have heard from him. If not, they are bound to be concerned, and may help us track him down.'

Abdul Qabid smiled to himself, his narrow lips not parting, his good eyelid, his left, lowering into a half-closed position. The empty socket of his right eye (lost in childhood when it was hooked instead of a fish on a badly cast line) was hidden beneath a loose fold of cloth hanging from his black turban. Abdul Qabid was a successful loan shark. Very few people knew of his connection to Omo Sharleen, although they had worked together for years. In fact it was mostly Sharleen's money that Abdul Qabid lent out. The Islamic proscription on usury was circumvented by having all the loans made out in the names of his Jewish clerks.

Abdul Qabid's method was simple but effective. Loans were made on the basis of a modest fixed fee for the first month, or part thereof, usually one perecent of the capital. Interest was calculated from the first day of the month during which the loan was taken out. If the loan wasn't paid in total within a month, interest immediately became due at a rate of two percent for the first month already passed, and then four percent for the second month (which had just begun). If the loan went unpaid, the rate of interest rose to eight percent for the third month, and so on. Loans were available any given day before midday. Repayments were handled after midday.

It was surprising how many people, believing that a loan taken out before midday on the 1st of Muharrem would be payable before midday on the 1st of Safar, would forget and arrive at Abdul Qabid's office on the 1st of Safar to pay their debt, only to discover that they should have paid on the previous afternoon, the last day of Muharrem. Not only would the debtors now incur an increase in interest rate to two percent for the month just passed, but also, because the contract then stipulated interest to be paid monthly for any part of a month in which the debt remained unpaid, they would have to find another four percent on top. Of course, as Abdul Qabid would point out, they would have a full 29 days to find this extra money. The matter of loans was further complicated by the fact that people were never quite sure exactly when the new month would begin, as this depended on the actual sighting of the new moon, something which varied according to the weather. In addition Abdul Qabid's office was closed on Fridays, and the Jewish clerks were never seen on Saturdays.

Now, if after a while it became evident that the debtor was unable to pay... well, this was how he got the name 'the Squeezer'. While Abdul Qabid's threats were dire, they were always accompanied with suggestions as to how the debtor might just be able to cover the interest for that month. Perhaps a smuggling run, or a little theft, or, if the unfortunate victim was privy to information which might be useful to Sharleen's organisation, a little espionage. But simply paying off the interest did not reduce the rate charged, which increased exponentially like the legendary grains of rice upon the chessboard. Having fallen within Abdul Qabid's grasp, the grip would gradually tighten, until the sum owed grew so great that only the performing of a capital offence would suffice to pay it off. A few miserable souls would depart quietly in the night, having already signed over the title deeds of their property to the loan shark. Others would despair and be driven to suicide. Some of the wealthier ones, invariably young gamblers abandoned by Lady Luck, turned to their fathers who reluctantly paid up in full, rather than suffer the shame upon the family name. Many remained in ever-growing debt and lived thenceforth in the service of 'the Squeezer'.

Omo Sharleen now turned to a second man. Abdul Qahhar wore the garb of a desert herder, black cloak, sheepskin waistcoat, face bearded and sun-darkened. He was Omo Sharleen's private assassin. To anyone else he was just the man who trained Omo Sharleen's hunting dogs. An expert tracker and an inhabitor of the wild places, Abdul Qahhar was rumoured to be half jinn, because of his way with animals, and his habit of shunning the company of men. He preferred the company of dogs, and spent most of his time on Sharleen's desert estates. Here he trained his master's prized Salukis and spied on passing caravans. He was central to Sharleen's spy network, communicating with the nomad camps which tracked between the Negev and the mountains of Iran, from the Jebel Lubnan to the markets of Baghdad and Basra. When not directly employed on a job for Omo Sharleen, he spent his time hunting deer and lion, for killing was what gave meaning to his life. It wasn't a blood lust, and he never killed in anger; for lust and anger clouded the necessary cool perception for this business and caused mistakes. The pleasure was in the art of execution: the preparation, the tracking down, the chase, and then the denouement. And he was always successful. In matters of death, there was no room for chance or accident. In this, the two men were of one mind. If Omo Sharleen trusted anyone, it was Abdul Qahhar.

'Abdul Qahhar, first I want you to visit our colleague Taymir al Bad. It's time he received his pension… A golden handshake perhaps? After all, he's been in the job a long time. His retirement would suit everyone. Then go over the area where the caravan passed. It could be that our elusive share-holder is still around. Perhaps he is lost. Perhaps he has died. But should you find him, I'm sure you will take great care of him.' There was the rarest hint of sincerity in Omo Sharleen's eyes as he smiled at his assassin. Abdul Qahhar, for his part, returned his glance without emotion, with the look of a cat whose spirit is occupied elsewhere.

The third man was balding, pudgy and bespectacled, and though wearing a *yarmulke* he was not actually Jewish. While indeed nursed on the bosom of Abraham, he was however of the line of Ismail, and merely affected Jewishness as a cover, better to infiltrate the trading entrepots of the east Mediterranean. Known as Haywani the Jew, his given name was Al Muntaqim, the Vengeful One. A gatherer of information, he practiced his profession in the brothels and private drinking clubs of the Levant. He understood the compulsion men have to confide their innermost thoughts in the calm aftermath of a passionate encounter, especially when lubricated with strong Bekaa wine or arak and encouraged by flattery and solicitous after-play. He paid his female informers well for these snippets, and in spite of his repulsive appearance, his wealth gave him entry to most of the Beirut hotspots.

Haywani's trading connections meant he was well placed to look after the disposal and export of Sharleen's stolen goods, and he was involved with smuggling on a grand scale. He had transacted deals with Daud's agents on a number of occasions, and having got wind of Daud's caravan and its valuable cargo, it was Haywani who first suggested this possible source of revenue for the Sharleen estate. He had never met Daud, but knew many who had. If the truth be told, he had always been rather envious of the man.

Haywani had met a very beautiful girl in a Beirut brothel. A fair-haired blue-eyed Circassian, he had fallen head over heels in love. Again and again he had paid the enormous price she asked, until he was intimate with every curve, scent and texture of her body's landscape. Yet, in spite of the *laissez faire* she granted him through all the gates and byways of her corporeal city, and although she smiled a smile which melted hearts, nary a glance had Haywani been permitted of her soul; not a hair's breadth had her heart opened to his advances. And in the depth of his carnality he fell into dangerous obsession.

One day Haywani arrived to find the beautiful Circassian gone. A trader from Arwad had visited the brothel, and the moment the girl had laid eyes on him, the ramparts of her inner sanctum had collapsed as a sandcastle before a wave. That trader was Daud. He had paid off the brothel-keeper and set up the girl in a villa in the hills above the city. Haywani buried his distress in a riot of indulgence with the city's whores. His hurt pride had been partially assuaged by the plan to take Daud's caravan, but now the opportunity for revenge awakened in him thoughts of the girl, and he gleefully awaited Sharleen's instructions.

Sharleen looked at Haywani with a mixture of pity and disgust; intrigued to discover how he could manipulate Haywani's passion for his own ends. Sharleen addressed him enthusiastically:

'If the Arwadi is alive, he'll want to see his women eventually. Maybe one of them is hiding him. Check out the ports, watch all their apartments, speak to their friends, visit the brothels, I'm sure you can discover things, as it were, 'between the sheets.' Omo Sharleen exchanged a smutty school-boy smirk with the loathsome Haywani before adding, 'and then, I believe you have some unfinished business with our Shareholder?'

'No worries, Boss.' Haywani responded, with a chuckle.

The fourth and final figure was dressed head to foot in a grey burqa, the all-covering garb of a woman of Arabia. Not even the eyes could be seen through the fine mesh of the head covering. Whether it was to hide the person's identity, or simply feminine modesty, was not disclosed. Sharleen spoke briefly:

'Your domain is Damascus. Be my ears and my eyes, and if a situation offers itself, be my hand.'

The grey-clad figure nodded, and immediately took its leave. No name, no pack drill. It was known that Sharleen had spies in places other criminals were only dimly aware of, if at all. Of the other three, only Abdul Qahhar was part of Sharleen's inner circle, whose members were never introduced to each other. The infamous circle might have included the maid, the cook and the gate-keeper; or equally the Governor of Jerusalem, the Harbour Master at Tyre or the wife of a Damascene Pasha. Perhaps the figure in the grey burqa was such a one, but they would never have known.

A servant appeared shortly afterwards bearing a polished silver tray of tea in small glasses on tiny porcelain saucers. He handed one to each man and left with the tray. This was the normal procedure. They drank their tea. Sharleen handed each man a small but heavy purse, and the three cronies departed.

Soon afterwards, the servant re-entered the room. Instead of picking up the glasses as one might expect, he walked over to the desk, took a cigarette from the silver case on Omo Sharleen's desk, lit it from a candle set in the wall and sat down in one of the many gilded armchairs around the walls of the room.

'Well, what do you think,' began Sharleen. 'Can we trust them?'

'That depends. No problems with Abdul Qahhar of course. He's in it for the sport. The others, of course not. Abdul Qabid is only ever out to save his own skin, and as for that fat, spineless, would-be Jew….' the man grunted in derision, 'But can they do the job? That's really the question. Abdul Qabid is squeamish. If he finds the Arwadian he'll put the squeeze on one of his marks to do the dirty, so to speak. If Haywani finds him, it'll be a case of who kills whom; and if Haywani does get in first, he's bound to leave a trail. Is he expendable?'

'They're all expendable. But my feeling is that our man is in Damascus anyway, or at least on his way there. I sense it somehow. But why haven't we found him?'

'You know, the slowest caravans bring home the biggest treasure.'

Sharleen smiled, 'By the way, most becoming, the grey burqa. You cut a fine figure.'

Grey Burqa Man just picked up the tray, and with an almost imperceptible tossing of the head, said, 'See you in Damascus' and walked from the room.

ELEVEN

The Drum speaks

AUD sat outside the coffee shop in an alley behind the great Umayyad Mosque. Here under the high window he could listen to the sing-song voice of the *hakawati*, the old story-teller inside the cafe. Nursing a hangover from the previous night's drinking, he didn't feel like company. However, it was a shady spot, and he always enjoyed the wonderful tales that the hakawatis told.

Dozing off in an effort to rid himself of the painful throbbing in his head, his dreams were sweet. He saw again that delightful face which he had encountered in his recent wanderings, the love-inspiring beauty which made his heart expand and thoughts vanish. He tried desperately to address the vision in his slumber but his ardour remained in his chest. No words came. The vision fled.

When Daud awoke his head was clear, but his throat was dry, so he went inside the coffee house. He found a seat near the door and signalled to the waiter, who brought over some coffee and water. The hakawati was sitting nearby with some friends discussing the flaws and bad character of people from Beirut. Daud understood from their conversation that their complaint related to their Beiruti landlords, who lived a life of ease on the high rents they charged the tenants of their Damascene properties. The talk was light-hearted, a way of venting spleen from the underlying

disgruntlement. After a while the hakawati returned to his pulpit.

'*Ya Shadid al Batsh! Ya Jemil! Ya Rabb!...*' 'O Thou the most Forceful in Assault! O Most Beautiful! O Lord!...' The old hakawati chanted in Arabic, and waved a crude metal sword above his head, crying 'Blessings on the Prophet!' which evoked the response from his audience: 'And upon his family and companions, and peace.'

The hakawati sat upon a gaily painted wooden throne, set on a raised plinth covered with carpets. He was about sixty years old, with a dark moustache, grey-haired beneath his wine-red fez, and silver wire-rimmed spectacles bridging a narrow but well-shaped nose of good length. He wore a pale cotton shirt beneath a bright red and white woven waistcoat, and over his shoulders was draped a cream cashmere shawl. A white cummerbund and brown pantaloons completed the ensemble.

The storyteller began to recite in a very dramatic voice as if repeating a chant, in phrases of regular metre and equal length. Although he had a large book open on his lap, he only glanced at it once or twice to pick up his place from the day before. From time to time he slammed down with the flat of his sword, *whack!!* onto a metal stool to emphasise a point. Occasionally he would pause, giving time for the narrative to sink in, pick up his glass of tea from a little ironwork table by his knee, and take a few sips. Then replacing the glass on the table, he would continue his recitation.

'*Wa la hawla wa la quwatta illah billah!*' the hakawati repeated the holy phrase, 'There is no power nor strength save in God!', at the same time peering conspiratorially over his glasses at the gathering of urbane Damascenes, sipping coffee and puffing lazily on water pipes.

A fresh glass of tea arrived, and with a small spoon, the hakawati stirred in the sugar. Then, carefully so as not to spill any, he lifted a couple of spoonfuls to his lips, revealing a large gap between his lower front teeth, just as some people have in their upper front teeth. For Daud this feature had a strange and powerful significance.

Daud studied the pictures on the wall above the hakawati's little throne. There was a carved wooden calligraphy in a gilded frame, typical Damascus decorative woodwork. This piece was flanked by two old paintings: one of a gallant Arab warrior, in a gold helmet and sporting the most extravagant moustache. He was holding in his right hand a long lance, while with his left he was pointing to the sky. The knight was mounted on a black horse, gaily bedecked in golden straps and tassels and prancing light-footed and proud. The second picture showed an almond-eyed maiden who held in her hand something which looked to Daud like a pine-cone with a bird sitting upon it. Or maybe, he thought, it could be a pomegranate. Her horse was a bay, pale golden in colour, and dancing skittishly. The eyes of both knight and maiden gazed directly at the audience, compelling attention. These two were the chief protagonists of the story that the hakawati was now telling, the famous tale of Antar, the darkly handsome, brave but lowly born warrior, and the fair and beloved Abla, for whom Antar must constantly prove his love to Abla's family with impossibly heroic exploits.

A waiter wandered among the customers with a large brass coffee pot, pouring out small tastes of bitter coffee into tiny cups for anyone who wanted. Daud took a refill. By now the coffee shop was quite full. Another waiter wove carefully between the tables carrying a bucket of glowing charcoal, and with tongs he replenished the fires of the narghilehs. Each smoker had started off with a mound of tobacco as big as a hen's egg, which would take more than an hour to consume.. The air was wreathed in mellow contentment.

The story teller resumed, becoming even more expressive as the episode built to its climax, and leaving the assembly hanging over an abyss of uncertainty until the next instalment. This story would be more than six months in the telling. Everyone applauded, including the hakawati, who, relieved of his tale for the time being, rose to join his friends in more coffee, tobacco and conversation.

'Thank you all,' he said. 'Now, if any of you here know the stories, or if you can spin a good yarn yourself, the chair is free.'

Daud felt the Drum twist gently under his arm. A strange compulsion made him tap lightly on its taut skin, and before he knew it he found himself in the storyteller's seat. Daud beat strongly upon the drum six or seven times and began telling a story. From where it came he had no idea. The story was about an eagle who had lost his wife and children to a hunter. In his misery, he tried to end his life, flying so high into the sky that he went unconscious, and then dropped, crash landing in a dove's nest. This dove had been abandoned by her husband, a fancy tumbler and ne'er-do-well rake. She had then fractured her wing defending her young brood from an attack of jackdaws. The eagle, in a state of amnesia, took the fearful dove

under his wing, bringing her food and water and serving her every need. In time he came to believe he too was a dove, and began to fall in love with his hostess. When the lady dove's wing was mended she had to reveal to her lodger his real identity by taking him down to the lakeside to see his reflection. Then a lone female eagle appeared in the sky, and everything was resolved to the satisfaction of both eagle and dove.

It was a simple story, but as the words came from Daud's mouth, it appeared layered with meanings. Outside the coffee shop the evening call to prayer sounded from the Minaret of Jesus in the Umayyad Mosque opposite. Daud took a sip of water. The audience, still rapt in their imaginations, muttered their appreciation. The hakawati came over chuckling, and helped Daud down from the pulpit, congratulating him on his efforts. There were calls from many tables for Daud to join their company, but he proffered an acceptable excuse, and promising to return soon, slipped out of the cafe.

As he walked through the narrow streets in the cool night air, he thought how strange it was, the way the story had come, appearing in his mind out of thin air, like a picture he was walking through. All he had done was to describe what he saw. He had picked words as if he were gathering scattered beads which then he strung as sentences on the thread of his breath. For now Daud just wanted to sit quietly somewhere and let it all settle.

Back at Touma's store, Daud lay on his bed daydreaming and gazing at the round face of the Drum, 'You are a funny thing,' he said, musing out loud, 'that story, where on earth did it come from?'

As he gazed, he became deeply relaxed, slipping into that in-between state on the edge of sleep and wakefulness where revelations from our deep interior issue forth in tenuous form. It was here, upon the transformed luminosity of the drum's skin, that the face of a shaggy-haired, tufty-bearded old billy goat appeared. And the goat spoke:

'Funny? I'll give you funny! Just look at yourself! Lying there like a teenager in love. As for where that story came from, don't you even know that? It came from where all stories come from, the realm of possibilities. You have heard about the Realm of Possibilities, haven't you?'

Daud opened his eyes and looked at the face in the drum, speechless. Then, with an air of complete disdain the goat condescended to expound upon his own question:

'No? ... and I thought you humans had all the knowledge. But far be it for me, a humble denizen of the animal realm, late thereof, to pass judgement on the ways and the world of men.

'As for the world of possibilities, well quite simply, everything is possible, in one sense, and impossible in another sense, leaving us with the necessary. Remember that, the necessary, and the impossible. Don't mix them up. Anyway, we'll let it go at that for now.'

And with that the apparition of the goat, revealed in the aspect of the scolding schoolmaster, faded. Daud was left gazing at the skin of the drum, wondering what on earth this was all about.

TWELVE

Daud wakes up and smells the coffee

HE following morning found Daud ambling through the market just beyond the Street of the Apothecaries. The panoply of goods appeared as a delightful spread of impressions on all his senses: neat pyramids of tomatoes and potatoes, bundles of long-stalked herbs, peppers green and red, lantern-shaped or dagger-slender; the dye merchants sitting impassive before perfect Vesuvian cones of indigo, scarlet and saffron-coloured powder; the rigorous smells of olive oil soap, alum and raw tallow identifying the laundry suppliers. Iron-buckled leather halters, martingales with blue bead decorations to ward off the evil eye, and saddles cobbled from wood and old pieces of carpet were all laid out on hempen sacks along with knives and hatchets, in the middle of which a grime-faced Kurdish blacksmith beat red-hot iron into horseshoes on a portable forge.

Nearby smoked a small charcoal brazier where an itinerant food vendor was grilling kebabs which he served up wrapped in warm, flat bread with a charred hot pepper and a nosegay of parsley. Daud was ravenous and easily succumbed to the delicious smell of roasting lamb seasoned with lemon and fragrant oregano. He joined a throng of merchants and shoppers all munching away in the shade of a nearby warehouse.

Amidst the lunching crowd a heated debate was taking place between three men. The discussion – really more of a series of rants – centred on the merits of their respective belief systems, prophets and supreme deity. Daud had heard this one before. In every port and city, in every market place in the Middle East it seemed, there were people with nothing better to do than to sound off in most authoritative and categorical tones on deep matters of religion and philosophy. They might well have been comparing the finer points of their fields, their livestock, or even their wives. The hammering tone of their speech irritated Daud and he quit the market before losing his appetite.

His stroll took him back to the coffee shop, scene of the previous day's bizarre occurrences. Ordering coffee, he sat and listened to the final minutes of a tale about a monster of the deep seas whose hunger not even the efforts of Solomon could satisfy. The coffee was delicious, a sweet and perfect complement to the kebab. Daud felt most comfortable. Life was good, whiling away time in the coffee shops of Damascus. 'I could get used to this,' he thought. But as he savoured this notion, the Drum twisted against his knee. He was instantly filled with dread, and with an inner compulsion to move. He thought of taking his place again at the storyteller's pulpit, but that didn't seem to be what was needed. He stood up and immediately the stress in his mind fell away. He left the coffee shop and wandered up the street and around the south-west corner of the Umayyad Mosque.

Seen from above, the great Umayyad Mosque of Damascus is likened to an eagle. Its roofs spread as sheltering wings to enclose the wide prayer halls unfolding on either side of the central body, above which rises the dome, a many-windowed orb encompassing all within its imperial view. As sceptre, mace and spear, three tall minarets anchor its flight in emblems of dominion, might and power. Daud entered the mosque's protective presence by the western door, the Bab al-Barid.

The prayer hall is cool and reflective, its high wooden ceiling supported by great white-painted beams which sit on two double-arched colonnades of pale stone. Pigeons scribe these lofty spaces like trapeze artists on unseen wires, an arcing dance on skeins of light from windowsill to architrave, from capital to chandelier. Here prayer has many forms. People take their ease, some lying full stretched upon the floor and maybe asleep. On the raised sections along the back of the mosque, small groups of women lounge, black bundles of cloth chatting away on the soft pile.

Daud too reclined, propped on an elbow in a corner of the carpet which flowed before him as a sea of red. A marmalade cat stalked the back wall, but the pigeons were safe, roosting in the high beams and upon Corinthian ledges. On his left, a thin sage in a camel-wool cloak and white skull cap was discoursing to a group of young students. Within the mosque is a small building, the domed mausoleum in which is interred the severed head of the Prophet Yahya – St John the Baptist. Nearby sat two sheykhs, wizened old men in red fezzes wound with turbans. They leaned on their walking sticks, one telling his rosary in mental invocation of the names of God, the other singing a low chanting hymn. Looking up, Daud felt he would not be surprised to hear the beating of angels' wings, gold and green among the beams, competing for space with the pigeons. He remembered the lines of his prophet, *'the freshness of my eyes is given to me in prayer'*, and sat a while contemplating the question of what lay beyond the veil of his self-consciousness. It was then that the goat chose to reappear, a glowing apparition once again upon the face of the Drum.

'Now where were we?' he began, taking up where he had left off the day before, as if he had just paused for thought and no time at all had elapsed 'Ah, yes, the world of possibilities. Or, put another way, nothing ever really happens for that would imply that there were two beings in existence, a logical impossibility. As one knows, there is only one. But I'm getting ahead of myself. Let's just leave it at that and get down to the business in hand. After all, nothing really ever leaves the realm of possibilities, because there is only ever what is necessary, and the rest is impossible, in spite of appearances.'

'I know you!' exclaimed Daud. It had finally clicked, where he had seen this goat before, that is. And he was not really surprised to hear it talking to him in this way now, given recent happenings. 'What's your name anyway?'

'Call me Shams,' announced the goat, and paused, as if to let the true weight of this momentous fact sink in. Then, in a serious, even earnest tone, he continued, 'For some reason which I cannot fathom, and which in the wisdom of my current position I have no cause to question, I have been given the task of acting as your guide. And at the moment, for today at least, guidance is what you require. You see, you are in fact in some danger. Not insurmountable, I admit, but nonetheless unavoidable. There is a little unfinished business to attend to following your recent disencumbrance from material goods. You remember that lovely Circassian, the one you so valiantly rescued from the fleshpots of Beirut and set up in the villa in the Lubnan? Well, she's fine. For the present, that is. But it would do well to pay her a visit. Unfortunately in your absence she is again attracting the unwanted attentions of a certain Haywani, the one who fashions himself a yahudi, but who is

nothing but a puffed-up godless reject of an oily Levantine spewed from the pits of Sodom. I think you need to ask him some questions.'

'But what about?' asked Daud.

'Oh, don't ask me,' grunted Shams, 'That's none of my business. But perhaps you should find out why he's visiting the Circassian.' And with that the image of the goat faded, and Daud found himself staring into the blank skin of the Drum.

Outside in the courtyard of the mosque, the heat had gone out of the day. A cool wind blew around the pillars. A tired sun glinted over the edge of the enclosing wall and reflected dully in the gold mosaics. Late afternoon light spread in the white marble paving, giving it the translucence of cold skin, revealing the veins of the stone. Pigeons carved the sky and lined the roof eaves between the mosque dome and the Minaret of Jesus in the south-east corner. Daud looked up at this noble tower and sensed a distant expectancy. He knew that from here, according to tradition, Jesus would descend again in future days to kill the Dajjal – the lying impostor whom others call the anti-Christ – and usher in a new era for humankind. Below, where the last rays of the sun still reached under a little domed kiosk at the far end of the courtyard, a sack of golden corn had been spread out for the birds. Little children who had never seen the sea had made a beach of grain here, heaping it in piles as if sand, following their nature to gather and collect, to order and possess.

From beyond the cloistered court Daud could hear the camel bells of a departing caravan. The slow, distant ringing reminded him of Shams' warning. It was time to move on. He hastened back to his lodgings to collect a few things. He borrowed a little money from Touma, who asked no questions, and then snuck out of a back door into the night. Down the Street Called Straight, he left the Old City by the Bab-i Sharqi, the Eastern Gate. A little beyond, in a dark place in the road, he slipped into an alley and waited a while to make sure he wasn't being followed. He then made his way north-westwards around the outside of the city walls by way of Salihiye, until he reached the road by which he had entered Damascus.

Daud took the Beirut road, mingling with the country people leaving the city at the close of day. He fell in with a goatherd returning to his village. The man had sold all his milk and cheeses, and most of the year's offspring from his herd. A pair of kid goats, one of each sex, had remained unsold. He offered them to Daud at well below market price. Daud could not imagine why he should want to encumber himself with a pair of young goats, and laughed at the goatherd's offer. Then the Drum, which had been quiet and well-behaved all this time, twisted perceptibly under his arm and let out an audible sigh, so that Daud almost dropped it on the road. The goatherd showed no sign of alarm, and just smiled. For Daud, this was a sign, certainly, but why?

Why indeed? Why was he here walking in the middle of the night on the road out of Damascus? Why did he feel just then a queer tightening in the pit of his stomach as some of his fellow travellers turned off in the direction of Seydnaya? Something was compelling him, moving him along in ways that seemed beyond his control. It wasn't just the Drum. Yes, that did effect things. But the Drum was simply a mirror to his soul, ordering the thoughts which he couldn't formulate clearly, throwing light on decisions which needed confirming. Even the apparitions of the goat felt quite natural. Daud found himself operating on two levels. There was his normal thinking processes, endlessly circular and repetitive. And then at other times his mind stilled and a different perception took over. This was like watching a pool of water, and distinguishing between the surface reflection and the details underneath. It usually happened when he was relaxed and allowed his mind to drift. Or sometimes like now when something needed to be heard the Drum simply brought him to attention. Then he knew something was required of him, whether action or inaction. Right now he knew that it would be a very good thing to purchase these two goats, and so he did.

THIRTEEN

A scorpion tale

EIRUT, pearl of the eastern Mediterranean, a black pearl to some. Natal earth to St George, who is a resonance of Al-Khidr, seer of unseen worlds, verdant guide of those to whom Reality reveals Itself without intermediary. Al-Khidr is the Green Man, and also Elijah – and St George, dragon slayer for a maiden's virtue, gritty captain in the oyster shell of the Roman army, whose legend has him martyred three times before his body vanishes; St George, whose namesake is carried in that opaline band of sea crowning the northern shores of the city of his birth, Beirut.

Gülbahar gazed down from the balcony of her villa. Far below the creamy blue shallows of St George's Bay spread out to distant, darker seas. A light breeze lifted up from the waters, rustling through the pines and cypresses which clung to the slopes and filtered out the noise and dust of the city, cooling the midday heat of her secluded home. It had been many months since she had seen her Daud. That was not a problem. She knew not to expect anything from him, and was thankful to be removed from the squalor of her previous existence. The deeds for the villa were in her own name – Daud had insisted on that.

Bad news travels quickly in the east, especially where it concerns money, and both Gülbahar's and Daud's bankers were aware of the caravan's disappearance. Gülbahar's stipend, arranged through a Greek banker in the city, had not been paid that month. The Greek had not heard from Daud himself, and rumours were rife. Regrettably, the Greek had informed Gülbahar's banker, although Daud's credit was good, for the present his bank would not be making the usual payment.

Gülbahar wasted no time. Of course she could have survived by selling odd pieces of jewellery and fine garments – gifts from past admirers – but no one knows what the future will bring, and she didn't want to dip into her pension. In any case, she still possessed attractive tangible assets, with options which could easily be realised if necessary. 'A girl's got to do what a girl's got to do.' she told herself, having decided to return, strictly on her own terms, to her earlier profession, and quietly let it be known that she was in the market again. She would have no trouble attracting some of her former preferred patrons for discreet awaydays from Beirut.

Gülbahar had lost none of her beauty; the quiet and orderly life as mistress of her own house, combined with the pure air of the hills, had given her pale Circassian complexion an affectionate bloom, such as one finds in the skin of a white peach. There had begun to germinate in her the seeds of a simple appreciation of life's gifts, seeds planted in the carefree days of her childhood in a mountain village in the Caucasus. Gülbahar was no stranger to the earth, and in no time at all she had transformed the terraced garden in front of the villa into a small vineyard. Between the vines she planted tomatoes and peppers, salads and herbs. Olive trees interspersed with citrus – lemon, orange, grapefruit and bergamot – covered the slopes above. Flowers surrounded the house, leafy wisteria and fragrant honeysuckle trailed the walls, while potted geraniums flanked steps and balconies.

It was quite natural then, on seeing a vagrant goatherd hauling up the path with a couple of young kid goats, for Gülbahar to wonder if the time hadn't come to introduce livestock to her estate. She went down to meet the ragged wanderer. As their eyes met, Daud put a finger to his lips, to suppress her anticipated cry of recognition.

Gülbahar frowned in puzzlement, and intrigued said nothing. Only when Daud spoke did she realise that this lean and bearded man was her former lover, so drastically changed was his appearance.

'Yes, it's me. Can you believe it?' he said softly, smiling with friendly familiarity into the powder blue pools of her eyes. She remembered that cheeky smile of his and instantly the eye of her heart opened in recognition.

Daud explained in brief the reasons for his subterfuge, without disclosing any information that might compromise her. Then on the pretext of entering into negotiations for the purchase of the goats, she offered him some food and they went inside where they could talk without the risk of being overheard.

'Look, I've been warned that this Haywani chap is going to try and see you. It's something to do with the bandits who ambushed my caravan, and I need to know what he's up to. Is there any way you could help?'

Gülbahar gave Daud a sheepish look, and said quite matter of factly that in her current circumstances she had considered returning to the 'entertainment business'. 'In the best possible taste, you understand.'

'Of course, in the best possible taste. You don't have to explain.' A shadow of memory invaded his consciousness. A face. A scent. But it was not Gülbahar's. It was as if his very being had departed, and Gülbahar understood at once. She felt a mixture of sadness tinged with relief. It was just a moment, then Daud was back, concentrated, resolute. 'Look, this gives me an idea,' Daud continued. 'Haywani would be up here like a shot if he thought he had the chance of another slice of cherry pie. Maybe if...'

'Ugh!' spat out Gülbahar. 'He disgusts me! You disgust me!' Then she laughed. Something of the old relationship, the warmth and ease of the friendship they enjoyed, returned. 'I think I may have an idea. But you'll have to keep out of the way. If he suspects for an instant that you're still alive, or that I know anything, the game will be up.'

'Don't worry, I'll hang out somewhere nearby, just another lonely goatherd high on a hill. No one takes any notice of us.'

It had been Haywani who, through discreet enquiry and careful analysis of market information, had originally discovered Daud's plan to liquidate his assets and secretly transport his fortune in gold to Damascus. Haywani believed that a similar line of investigation among his contacts in the Levant ports would also yield fruit now. But so far his efforts to find Daud had drawn a blank. Yes, there had been rumours in the past that he was moving his business to Damascus, or was it Aleppo? But nobody had seen or heard anything of the Arwadi for months. As Daud hadn't left any debts, no one was unduly concerned. That's Beirut. No questions, no lies.

Haywani was definitely not on the list of Gülbahar's preferred patrons. However, men will boast among themselves where women are concerned, and it was not long before news that Gülbahar was again plying her trade came to the ears of the loathsome Levantine. 'Does this mean the Arwadi really is dead?' he wondered. 'Maybe the girl knows something. And if she is…' Here the smog of lust clouded what little light of judgement remained to illuminate his addled mind. So convinced was he that the beautiful Circassian would welcome him into her arms that he was emboldened to journey up into the hills at the earliest opportunity.

Haywani had to beat his donkey throughout the steep ascent to Gülbahar's villa, the poor beast being accustomed only to the gentle avenues of the city. In thrashing his mount Haywani fought off any remaining doubts regarding Gülbahar. 'She must know something.' *Whack,* 'Otherwise, why would she need to be taking clients again?' *Whack! Whack!* 'He must be dead.' *Whack,* 'I'm back in the saddle!…' *Thwack!* Gradually, though, all thoughts for the real object of his mission vanished in the dust and sweat of his ride, and with the rising passion of anticipated congress.

Gülbahar looked down on the steep winding track that led through the grove of cypress and pine below her villa. She beheld this not-so-unexpected visitor, red faced and grimy, astride a miserable donkey which staggered beneath its rider's weight. She felt revulsion as she remembered her past experience with Haywani. Then she remembered Daud, and the danger he was now facing, and she became resolute.

She called out to her maid, a young girl, another Circassian whom she had brought with her from the brothel. 'We appear to have a visitor. Go and welcome him. Show him to a room, let him take a bath. Tell him I'll be down shortly. Make him feel relaxed.'

The day was getting hotter. Although Haywani's intemperate passion had wilted under the strain of the climb, he was encouraged that his unannounced appearance had not been cause for rejection. He now welcomed the suggestion of a bath, and as he relaxed in the steamy atmosphere of the small hamam, sluicing himself with a silver scoop from the white marble basin, his fantasy slowly revived.

The maid returned with towels and a jug of *ayran,* and suggested that Haywani make himself comfortable in the bedchamber next door. It was an old wooden house, formerly the country retreat of an Ottoman bey. The room had cedar panelled walls and a wooden ceiling with cross beams and starred panels painted in green, gold and red. The midday sun cut through the slats of the shutters sending bright shafts deep into the room. Haywani drank the cool yoghurt drink, gave a self-congratulatory belch, and lay down on the low divan. The young girl returned and began the massage. 'Ah!' he sighed to himself, 'I am in heaven, and she is surely a houri.'

The maid's strong fingers worked along his back from the base of his spine to his tired shoulders and into the base of his skull. Haywani drifted into a state of deep and pleasurable relaxation. He did not notice as Gülbahar slipped in quietly and replaced the maid's hands with her own upon his disrobed corpulence. He felt only a mild stirring in that pit of pain and pleasure which sits below the navel as she stroked firmly from the soles of his feet and along the back of his thighs, upwards towards the seat of this warmth. Haywani groaned faintly, 'Second heaven...'

Gülbahar giggled. 'Oh, is that nice?' she asked solicitously.

'O Gülbahar, it's you...you have no idea,' said Haywani, sinking into bliss and groaning even more. 'how much I have missed you.'

'Come on, Haywani, I bet you say that to all the girls.'

'No really, Gülbahar, there's no one like you, not in all Beirut, nor Tyre nor even Sidon.'

'Oh, you're so charming today.' She purred, feathering his back with the tips of her fingers, making the soft hairs over his shoulder blades rise in delight. A shiver ran through his whole body.

'I've been so miserable since you left Beirut with that Arwadi. I didn't know what to do at first, I tried all the other brothels, but none of the girls were anywhere near as good as you, not even the Egyptians. Didn't come close. Not even those big girls from the Sudan.'

'O bless! You're too sweet' and she began to press gently over his skull with her fingers, across his forehead to his eyebrows, and with the cool flat of her hands she slowly swept the tension from his closed eyes and puffy cheeks.

Haywani sighed, 'But I suppose you're still with him, are you? Expecting him soon?'

'Him? Oh, you mean the Arwadi? No, he left and never came back. Why do you ask?

'No reason in particular. I was just thinking, hoping really, that maybe, you know, seeing as… well… if you're not with him any more… and well, we had such fun… maybe we could… again…'

Perhaps because he was now so relaxed, his immediate desire abated. He became a child in Gülbahar's arms, a patient in skilful hands, subject both to her charms and her devices. She leant over and breathed softly in his ear.

'But was that the only reason you came here? Surely not just for me?…' she whispered, gently diverting Haywani's train of thought, while at the same time delivering subtle pressure, some might call caresses, in ever more sensitive areas of his person. 'And anyway, you must have heard that the Arwadi was not here… the money stopped coming ages ago. The banker said he'd not had any funds. And the caravan didn't arrive… He must have been killed.'

'The caravan, you know about the *caravan*…?'

'You know about the caravan?' Gülbahar's ministrations became more intimate, and Haywani let out another sigh.

'Aaaah…Well, yes, you know, one hears things…in the market… gossip…'

'Oh really, like what? What things have you heard?' Gülbahar once more lowered her head to his ear. The warmth of her breath and the delicate scent of her skin so close softened his will like wine. She rested her head besides his and gazed innocently into his eyes.

Haywani's desire for intimacy now reached bursting point. Something had to give. The yearning in his soul had grown beyond simple lust, but he was out of his depth. While the soul of Gülbahar was that of an empress, Haywani's was but a slave prostrate at her outermost gate. He felt an over-powering urge to unburden himself to her, and he didn't hold back. Loyalty to his previous life, such as fear and vanity may have inspired, was abandoned to a kind of love. His inhibitions flew out of the window as he gave chapter and verse, in so far as it was known to him, of the business of Omo Sharleen, including the ambush and the seeming failure by Taymir al-Bad and his gang to dispose of Daud, and the recent meeting with Sharleen and the three other henchmen.

'Well, that's the long and the short of it.' said Haywani in conclusion. 'So you really think he's dead?'

Gülbahar feigned a sorrowful look, and turned to gaze wistfully out of the window, letting her glance rest in a nearby olive tree, its branches threading skeins of light in the spinning silver of its leaves. She was so taken by her own theatrical display that she failed to notice, lying along one of the branches, chameleon-like among the darker leaves, the slim figure of her maid. Gülbahar turned back to the deflated heap upon the divan.

'If Daud was alive, he would have come to me. I'm sure of it.' She spoke with deadly certainty, clutching her hands to her bosom.

Haywani took her hands and pulled her towards him, a pitiful look in his eyes. 'Please, please, let me be your lover. I could love you just as much as he. I would never abandon you.'

It was a sorry sight, and though Gülbahar found it difficult not to be affected by the pathetic spectacle, the thought of him as her lover repulsed her. Nevertheless she continued to play her part, firstly falling into his arms, as if willing to yield, then gently pushing him away.

'Oh that I could, but it's the wrong time of the month. It's such a nuisance, you know how it is. And it's so hot today, let's just rest here a while. Who knows ... another day... what might be possible ...?'

Haywani was initially crestfallen, but the emotion of his newfound yearning had taken the heat out of his randiness, and he became philosophical. Being philosophical was a novel experience for Haywani, but he fumbled away heroically, pouring out epithets and couplets, a veritable Saki of love talk and wisdom words.

Meanwhile the maid had climbed down from the olive tree and was busy in the kitchen garden, crouched down, carefully upturning rocks with one hand and holding a jar and a lid in the other.

Gülbahar eventually left Haywani, failed assassin, and failed seducer, dozing in the heat of the afternoon. When the day began to cool a little, the maid brought him his clothes and served him coffee, cold water and some baklava. Suitably refreshed, he said goodbye and set off on his donkey.

Haywani could not have been gone more than three or four minutes down the Beirut road when a loud scream rose up through the trees below the villa. Gülbahar and the maid rushed out to discover poor Haywani rolling on the ground. He was in evident agony, clutching at his nether parts and desperately pulling away the folds of his robe.

'Help, help, something stung me.' Haywani was weeping now, his face smeared with dust and tears.

'There, there,' Gülbahar cooed soothingly, 'You'll soon be right as rain.

Let me see.'

And with that, she parted his reddened, flaccid thighs in time to see a scorpion lift its tail and sting away heartily in the dark conjunction of his limbs. Haywani lay there and shuddered, sucking in his breath in fits and moaning softly. The maid reached in and carefully removed the creature, returning it to under a stone. Then quick as a flash she took a small knife from under her skirt and made a small but deep incision where the scorpion had stung. The blade cut curiously close to his nether parts. Gülbahar looked at her maid with surprise. Then for a brief moment a picture came into her mind, it was the olive tree seen from the window earlier, but this time she saw a figure on the branch. She understood. The maid had heard everything. She was fiercely loyal to her mistress, and to Daud who had saved them both from the brothel. This was her way of paying a debt of gratitude, a scorpion in the folds of the fat man's robes, a quick snick of a knife to leech the poison and to relieve him of the burden of his desire. Nothing could be simpler.

For Haywani, the shock was too great: the climb up the hill, the heat of the day, the excitement of the afternoon with Gülbahar, and then the scorpion making a feast of his manhood. In the end it was simply his heart which gave up. At least, that was how the event was reported. Gülbahar and the maid had lain Haywani's corpse on his donkey, covered, and taken it a mile or so away from the villa, where they unloaded it again onto the road. Gülbahar made a courtesy call on the chief of police who happened to be one of her 'preferred clients', and that was that. Case closed.

Back in Beirut, Haywani's wife received her husband's corpse, tied to the donkey, late at night, with a death certificate from the police chief. It simply read: 'Cause of Death: heart failure due to scorpion bite while riding. Attempt to bleed the wound failed to revive.' It was never questioned. Why should it? Fat men falling off their mounts, an everyday occurrence. When Omo Sharleen eventually heard of Haywani's passing away, events had moved on and it was old news.

Daud had observed the death throes of Haywani at a careful distance. That evening, Gülbahar repeated Haywani's confession word for word. So, Daud was a very wanted man. This news did not entirely surprise him. He was beginning to take Touma's, and Shams' warnings seriously. The strange turns his life had taken since setting out from Arwad: the caravan ambush, his mountain and desert wanderings, the meeting with the girl by the pool, the goat, the drum, the musicians and the stories, all these events had given him a depth of experience which had more than compensated for the material loss of his gold. However, although he was not in fear of his life, it was tedious at times maintaining his incognito. And now he had a bunch of assassins on his trail. He could only be vigilant and be prepared for any eventuality. 'Oh well,' Daud mused, 'one down, three to go, I suppose the odds are improving, and so far I haven't had to lift a finger.'

Later, as they sat down to eat, Gülbahar looked over at Daud fondly, and Daud smiled back.

Daud put her at her ease saying, 'And now you have saved my life, and I have nothing to reward you with but my gratitude.' She understood that there was no obligation in this relationship now, if indeed there had ever been, other than the natural responses of love. She recognised a sincerity in Daud that she had not been aware of in earlier years.

'I'm sorry I'm not in any position to maintain you as before.' he said, with a mock-sheepish look.

She laughed. 'Don't worry, I have some keen admirers whose needs are as modest as their hands are generous. But of course, you will always have 'droit de seigneur' in my heart, and my body too if you wish.' She gave him that familiar loving look, letting her eyelids droop ever so slightly.

Daud took another swig of the rich red wine, produce of Gülbahar's vineyard, as the memory of an old pleasure came momentarily to mind. His reverie was interrupted by the image of a goat's face appearing in the doorway opposite – a shaggy, red-bearded, old billy wearing a frown of disdain. It was gone even in the moment he registered it, but the suddenness of the apparition sobered him instantly.

'Would love to, my dear Gülbahar, but I have to move on tonight. And please accept the kid goats, as a keepsake if you wish.'

Gülbahar had the maid pack him a swag for the journey, some bread, a little goat's cheese and some olives. They embraced, in friendship now, and under a bright moon Daud set off into the mountains.

FOURTEEN

The song of the flutes

THE bright star Antares, the "Heart of the Scorpion", shone red like Mars above Daud, guiding him east over the Jebel Lubnan.

Despite the dangers threatening him, there was no conflict in his own heart, only peace. He felt sure that he could answer any questions which might present themselves, simply by looking within, for that still point of beginning. Yet the mountain paths of the heart, which seek and hide the summit of our striving, wind steep. The way is treacherous, traps are laid and wild beasts wait in ambush; rock falls and avalanches, snakes and scorpions, danger above and below. In travelling the pathways of the heart, all is at stake.

As Daud contemplated the heavens from a dusty mountain track above Beirut, another nocturnal wanderer was setting forth from the very same city. Abdul Qabid, the Squeezer, one hand gripping the rail of the little wooden coaster moored at the quayside, put his finger down his throat and vomited into the harbour his dinner of chilli and garlic prawns. He rinsed his mouth and spat overboard, then looked on in amusement as delighted small fry appeared from nowhere, indulging in a minor feeding frenzy amidst the semi-digested jetsam. Their excitement prevented their seeing the sleek, dark shape of another lone shark slip up and snatch a mouthful of minnows, just as one might idly stretch out and scoop a handful of pistachios or sunflower seeds. Abdul Qabid watched the sharp dorsal fin scribe the obsidian sheen in a long and silent *alif*. He then headed below deck to the boat's only cabin which was reserved solely for him. His self-induced retching had been a prophylactic measure against seasickness, and with the alcohol of a bottle of arak already well absorbed into his bloodstream he fell into a sound sleep. While Abdul Qabid snored loudly, the crew cast off, raised the sail and headed into the dark of the open sea.

The shark now had the flavour of garlic in its gills, and if anyone had looked, they would have seen a long grey shadow cruising astern of the boat. It was following north, savouring the pungent odour which wafted on each rasping breath from the cabin porthole to permeate the foamy wake.

Safe on land, and unaware of anything but the sweet night air and the majesty of the sky with its bright celestial beacons guiding his way, Daud walked until the dawn. The horizon lightened before him as his path descended into the Bekaa. Reaching the banks of the Litani River he slept a while, then hitched a boat ride across and onto the Damascus road. Late in the evening he descended once more into the city.

In the heat of the following afternoon, Daud took up his old position outside the coffee house, below the storyteller's window. He nodded off to the click-clack of counters and dice smacking down on the backgammon boards, and dozed through the storyteller's rendition of a tale from A Thousand Nights and One Night, of the girl called 'Freshness of the Eyes'. Here Sheherezad tells of Abu Isa who falls in love with one of his cousin's female slaves, and the trials he undergoes to persuade his cousin to let the girl go.

As the storyteller recited, 'Only one schooled by the genii could pierce a heart from an unstrung bow...' Daud's heart too was penetrated. At that instant Daud beheld a vision of that face he had sought so long but to no avail in the feeble transcript of his memory, the face of his ravishing desert encounter. This was no idle daydream or wishful thought. The face that appeared to him now was more real than life itself. No angel, no imagined beauty, she was form, moving and more tangibly present to him than he was to himself.

She smiled, and her look left Daud caught between simultaneous desires. On the one hand he experienced an insatiable yearning to gaze endlessly upon her beauty, while on the other he desired profound and annihilating union with her. The tide of love now moving him: that delicate oscillation inclining him first this way, now that. It was as easy as walking,

Daud came back once more into the poorer dream of this world, and found himself still sitting in the corner of the coffee shop wall. The feeling of pain was gone, and there remained a sense of lightness and keen joy, such as that which cloaks a traveller departing in the dawn for an unknown but auspicious destination. He was just in time to hear the storyteller inviting anyone from the audience to bring a tale. He needed little urging from the Drum which twisted slightly under his arm. As he entered the coffee shop, the storyteller welcomed him, recognising him from before and beckoned him to the chair. With barely a pause, Daud launched straight into his tale:

'This is a story of longing and lost loves ...'

Daud beat gently upon the Drum, and a low boom echoed from the skin like the sound of crashing surf upon a distant shore. He continued:

'There once was a time, or a time will come, on an island far, far, further to the east even than Screndib, a jungle island where lived a people who never lost touch with the spirits of their ancestors. For they were a people who had found a voice to bridge the worlds of the here and the after. It was the bridge of music. For does not sound form the very spheres of existence we call the universes? And so is it not with sound that we return again through the veils of those spheres to the eternal dwelling of souls themselves... through prayers and sacred words, songs of love and longing?'

As he spoke, Daud kept slowly beating the Drum, which continued to roll out its deep, booming wave of sound. A sound which vibrated like breath in the chests of all those present, so that their attention became rapt on his every word. Daud spoke with closed eyes. He saw himself walking in dappled glades of green and golden shafts of sunlight, among outrageous blooms of red, white and orange, under dripping palms beneath a towering canopy of treetops which all but hid the sky. He heard the screeching of birds, the click-rattle of insects, the chit-chatter of monkeys.

'And in this green and mountainous isle the people had discovered that in the music of their bamboo flutes, they could hear again the voices of their loved ones who had departed from their worldly forms. Whenever someone died, a close relative would go out and cut a piece of bamboo from which they would make a flute. The size and tone of the flute was determined by the character of the person who had died. By playing on this flute, they would invite the departed one to return. Then it was as if the flutes played themselves, returning the breath back to the people with news from those whom they had thought lost. The flutes sang of the new world where their ancestors now lived, and in this way, through the music in the flutes and the breath which came in and out, the people always remained connected with their origin.'

'The flute playing was not just for keeping in touch with the dead, but for bringing into life also. When a couple wanted to have children, they would make a flute and play it before love making, to inspire a good spirit to come into the woman's womb. And this flute continued to be played throughout the confinement to help the newcomer become accommodated in its new environment of earthly time. It was very important that the flute was played with gentleness and love. If a miscarriage occurred, it was said that the flute playing had not been kind enough, or sweet enough, or generous enough, to persuade the spirit to stay. Or it had been played in anger or mistrust. If a newborn baby was particularly bonnie, then it was murmured, 'Ah, good flute playing!' If the child was difficult, then the state of the flute players was ultimately to blame. But difficulties could be remedied, for there were also healing flutes, played to the sick by the priest doctors to calm the patient's mind, tune the organs and strengthen and harmonise those subtle bonds through which a person's soul animates the body.

'One day a visitor came from a far away land, a *ferengi* from out of the west, a travelling scholar like Ibn Battuta, but not so sympathetic. He was a novelty to the islanders who had never before seen pale-skinned people, with their strange robes and stranger eating habits. Nevertheless, they treated this foreigner with the proper respect due to a guest; and as he seemed not to be a threat, they allowed him to live among them. The visitor stayed a long time, learning their language and their ways. He too was very curious, always questioning the islanders on this or that, scratching away in his notebook, and making drawings of the simplest of everyday objects found on the island. He was fascinated by the flutes and the stories the people told of the flutes' power to communicate between the worlds.

When the visitor asked to be allowed to play one, the islanders were at first reluctant, but he kept on at them and eventually they were persuaded.

'The stranger from the west was quite surprised when he discovered that the flutes really did play themselves. All he had to do was put his lips to the mouthpiece and blow gently. His fingers seemed to find their way across the holes easily without any conscious guidance from him, stopping and unstopping, lengthening and shortening the flow of air, as a sweet sound rose from within the hollow reed pipe. It was as if he was being led in a dance by a silent and invisible dance master, and he was entranced. But what were the flutes saying, he mused to himself. Surely they weren't really the mouthpiece of the dead, such beautiful, heavenly sounds couldn't possibly have any connection with dead people.

'You see,' Daud looked up and addressed his audience for a moment open-eyed, 'the man didn't believe in the invisible worlds. He certainly had never seen, let alone ever had an inkling, of what moves beyond the coarse veil of this physical reality, and so had no sensitivity to the subtleties of life apart from this low world of weighty struggles and shadowy sadnesses. The visitor from the west was susceptible only to the calming effect of the flute playing on his general sense of being. He was not, as one might have hoped, transported in his listening to the kind of visions the islanders spoke of, but merely reached a point of comfortable and pleasurable self-satisfaction.

'Nevertheless, the desire formed in his mind to acquire some of these flutes and bring them back to his own country, where he was a professor in a famous *madrasa*. He told himself that the flutes were an essential part of the study he was undertaking with regard to the islanders, and he was determined to possess some examples. So, during the final weeks of his stay the visitor dropped hints to the chief of the islanders, to the chief's counsellors, their wives, to anyone who would listen, about how important it was that he should be able to show the flutes to people in his own country.

'You see,' he explained to the islanders, none of whom had ever been known to leave their island, (for why on earth should anyone choose to leave paradise?) 'it would be as if you were travelling, through the flutes.'

This kind of logic was lost on the islanders who knew many ways of travelling besides the physical way. But the visitor had always appeared sincere in his dealings with them. He had stayed among them a long time and had never upset anyone. He had not stolen anyone's wife or possessions. He had brought them iron fishing hooks and axes, things quite unknown to them before he arrived. So they trusted him, and eventually they surrendered to him a number of flutes which he promised to play regularly.

The night before the visitor left, the elders gathered together the flutes which were to be taken away, and began to play. One of them remarked how well made the flutes were. Another elder said 'These are like beautiful birds singing love songs to each other.' Another noted how the bamboos warmed to the touch, like the hands of old friends. And the elders played the flutes through until the dawn. The visitor was now ready to take his leave.

'What will you do with them?' asked one man, who looked sadly at the reed pipe in his hand.

'I will take the flutes back to my school in England, to the great *madrasa*. They will be displayed there in the museum for all to see,' said the visitor. 'We will teach people to play them, so the voices of your ancestors will continue to be heard in this world.'

The islanders were reluctant but did not know how to refuse this request, and so they allowed the visitor to depart with the flutes. But perfidy sits in the hearts of those who seek knowledge for personal gain. Just as people steal from the cultures of others, hiding them in unread books, in dark cabinets and museum cellars, so too do selfish fears rob the treasure of possibilities in our own hearts.'

And here the Drum in Daud's hands sounded loudly, deep and booming across the coffee house, and the shivering of the little metal chains in the drum's rim made a tinkling sound, like shingle rolling on the shore as a wave draws back.

Daud continued: 'The visitor certainly brought the flutes to his homeland, where to this day they lie unplayed, gathering dust on a museum shelf, waiting for the sweet lips of a sympathetic player to release their voices once again and give life to their longings in this world.'

As Daud concluded his tale, the sound of a reed flute rose from the back of the coffee house. He looked up and saw it was Nefsi, the *ney* player he had met that night at 'Umm Harun's house in Salihiye. Beside him sat Refik, who, as the flute's plaintive cry slipped over the top of its airy crescendo, and gently diminished, began to recite in Persian, the opening poem of the Master Jelaluddin's Mathnavi:

"Listen to the story of the flute, how it complains of separation
'since I was torn from my bed of reeds, my song makes mankind cry...' "

A sigh rose from the room, and the famous poem of separation, love and longing for mystical union was recited, couplet by couplet by different members of the assembly, until the lines in which the Master Jelaluddin bids the hearers farewell: *'wa-salaam'*.

FIFTEEN

The heart of Damascus

AUD spent the next few days hanging out with Refik and his musician friends. It was late spring, the afternoons were lazy, the nights warm, and they filled their time with music, poetry, wine and conversation. Sometimes, when Daud visited the coffee shop, a tale would arrive as if out of thin air. They were strange tales, and he knew they meant something, but what? They were orphan tales for whom he was their surrogate mother, the Drum the midwife and the listeners their vagabond foster homes in whom they would journey God knows where.

Since visiting the Circassian and the subsequent revelations by Haywani, Daud felt disturbed. Not so long ago he would have relished the challenge of confronting the odious Omo Sharleen, but lately he had lost the yen for madcap adventures which had coloured so vividly the days of his youth. Something had changed. It was that affair in the mountains, with the girl, and then the goat and the Drum, the visions and the stories. The matter of Omo Sharleen just didn't seem relevant any more. Yet there it was, trailing along behind like a bag of unfinished business that wouldn't let him go.

He could have played them at their own game – with the help of his Arwadi compatriots he knew he could deal with Sharleen and his gang.

But other matters interested him now; and it was this which disturbed him. He was beginning to relish the conversation that occurred, infrequently and without any warning, with the Drum, or rather, the spirit of the Drum through the image of Shams the Goat. Even more Daud ached for the unworded discourse with that elusive beauty, who came and went of her own accord. No lamp *jinn* of Ala'uddin to appear at his elbow at the slightest rub, she was a free spirit and no one's slave, this girl. Her memory could still provoke in him a twinge of visceral anxiety.

Deep down, however, Daud knew he would not find ease until the business of the bandits and Omo Sharleen was resolved. As long as he kept up the disguise of the goatherd, with his beard, his worn-out country clothes and his little band of goats, he could pass unnoticed and unrecognised throughout the land. However, in order not to be drawn into the game, he had to stay ahead of it; and to stay ahead, he would need some moves.

So, what to do? Daud looked at the Drum. But the Drum just lay there, a piece of dead skin and wood. He picked it up, started tapping it. Nothing. Even its tone was dull and lifeless, the skin cold and sagged, not taut or vibrant. Why, it was just a drum. Daud knew it was simply reflecting his own state; that he needed to get out and get some air. He picked up the Drum and slipped out of the khan. It was mid-afternoon and those who had not gone to their homes to eat were snoozing off their lunch in the shops and khans of the Street of the Apothecaries, in shady corners cradled on sacks of pistachio nuts and pillowed on bales of soporific herbs.

Daud headed up into the Salihiye district, to where he had spent that first evening with Refik and the musicians in 'Umm Harun's waterwheel house. He remembered Refik saying that below the garden behind the mosque was the tomb of a great saint which was known to be a place of great help from beyond the veil of worldly predicament. Whether by intent or seeming accident, wayfarers on the roads of Damascus find the way here at some time or other.

Daud was not religious in the conventional sense. This is not to say that Daud had no moral sensibilities, no sense of right and wrong – on the contrary, his schooling had been the *madrasa* of the trading floor and market places. He had come to know his fellows just as they were, with their troubles and woes, their joys and successes. By keen observation of others and honest self-reflection he had developed an insight into human nature which was both compassionate and generous. Not for Daud the confined judgements of textbook scholars or literalist religious authority. His way was according to the self-evident truths of a life grasped with both hands and lived with an open heart. And saints, who serve as conduits between the world of appearances and world of unseen realities, who do not divide between the image and the essence of a thing, were well within the compass of Daud's asking.

But Daud knew to choose his saint carefully. For it was no good, he would have said, if one's ardent desire was to attract the amorous attentions of a young lady, to seek aid from a known celibate. It just wouldn't have been tactful. And, he imagined, one would get short shrift in asking for assistance in one's financial affairs from a confirmed renunciate. And could one expect to be saved from imminent death by plague, famine or war by applying to the holy ones who suffered uncomplaining as they were torn limb from limb by the Mongol hordes or in silent acceptance went to their graves sick and deprived, requiring nothing but God alone? All these sanctified people Daud respected highly for their single-mindedness and unflinching devotion, but he needed something more in a saint. He needed the kind of 'man of the world' saint who would understand his situation, and be able to give him sound advice; a saint who by the strength of his gaze would illuminate within Daud's own heart events as they arose and help bring them to the most suitable conclusion, if it should so please God. Yes, Daud was in need of a saint who had that little bit extra. And so it was that he fetched up at the mausoleum of that most wise teacher, the Great Sheykh Ibn 'Arabi who is the Heart of Damascus. It is said that when this saint came to choose the place for his burial, he had a number of pieces of raw lamb meat hung in various places throughout the city until they began to putrefy. In some places the meat went off in hours, elsewhere in days, but the piece of lamb left in the good air of Salihiye was still fresh after a week.

Daud descended from the marble-paved courtyard of the mosque and entered the mausoleum of the saint which was built into the side of the hill. It was the hottest time of the day and he felt immediately the cool of the place. The building was empty but for a white-robed keeper who dozed in a chair just inside the doorway. Daud made his way past a half dozen small tombs to a large sarcophagus enclosed in blue and white tile work and silver grill. He stood at the head of the saint's tomb and closed his eyes. His

THE HEART OF DAMASCUS

pulse had risen in the climb up the hill, but now in the calm of this sanctuary his heartbeat slowed and he relaxed. He didn't really know what to ask of the saint, or how. So, he started by giving greetings, then he explained his dilemma and asked for help in sorting it all out (Daud knew well that the saint could read the lines in his own heart better than he could put them into words). He relaxed even more and let his mind go. Feeling himself to be in a bigger place, bigger than all his problems, his worries just seemed to evaporate. He was confident then that the difficulties of his situation would be resolved in the end. Suddenly it became very simple. It was just a case of putting one step in front of the other, all the way to that end. There were direct ways, and less direct ways. Right paths and wrong paths. But even the wrong paths eventually reach the end, and so become the right path. Daud prayed for the discrimination to choose a direct way.

Daud thanked the Sheykh, whose presence he felt as simply an atmosphere of wholeness, clarity and extreme kindness. He then went and sat a little way off, leaning up against the wall, resting his back on a cushion. His eyes closed, and in his contemplation the face of that shaggy old goat flashed momentarily into view, laughing that goatish laugh, big, confident and expansive, but also kind and caring, even fatherly. In the next moment Daud had the strange sensation that he was falling, as if from far out in space, through a vast sky towards the blue and golden earth. As he regained his focus there appeared below him the island of his birth, Arwad. A large black bird of prey was circling the island in wide sweeps. Then, as the bird approached to land, the island turned to fire and the bird flew up in flames and fell into the water. The island then returned to normal, resting jewel-like in its turquoise setting.

Daud awoke to feel the Drum twisting insistently under his armpit. The light was fast departing the day. As he reflected on the strange images he had seen concerning Arwad, he remembered what Haywani had said to Gülbahar, that Abdul Qabid had been sent by Sharleen to look for news of Daud on his native island. Daud knew it was time to head north. He made his silent farewell to the Sheykh in his grand throne-like sarcophagus, gave a piastre to the tombkeeper, who was by now fully awake and keen to provide his only visitor with a tour of the mausoleum. But the game was afoot and he had the scent. Daud departed the city like a thief, covering his tracks as before by heading off east on the Baghdad road before circling back round the city. Eventually reaching the turnoff to Seydnaya, the thought occurred to him to revisit the convent and pick up some of the kid goats that were his due. But a thump from the Drum reminded him they would not have been weaned yet, and besides, there wasn't time to dally in bucolic pleasantries. So instead, when he encountered a small herd of goats being driven to the city market, he made another investment, and headed off with his new flock on a different route north through the mountains to the richer pastures of the Mediterranean coast.

SIXTEEN

The nautical adventures of Abdul Qabid

VENTS in time generally occur each related one to another, as if in mutual cause and effect. The vast earth extends, the pace of life seems slow, the marriage of events requiring a measured betrothal. But that is just a quirk of time itself. Each day has been long in preparation, yet, when matters come to a head, its execution in time is instantaneous. The event is the moment. It breaks through time's

barrier, announcing 'Here am I!' with an infinity of faces, an endless procession of places of perception, united in living, knowing, willing, enabling,
seeing, hearing and speaking in response to the creative word, 'Be!'.

But what patience! Light measured in the years of its travelling from
inconceivable source to summum of matter, and then to dwell, flourish
and bloom for the so short day of its shining forth. Shining and shone
upon, journeying through universes of meanings and similitudes in forms
of light and fire to step down tentatively into this realm of water and clay.
Each person arriving in perfect co-incidence at this marriage with destiny,
and then turn, at the point of greatest distance from and closest vision of
the object of its desire, the whole of its encompassing movement from light
to light. But standing on the shore, how can we know the ocean's depth?
And if our gaze attains but the mundane horizon of our past and future,
how can we comprehend the immensity of the present in the frantic mirror
of its unstilled waves?

It was with comprehensive denial of such universally expansive
emotion, and none of cosmic patience, that Abdul Qabid greeted the dawn
on the third day out from Beirut. Although he spent a sound enough first
night in alcoholic slumber, the following morning an untimely offshore
squall set the little boat bouncing off-course in the direction of Cyprus. All
day the winds blew from the south and east, setting the little coaster
pitching and rolling in turbulent seas, until by nightfall they were within
sight of the island's Monastery of Cape St Andrew. In a little while they
were sure to be dashed on the rocks off the headland which the Turks call
Zafer Burnu, Victory Point.

Captain Ali was devout, as well as courageous. He strapped himself to
the tiller and struggled to steer the vessel away from the shore. Then, in full
voice as he might deliver commands to his seamen, he cried out the Litany
of the Sea, that he might drown out his and his crew's fears in the power of
these holy words:

'O Allah, make us steadfast, give us the victory, and subject to us this sea,
as You subjected the sea to Moses, the fire to Abraham, the mountains and
iron to David, the wind and demons and jinn to Solomon... And give us a
goodly wind as may be in Your knowledge, and release it upon us from the
storehouses of Your mercy...'

The captain also prayed to St Andrew, who has a special place in his heart for seafarers.

In any event, the winds changed as they rounded the Cape to the north and the captain and crew breathed easy again. The boat turned its barnacled prow back towards the Syrian mainland. Throughout that tempestuous night the flames of St Elmo's fire licked the masthead, and the crew, all honest sinners to a man, muttered their prayers. Abdul Qabid, however, remained frozen with fear, barely moving from his bunk. He hid beneath the covers, only emerging to retch bile onto the cabin floor. He prayed to no one, although his continual moaning and rocking from side to side might have been mistaken for some primitive religious ritual. Even when Captain Ali called upon all hands to bale out the vessel's hold, flooded from the waves coming over the decks, Abdul Qabid refused to budge. The crew would gladly have thrown their passenger overboard but the captain pointed out that this would have been tactless considering the timely intervention of God and St Andrew which had saved Abdul Qabid's wretched skin as well as their own.

The following dawn saw them battling down towards the Syrian coast, again trying to avoid being driven onto rocks, and again baling for all they were worth. Though there was little remaining for Abdul Qabid to bring up but his own miserable soul, the mingling smells of dried fish, tar and his own vomit did little to relieve his nausea. When the crash came, he went into a state of catatonic shock. Abdul Qabid fully expected to be drowned the next moment, and was surprised when the rocking ceased, the wind dropped and he heard all the crew cheering up on deck. He crawled from the cabin to discover that to ensure their safety Captain Ali had beached the ship in a deserted bay somewhere south of Arwad. The storm was abating and the crew spent the next week making the vessel seaworthy once more.

Two weeks after setting out from Beirut, the sun rose in a cloudless sky above calm waters, and Captain Ali steered his trusty coaster in behind the breakwater of Tartous harbour and made her fast. Immediately captain and crew went as a body to thank the local saint, Sheykh Ibrahim of Tartous, whose little green-domed *kubbe* at the end of Harbour Street looks down benignly upon seafarers and landlubbers alike.

Abdul Qabid was done with voyaging for the present. He tottered ashore, too absorbed in his own discomfort to notice the sound of swishing water below nor the cries of amazement of the fishermen on the pier. He also failed to see the great dorsal fin of the shark which circled among the moored boats before sliding back out to sea. Abdul Qabid skulked off to find a hotel. If he had hoped to keep a low profile in this busy port community, he was mistaken. The story of his cowardly behaviour during the storm was subject to a degree of exaggeration over the next few days as the seamen underwent some liquid post-traumatic stress relief in the local hostelries.

The tale of the Frightened Gentleman of Beirut crossed the short sea strait to the little island of Arwad well before the eponymous subject of this salty ballad dared embark again upon the waters. So Abdul Qabid was quite put out when, stepping ashore on the quayside of Arwad's little harbour, the local urchins gathered about him singing a ditty about a man from Beirut. He couldn't really follow the strange accent of Arwad, with its mixture of Arabic, Greek and Phoenician words. He could just about make out the refrain which referred to *al-Beyruti,* 'the man from Beirut'. Had he been conversant in the local patois, he would have heard a vulgar tale of how this one-eyed garlic-muncher left a trail of vomit from Cairo to Constantinople, causing all but the most resolute of tutelary saints and guardian angels to abandon ship; then, persuaded by sincere prayers to return, they did so with their holy noses, more used to the odours of sanctity, bound up with blazing veils of light as prophylactic against the spirit-repulsing stink.

Only when ashore did Abdul Qabid realise his mistake. He had imagined the island to be of sufficient size to allow him some degree of anonymity while he gathered information on his quarry. But Arwad is quite tiny, and very much a single community, a large, extended tribe inhabiting a jungle of alleyways, a kind of *kasbah,* walled in by the sea. Now, as Abdul Qabid entered a narrow lane leading in from the harbour front, it was as if the islanders had been forewarned of his coming. Everywhere he was met with knowing glances, nods of recognition and muffled guffaws behind cupped hands.

A quick change of plan. The direct approach, Abdul Qabid decided, would be least likely to arouse suspicion. If asked, he would simply say that he was looking up his old acquaintance in order to settle a debt. He asked a passer-by for the address of Daud the Timber Merchant and was directed to an area of shipyards just north of the harbour. There, between the slipways where bare-ribbed frames of boats sat propped on wooden blocks, was a large timber yard with a small shop. A sign read: 'Daud – Timber Merchant and Ships Chandler'. Abdul Qabid glanced around. It was lunchtime; the shop was shut, there was no one about. So he sat down on a cedar log and waited.

Abdul Qabid's movements did not go unnoticed. Invisible behind the lattice-work *kafes* of a window in one of the tallest houses backing onto the shipyards, two pairs of eyes gazed down upon the foreigner. One pair belonged to a tall woman of evident wealth and a certain elegant grandeur. Hadida, the deserted wife (as she saw herself), retained the essential good looks of her youth. Her long hair still shone with golden highlights though now it needed an occasional refreshing with lemon juice. And while the sylph-like figure that had been for Daud the joyous garment of many a night in their younger days had matured, the billowing curves of her generous hips and breasts still held a definite allure. Her face however, showed time's theft of innocence. Where once she had appeared demure and believing, experience now showed in the resolute set of her mouth and the penetrating look in her eyes. Hadida carried herself with the haughtiness of one who, abandoned, discovers her freedom and makes her own way in life. She wore her modest jewellery like an empress.

'What an ugly looking man,' hissed Hadida to the roughly clad, small boy standing beside her. 'What on earth is he doing in our shipyard?'

'It's the guy from that song everyone's singing, 'the Frightened Gentleman of Beirut'. You know, that skinny fella Captain Ali brought to Tartous? Who puked all the way and led the big shark up here?'

Hadida had overheard smatterings of the obscene verse in the past few days, but didn't admit to it. 'Ugh, he reminds me of… of… I don't know, something really snakey. I wonder what he wants.' She shuddered. 'He gives me the creeps.'

Hadida had a need to be suspicious. She had accepted her husband's disappearance with the equanimity of one grown used to the unpredictability of life, with its sudden deposits and swift withdrawals of fortune. Her marriage had always been like that. In the early days Daud had been horny, and so had she. The deposits were frequent and fertile, and there were five fine children to prove it. But as Daud's potency in the world of commerce grew, so too did her time alone. The deposits then came in monetary form. Rather than moping about, Hadida had busied herself with raising her tribe. Of course, the presence of a father would have been useful, but Daud provided substantially for them, and in this close-knit community there were ample male role models among their extended family.

Daud's disappearance, accompanied by rumours of a bandit attack, had concentrated Hadida's mind. That he might be dead never occurred to her. In fact, her thoughts about Daud were rather vague. If pressed, she said she thought he'd just gone off and started a new life somewhere and that was that. People did this kind of thing, and Daud had always had his mysterious side. As for the possibility that he might have left her for another woman, personally she thought not, although it suited her to let others think so. Hadida knew women were a pastime for Daud, not the main event. Daud's real passion had always been his business.

Hadida had no financial worries. Her father had provided her with a dowry more than adequate for her and her kids' needs. The children, however, were the legal heirs to her husband's business. As Daud had vanished, she was legally entitled to act as agent in his affairs, and to take her slice of the action. This she now managed with remarkable efficiency. First she inspected the accounts, where she discovered that in the months preceding his disappearance, Daud had converted the greater part of his assets into gold. She immediately stopped all those unexplained monthly payments to lawyers in various ports from Tunis to Alexandretta. Then, with her husband's closest advisors, she made a detailed analysis of Daud's businesses and gradually began to re-invest in the market. Hadida proved a quick learner and soon gained the confidence of her colleagues. Emboldened by her success she expanded into new markets: Benares silks, Kashmiri brocades, cloth from Manchester woven with her own Egyptian cotton, finest hose and woollen goods from the stocking shops and mills of Hawick in the Scottish Borders; spices came by dhow from the Moslem Indies, or across the seas from the steamy Caribbean and out of the deepest Amazonian forests. Of course, little of this actually passed through Arwad. It might spend a day or so in the Tartous warehouses before being transited to Constantinople. More often goods were shipped direct to the company's agents in Genoa or Cyprus from where they were distributed throughout the Frankish lands. In no time at all Hadida revitalised the links which had cooled following Daud's disappearance, and the business became more profitable than ever. Through the slatted window she eyed the newcomer with increased suspicion.

The young lad standing next to her spoke up. 'Yeah. He's a real mean piece of work, missus – you know he didn't even help the sailors bale the ship in the storm. I can have him got rid of if you like.'

'No...' She deliberated, sucking in air slowly between her tightly pursed lips. 'No, I don't think that's necessary yet. First let's find out what he's up to, then we can decide how best to deal with him. Go and chat him up. Maybe he knows something about Daud. But don't let on you know me, or anything about anything. Just play the dumb kid and get the information.' Hadida gave him a conspiratorial look, and the young lad scurried off.

The boy was the son of a distant cousin of Daud's. Hadida had employed him because of his family's poverty, but his wit was sharper and his aptitude for the game of business greater than any of Daud's own progeny. Most importantly, he knew how to listen, he remembered everything, and had the nous to make sense of it all. His name was Kush and he was quite fearless.

'Hey mister, what do you want?' Kush walked right up to Abdul Qabid and looked him in the eye.

'I'm looking for the owner, Daud the Merchant.' Abdul Qabid was surprised at the child's forthrightness and just answered him straight.

'Why you looking for him?'

'I've got business with him.'

'What business? You want timber? You want to build a boat? My uncle Farid has a boatyard, he can build you a number one boat.'

'No, I don't want timber and I don't want a boat. I want to see Sayyid Daud.'

'Ain't seen him. He's gone away. You want to buy his business?'

Abdul Qabid took the bait, 'Yes, yes, that's it, I want to buy the business.'

'Is it for sale?'

Abdul Qabid was getting exasperated by all this questioning and answered shortly, 'How would I know if it's for sale, I just got here.'

'Then why you say you want to buy it?'

'Did I? Well, what I meant was, I want to know more about it, maybe it is for sale. I'm looking for business opportunities up here.'

'You not Arwadi, are you? Where you from?'

'Beirut, where are you from?

Kush was puzzled. No one had ever asked him this question before. He was Arwadi, what else could he be. Everyone on Arwad was Arwadi, unless they weren't, like this foreigner, and then everyone knew it. Kush just stared at Abdul Qabid and after a while the boy smiled and asked another question.

'What's your name?'

'Abdul Qabid, what's yours?

'No, it's not. Your name's the Shit-scared Beyruti!' Then in a high-pitched voice Kush launched into the latest outrageous verses of the song the sailors in the harbour were singing.

'Now look here you brat!' Abdul Qabid had had enough of this ridiculous kid. He grabbed Kush by the throat and squeezed, 'I want to know what's happened to that Daud, you hear me? When did you last see him?'

Kush wriggled out of Abdul Qabid's grasp, and cowered on the ground, feigning terror.

'Don't hit me, don't hit me. I don't know anything. But I can find out. I know everyone here on Arwad, and in Tartous.' (He was lying here, though most Arwadis and quite a few Tartousis certainly knew Kush.) 'Let me go, I'll find out anything you want Mr Abdul Qabid.' And Kush blinked his eyes and did the cowering thing again, very convincingly.

Abdul Qabid was used to frightened people and felt once more in command.

'OK, if you behave, I won't hit you. Now, let's get one thing straight: no one must know you're working for me. You *are* working for me now, you know. You'll get paid, but only by results. And if there are no results, you'll pay me instead. Understand! So, secrecy, and then information. I want to know anything anyone knows about Daud's whereabouts, or if he's dead. Now, where can I find somewhere to stay here?'

Kush was again puzzled. No one stayed on Arwad if they weren't either Arwadi, or the guest of an Arwadi, in which case the question of accommodation never arose. If anyone got too drunk to sail back to the mainland, they usually spent the night in the tea house. Abdul Qabid didn't seem the sort who would want to kip down in the tea house. 'Tartous?' Kush suggested.

Abdul Qabid shuddered; it meant going on the sea again. He wandered back to the port to mull things over. Kush, meanwhile, returned to Hadida to report his meeting.

SEVENTEEN

An Odyssean return

ROUND the time Kush was kicking barefoot through the sawdust and shavings of the shipyards of Arwad, Daud and his goats were making their way into Tartous. He had crossed the mountains from Damascus to the coast, where with offers of fresh cheese and milk Daud persuaded a fisherman to carry him and his herd north in his boat. Even hobbled, the goats had been troublesome passengers. Daud still had a lot to learn about keeping goats. The fisherman didn't seem bothered by the smell, although Daud spent most of the trip cleaning up after his animals. They had avoided the worst of the stormy weather by hugging the coast and finding sheltered moorings at night, where ashore, Daud could cut fresh fodder and milk the she-goats without losing half the milk onto the deck. A few days later he disembarked just short of Tartous.

As he approached the town, Daud too began to hear the street-ditty of the 'Shit-scared Beyruti', and was amused by its tale of the drunk and seasick landlubber. The following translation does scant justice to the exotic language and inimitable music of an Arwadi sea shanty :

Now bold Captain Ali who's not known to dally
was sailing for home with his brave jolly crew
In the bay of St George's, under mountains so gorgeous
A traveller boarded whom he later did rue

(Chorus:
Sing hey ho for brave Captain Ali
and hey ho for all of the crew
sing hey ho for good St Andrew
and the wind that brought them home)

From Beirut he sailed on a warm summer evening
as storm clouds were gathering b'yond Cyprus' shore
he was smelling of garlic, and of arak was reeking
he'd puked in the harbour now he puked up some more.

As waves came a pounding the death knells were sounding
as the sharp rocks came closer he threw up again.
As the great shark was laughing the Beyruti was barfing
while brave Captain Ali prayed safe port to attain

The shit-scared Beyruti who'd no sense of duty
lay down on his bunk and threw up on the floor.
And when handed a baler he just turned even paler
The ship filling with water he then chundered some more.

The saints and the angels had covered their nostrils
and fled for the heav'ns to escape the foul smell.
All except for St Andrew without whom they'd be lost still
who blew the ship homeward on a westerly swell.

Daud knew Captain Ali. A man he could trust: he was an Arwadi too, related to him somewhere down the line. They had sailed the Eastern Mediterranean together often in the early days and got drunk in most of its ports. But who was this Beyruti? Could he be one of Omo Sharleen's men? Daud had to find out. He brought his herd down to the waterfront where, on the pretence of hawking milk and yoghurt, he chatted up the cook of Captain Ali's boat.

Brave Captain Ali

The cook enthusiastically filled him in on the story of the one-eyed Beyruti. 'We've scrubbed the cabin three times, and it still smells of garlic!' he chuckled.

Daud went off in search of Captain Ali. Before long he spied him in one of their old haunts, a coffee house on the seafront, tucked under the walls of the town and frequented by sailors and fishermen alike. He ordered a coffee and sat outside to keep an eye on his goats. Captain Ali stayed inside for ages shooting the breeze with other old seadogs. He was even persuaded to tell the story of his recent voyage and this he did with gusto, embroidering the tale in true Arwadi fashion by adding several fictitious characters and events. These included a mistress for the Beyruti, a couple of pretty young boys and a string of asses, all of whom jumped ship at various stages of the adventure – the boys swimming ashore on Cyprus where they were accommodated by leering monks, the asses eaten by sharks, and the mistress borne aloft upon a cloud of fire by a squadron of jinn. No one took it the least bit seriously.

Captain Ali finally took his leave. As he stepped outside, there escaped from the lips of the bearded goatherd sitting by the cafe door a whisper, a single word which carried the scent of bitter lemons and long lost love; a name which would establish Daud's identity, and at the same time guarantee his incognito would be maintained:

'Persephone.'

Captain Ali was stunned to hear the name of his long lost beloved spoken by a mangy goatherd sitting in the dust of the street. The events connecting the captain to the beautiful Persephone, a young lady of the island of Cyprus, were known only to the protagonists themselves. And also to Daud, for he had required Captain Ali to explain why he could no longer enter Cypriot ports. Persephone's father, an influential merchant of old island stock, upon discovering an infidel courting his daughter, had sworn an oath to defenestrate Captain Ali from a great height should he ever set foot on Cyprus again. Ali was not going to risk that fate. Perhaps also the memory of this threat had strengthened the fervour of his recent prayers to St Andrew.

Captain Ali noticed that the bearded vagabond was holding a finger to his lips.

'Good milk, good cheese and yoghurt!' Daud spoke loud enough for anyone to hear. Then in a mumbled whisper, 'I'm Daud, you know me. Pretend to be interested in buying milk.'

Daud got up and led the speechless captain to where the noise of the surf would cover their words. Renewing their oaths of mutual secrecy, Daud explained his situation and asked about the captain's passenger from Beirut. Captain Ali confirmed that it was the loan shark, Abdul Qabid.

'I need to know what this Abdul Qabid is up to. He's here to find me, or find the way to me, and he may use my family to try and draw me out.

Sharleen suspects that I am still alive. Well, I'm not alive; as far as you or anyone else is concerned, I disappeared on the road to Damascus. Hadida must be protected, but I don't think Abdul Qabid will try anything himself. Most likely he'll enlist some of Sharleen's men up here. Where is he now, by the way?'

'He went over to Arwad this morning, still looking pretty green. I suspect he hasn't a clue what he's letting himself in for, especially with Hadida.'

'What do you mean, especially with Hadida?'

'Of course!' Captain Ali laughed, 'You don't know! She's really taken on the business since you disappeared. She's become a real iron lady. Runs the whole show, and makes a good job of it. You'd better watch out. She may not take so kindly to your return.'

'Oh don't worry, I'm not returning. I'm dead, remember.' Daud paused. 'And men? Are there any men in her life now?'

'Dozens, but not in that way, no. She's become a sort of general of the army in your absence. All the commodores and captains are terrified of her. You'd be proud of her. Her motherly duty, she calls it. I'm sure she thinks you arranged the whole thing, disappearing with all your gold into the Yemen or somewhere and setting up with a harem of Nubian odalisques like some Turkish pasha. Well, that's what she says when she's in the mood to complain. I promise you, nobody has any idea what happened to you. Mostly people assume banditry, of course.'

Daud laughed. It was a relief to know that Hadida was well. 'But what about Abdul Qabid?'

'Leave that to me. I have an idea. Come down to the boat tomorrow; meanwhile I think I'll pop over to Arwad and see what the old Beyruti's been up to.'

Kush finished telling Hadida the details of his conversation with Abdul Qabid. She had viewed the whole meeting from her high window and watched the Beyruti heading back towards the harbour. She remained at the window deep in thought.

'If he doesn't know where Daud is, then he must think he is alive. That he didn't die in any ambush. That Abdul Qabid… I know his type, he'd squeeze the last drop of oil from an olive, and then chew the stone for a week before selling it on. Now he thinks he can squeeze the poor widow. We've got to fix him.' In her heart she remained loyal to her lost husband, even if in her mind she was still furious with him for disappearing without a word of goodbye.

A knock came from below. It was Captain Ali, who had just narrowly avoided bumping into Abdul Qabid on his way from the waterfront. Kush let him in and he joined the lady upstairs.

'What's going on, Ali, who is this character from Beirut? What's he nosing around here for? Is this some debt of Daud's I don't know about? You must have found out something, he was on your boat for three days. What a creep he looks!'

'Oh Hadida, perhaps he's come as a suitor. You know the Greek story…'

'Don't joke with me, Ali, this is serious'

'No, sorry. In fact, he's well-known around Beirut as a moneylender. But Daud was never mixed up with people like that. Most likely he'll pretend Daud owes him, and will try and get you to pay up.'

'But he seems to think Daud may be here, that he may be still alive.'

'Well, we'll have to dissuade him of that.'

'Then maybe I'll get to play Penelope after all!' she grinned at Captain Ali, who now blushed. Then she turned to the lad squatting on his haunches. 'Kush, you go after the Beyruti and tell him I want to see him here tomorrow afternoon.'

'Couldn't we just bump him off?' said Kush, trying to be helpful.

'Enough Kush!'

Kush disappeared, leaving the Captain and Hadida together speaking in conspiratorial tones.

The following afternoon Abdul Qabid set out once more from Tartous. The onshore breeze meant it was a rough crossing, and he arrived on Arwad looking as bilious as a barrel of jellied eels. He steadied himself on the quayside, and then asked directions to Hadida's house. The street urchins didn't harangue him this time, just eyed him cautiously. Kush had spread the word about the foreigner's temper.

'At least they've stopped singing that song,' thought Abdul Qabid as he made his way to Hadida's house. He was let in by a maid who led him upstairs to the reception room. The walls were lined with low divans spread with colourful rugs and silk cushions, and a table was laid with fruit: dried figs and walnuts from Anatolia, strawberries from Tartous and dates from Medina. There were little pistachio-filled, syrupy pastries and on another table stood a silver jug and two wine glasses.

'*Ahlan wa sahlan!* Welcome!' Hadida greeted her guest with open arms. 'Please, come, sit. Won't you eat something after your journey. The sea crossing can be so tiresome when the wind is from the west.' She sat Abdul Qabid at one end of a long divan. She put fruit and nuts on a plate, and poured him wine from the jug. It was strong wine from the slopes above Latakia which she had fortified with a little brandy. 'Here, drink!' It was an order. Hadida sat further down the divan by a luxuriant potted palm.

Abdul Qabid was unsure how to respond. He had never been offered wine by a woman in the privacy of her home before. In fact he rather avoided such situations which he felt were more suited to the whorehouse, a place he certainly didn't frequent, unless it was to collect rent or debt repayments, or to observe the comings and goings of the clientele as material for blackmail. In the end he decided that this must be the custom in Arwad.

He drank. And she drank. Or, at least, she did a fine job of pretending to match him glass for glass, holding the attention of his one eye, while slyly tipping her wine into the potted palm on his blind side.

'Now, you're probably wondering why I invited you here. Well, I understand that you may have news of my husband. You know he went missing, I suppose? And I hear you're interested in buying his business. Did you know Daud well?'

'No, not really. Our paths crossed of course, in business. Is it true that he has...' Abdul Qabid paused, feigning a look of extreme pity and condolence, 'passed away?'

'Oh, I've heard so many different stories: that he was ambushed and his caravan robbed, and no one left alive. But I think he just went off to Yemen or India with one of his mistresses. You do know he took a fortune of gold with him, don't you? Why, I ask? Only one reason, I tell you, he had another woman and wanted to set up a new life.'

Hadida looked imploringly at Abdul Qabid, leaning closer to him with every word. She was using the gaze of seduction, which never failed her in her business dealings. She lowered her head and looked out from beneath her eyelids, making her eyes look bigger. Then she blinked her long lashes, all innocent and beguiling. Resting the rim of the glass on her own wine-dark bottom lip, she tilted it gently up so the liquid spread catching the light in its ruby pool and casting a rosy glow upon her cheeks.

'You know, it's not easy managing without a man. Daud left me with such a mess of business from one end of the Levant to the other. It's all I can do to keep trading and pay the captains and the agents, the forwarders and the cargo handlers… and as for the customs officers – you know the bribes they expect! I really should have a man around to deal with such things, don't you think?' She breathed in deeply and sighed, her bosom rising and falling as she leaned her décolleté towards him. A drop of wine fell from the rim of her glass into the gorge of her cleavage. Hadida arrested its descent upon a henna-tipped finger which then she licked.

Abdul Qabid resisted a strong urge to flee. He thought of rebuffing Hadida, but he needed to be sure she really didn't know where Daud was. He drew a little closer and allowed her to rest her arm on his shoulder, her face now only a few inches from his. Hadida was still an attractive woman in spite of the rigours of raising five children. Her lily of the valley perfume married with her own natural chemistry in such a way it would have collapsed the defences of anyone susceptible to female seduction. But Abdul Qabid wasn't into women. It wasn't even that he preferred his own sex. Or rather, it was precisely because he preferred *his* own sex, and no one else's, male or female, that he found it difficult to dissemble now. But he did his best. He took Hadida in a fearful embrace and planted a rather dry and tight kiss on her full and expectant lips. 'Far enough,' thought Hadida, and she slipped her hand down the back of the divan and yanked the hidden bell- pull.

Seconds later there burst into the room the roughest-looking gang of bearded Arwadis, Tartousis, Baniyasis and other piratical types, all purporting to be Hadida's in-laws intent on protecting her honour. Hadida wailed and clung to Abdul Qabid. But the gang hauled him away. They gave him a sound beating, and only relented from slitting his throat because Hadida begged them to spare his life, saying it was all a misunder-standing, that in her grief she thought it was her husband returning. He was freed with the warning never to show his face within a hundred leagues of Arwad. Then he was unceremoniously hurled out into the street where a gang of yelling urchins pursued him down to the seashore.

From nowhere Kush appeared and pulled him over to an old rowing skiff by the water's edge. It was half full of water but the fugitive managed to drag it into the sea and scramble aboard as the growing crowd of young lads began to pelt him with pebbles, closing in on him like a pack of dogs. The boat had no oars, just an old copper baler which he used to scull the little craft away from the shore.

It was late afternoon, and the sun was low in the west. Abdul Qabid, bedraggled and bruised, shivering with cold and fright, looked across the mile or so to the mainland as he continued to paddle. But the boat was taking in water, and he regularly had to stop to bale out. The sun set. The lights were coming on in Tartous. A small coaster put out from Arwad and tacked north towards the mainland port. It passed Abdul Qabid on his blind side, but had he looked up from his baling, he might have seen some resemblance in the boat's crew to Hadida's 'in-laws', and he might have seen the laughing face of Captain Ali at the tiller. As it was, he was hard put to prevent the dinghy from being capsized by the larger vessel's wake.

It was an uneven struggle. Abdul Qabid was tiring and his rowing slowed; but whenever he stopped rowing, he drifted towards the island. He baled furiously, but it did no good, the water just kept coming. He was going nowhere but down.

Night fell and something bumped against the stern. 'A log in the water,' Abdul Qabid mumbled to himself. He continued to bale. It grew darker until he could barely make out the dinghy's outline in the dim light of the waning moon. The water level was getting higher. It was no use. He let go of the baler and the boat floated for a while as if suspended, weightless beneath him, a few inches below the level of the sea. He seemed to be supported too. The tide had turned and was carrying him away from the island, north towards the lights of Tartous. But it was an illusion. Once he had drifted into the strong current beyond the island's undersea shelf, the little craft which he had made his home that past hour – it seemed a lifetime – was swept beneath him into the deep. He floated awhile feeling helpless and bereft, slowly becoming numb with cold. He was frightened beyond fear, so that when the big old shark took him down, Abdul Qabid did not even struggle.

EIGHTEEN

Conversations and departures

HE fishermen of Tartous were setting up their stalls behind the harbour as Daud strolled in the cool of the morning. The sea was deep indigo with choppy white tops whipped by the westerly wind. Some broken timber in the distance caught his eye. It was the wreckage of a small dinghy washed up on the tide. There was no doubt about its origin. Carved into the boat's stern was the name 'Utarid' – the planet Mercury; the same dinghy in which as a child he had run away to Tartous after arguing with his father; and which he had given to his young cousin Kush when he too had wanted to escape the island at the age of seven. Kush had been found by Captain Ali weeks later hiding out in the old ruined castle of Qalat Marqab which guarded the coast to the north, where he had survived by fishing and stealing fruit from farms.

Daud looked at the wreck, and felt a wave of unease in his stomach. That afternoon, as he crossed the square by the walls of the Tartous citadel, he heard the local lads singing a new version of the Excessively Frightened Gentleman from Beirut. It told of the garlic-mouthed Beyruti's unrequited passion for a widow's gold, his discovery *'in flagrante'* molesting the widow in mock seduction, and his escape from the enraged Arwadis, only to be devoured by a monster of the deep. The song would already have come to the ears of Sharleen's men, who would report it as fact to their boss accordingly.

Daud passed among the derelict fortifications of the old Crusader city. Its high walls of pale cut stone, in some areas more than thirty feet thick, were pierced here and there by arched alleyways, barely wide enough for two laden camels to pass. High windows indicated dwellings carved out within the walls. Daud arrived before the high entrance facade of the Church of the Virgin of Tortosa, constructed by the Templar Knights in the days of the Crusader wars. Daud knew of these fanatical para-military Christians, and their rivals the Knights Hospitallers, from stories heard as a boy: how Saladin had bypassed the Crusader knights in their impregnable fortress Krak des Chevaliers, as he led the Muslim army north after defeating the Christians at the Horns of Hattin. The knights held on in Arwad long after the mainland had been cleared of Christian troops, and even now the Frankish features inherited from the island's garrison were remarked upon among the present-day inhabitants. This was either a compliment, affirming an individual's fierceness and resoluteness, or an insult, indicating ungainliness or foreign looks. It depended on the context.

Daud stood inside the doorway of the abandoned church, blinded by the change from bright afternoon to gloomy, high vaulted interior. Mote-filled sunbeams intersected the sombre verticals of stone columns, then melted into the floor in a splash of reflected light. The building was as much a fortress as a place of worship, a reminder of the rigorous aesthetic of those ancient warrior monks and their constant need to defend against attack. At the base of one of the columns sat the figure of Captain Ali. He greeted Daud cheerfully and they discussed the previous evening's escapade, in which Daud had also taken part, albeit in the background, heavily made up and veiled like a desert nomad.

'Do you think anyone saw through my disguise?' Daud was still worried he may have been recognised.

'No, none of the shore party were local men, I made certain of that. And with that beard, even I was hard put to know you yesterday. So, what's your next move?'

'Back to Damascus, I guess.' Then, from out of the blue 'But I might drop by Qalat al Hosn on the way.'

Daud was referring to the vast Hospitaller stronghold of Krak de Chavevaliers, long since abandoned. According to what Haywani had told

Gülbahar, it was the hideout of Taymir al Bad and his brigands. That's crazy, he thought to himself – what could possibly be gained from going anywhere near that den of vipers? Then he remembered the girl. Perhaps… but no, he put her out of his head. She must have been a dream. And anyway, what chance could there be of running into her again, even if she did exist? Daud had no idea where he had been at the time of their meeting, except that it couldn't have been too far from Seydnaya, a long way on from the Qalat.

'Qalat al Hosn? Is that wise?' asked Captain Ali. He knew that the mountainous area between Homs, Tartous and the Bekaa was rife with bandits and ne'er-do-wells who were not suffered by the good folk of the towns.

Daud smiled. 'Was it wise to dress up as pirates and scare that criminal into the jaws of a shark? Who knows what's wise? I certainly don't – all I can do is follow the clues as they appear. Something is drawing me that way. Perhaps I will find that something there, and maybe then I'll know. For now it just seems to be the next step.'

They embraced and bade each other farewell. Captain Ali stepped back out into the sunlight, leaving his friend alone the gloom. Daud walked down between the two rows of pillars, and crossed into the right hand aisle. Here he sat, upon the worn stones, out of sight of the main door. Above, in the apse, a large bird of stone looked down. Or would have looked down had not its head been missing. Daud gazed at the empty space, and in the half-light his anxieties faded as night shadows in the dawn. He was not surprised when there appeared in place of the bird's missing head the face of his old friend and erstwhile guide, Shams the Goat, grinning from on high.

'Oh Shams, what a mess I've got myself into. I really don't know what to do any more. Everyone is after me, and wherever I go, I seem to leave nothing but chaos and death in my wake.'

'Nonsense, it all seems fine to me.'

'What do you mean 'fine'? Don't you know people are trying to kill me? And when I try and do something about it, people end up getting killed. Really Shams, I've had enough.'

'Come come now, what are you getting so het up about? You say you don't know what to do. Well, I think you're doing fine thank you very much, doing nothing much at all. Just you be where you have to be, keep your eyes open and do nothing. What could be more simple?'

'Simple? What's simple about that?'

'Well, you for a start,' said Shams.

Daud didn't rise to the goat's sarcasm. 'But when's it all going to end? It's a nightmare.'

'Nonsense. If you think you had anything to do with the death of Haywani or Abdul Qabid, forget it. One killed by a scorpion, the other by a shark. It was in their destiny. It would have happened anyway, so stop whinging, there's nothing wrong with you.' Shams gave Daud what appeared to be a leery look and grinned. 'And anyway, what about that young lady?'

Daud was shocked. 'Young lady? What young lady? What on earth are you talking about?

'Come come now, don't get huffy with me. Not wishing to pry, but you don't imagine I wasn't aware of your little dalliance in the desert, do you? I mean, you weren't exactly discreet, out there by the pool, in the middle of the day.'

Daud flushed with irritation and embarrassment. He would have answered Shams sharply, but the recollection of the details of his meeting in the wilderness dissolved his anger into a feeling of loss and sweet regret.

'Oh Shams, what am I to do? Did I really meet her? Did we really… you know?… and she is so beautiful. What am I to do?'

'Again, do nothing, and remember, love conquers all. Though you could, I suppose, try and find her again.' Shams gave an approving if expectant look.

'Find her? But how? I mean, I'm not even sure if she exists. At least, not in this world.'

The hoary old goat-face atop the stone bird guffawed, 'Oh, you don't still think you've been visited by an angel, do you? Did it ever occur to you that there might be some gorgeous creature out there – someone real, of flesh and blood – that might also be longing for the vision of her beloved? Her beloved – that's you, in case you didn't catch my drift.'

This goat, thought Daud, is particularly obnoxious today.

'Well, if you're so clever, how do you propose I find her?' Daud snapped.

'There is a saying, among detectives and hunters, that if you want to catch your prey, you return to the scene of its last kill.' Daud smarted at the phrase and shot a murderous glance at Shams who continued, 'Which supposes, of course, that you know who is the hunter and who the hunted. Look back and learn…'

Shams' last words hung in the air as the goat's face slowly faded. Daud did not notice. He was thinking over what Sham's had said and was lost in the sweet memory that his words had revived. After some minutes, he realised he was still gazing up at the space where the stone bird's head might have been. The audience was over.

Darkness fell, and in the quiet of evening Daud and his troupe of goats headed out of the city. Krak des Chevaliers lies about forty miles to the south-east of Tartous. Daud was in no hurry. He needed time to take in recent events, and he needed solitude. Being around people got him into trouble. A period of gentle grazing would be good for his flock and for him; he was determined to shrug off the oppressive clouds that had gathered around him in recent weeks, and to find some clarity. So, he headed off into the hills, following his nose.

NINETEEN

Krak de Chevaliers

N THIS bright future, we shan't forget our past,' sings the minstrel in the court of Queen Bilquis. Appreciation of true value is seeing into the depth of things. To appreciate the future, Daud must now dive into the past. Not simply the brief span of his life measured in the rotations of planets, suns and galaxies, that geocentric perspective of time-created self, although this too indicates, in summary, the totality. 'Look back and learn' says Shams. So Daud looks to the place of beginning, where there is so much to discover. Always a story within a story. And therein a story. And then the storyteller.

And here is Daud, wandering under burning skies, beneath star-filled nights through the hills and valleys of the Jebel an-Nusayriyah, into a past that he never suspected. Journeying not in time, but as a stone cast in the ocean he sinks within himself. First through the layers of memories, which passage as a warm current below the surface of his thoughts. Then deeper into a world darkened only by his unknowing, which his material mind has no strength to illumine. He craves another light, and gradually,

becoming accustomed, he sees a world independent of referential dimension. A unified vision. For he sees a thing both from himself, and from
itself; everything appearing according to an interior volition; thoughts and
meanings transforming into bodies of light, radiant, shaped, formal. Daud
has entered a region of vastness, a passage between worlds in which
happenings are both defined and yet seemingly infinite. Between an above
and a below. Except there is no above or below, nor front, nor back, nor
even inside nor outside.

And when Daud returned to himself, this vision did not cease like a
fabulous dream which dissolves upon waking. Something remained,
adding a new depth to the topography of his wanderings. It became a place
to rest in, like a home in himself.

Summer wore itself out eventually and the world rested in the brief
and balmy days of autumn. The leaves on the fruit trees gathered dust and
desiccated, and the nights needed a blanket when sleeping out on the high
ground. Daud sat with his flock in the early morning, gazing over the
shadowed land to where the dawn light was creeping down the white stone
walls of the hilltop castle of Krak des Chevaliers.

Then something quite unexpected happened. The distance between
Daud and the castle just folded up to nothing, so he found himself, in
vision if not in body, sitting right before its gate. It was as if the two ends of
a piece of string, at one moment stretched out straight at furthest extent,
were suddenly joined together in a circle, and he and the castle inhabited
that point where the two ends met. Had he, through some interruption of
the usual order of things, been moved towards the castle? Or had the castle
been drawn to him? He had no idea what was going on, and it didn't seem
to matter.

This castle interested Daud. He looked at the smooth cliff-face of steep
walls and rising towers, the dark heights of laid stone blocks forming the
curves of its battlements. The old gate was closed, but broken. No locks or
bolts or armed guards. Not that it would have made any difference, for
Daud's new-found mobility took him instantly to wherever he placed his
attention. He entered. To his left was a long, barrel-vaulted tunnel,
enclosing a cobbled ramp, which led up inside the outer walls. The air was
filled with bats, but even their sonar did not detect Daud as he moved
freely among them like a ghost. Daud saw other non-physical forms: pale,
subtle creatures which cowered in corners or fled, perhaps sensing an

invisible presence. After fifty yards or so the tunnel turned abruptly in a hairpin bend and continued up. He took a short passage branching off to the left, and emerged into an open area between the outer fortification and the central bastion. The place was deserted.

The phantoms of the tunnel vanished in the bright daylight leaving only the hard rock and earth of the physical environment. The walls of the inner keep rose up from steep, sloping bases formed of smooth, tightly-fitted stones, now bearded in the stubble of dry weeds and shrivelled grass. Every thirty or forty metres circular towers interrupted the line of the wall at the point where the skirt of sloping masonry turned upwards to the vertical. The entire circumference formed a roughly oval-shaped citadel, surrounded by a dank moat; an impregnable mass, within and above a curtain of stone walls and towers which history had proved inexpugnable. The Krak had yielded only to deceit and the decay of time.

Daud returned to the tunnel and continued his ascent. The dark passage eventually insinuated itself, by rising twists and turns, into the main body of the inner castle where again he found himself in the open. He breezed around a honeycomb of nooks and crannies, winding staircases, round towers and lookouts over rolling hills to rainclouds gathering in the west. Back inside, he proceeded through interminable empty rooms and deserted halls. He came at last to a fine colonnade of gothic arches and rose window frames, now just bare, weathered stone bereft of timbered doors and leaded glass. In this shady arcade stood a number of donkeys and horses. The arcade fronted a large hall with a vaulted ceiling. Beyond this room opened an even larger space, more than a hundred yards in length, and half a hundred in width. In the first hall a dozen or so men were lying about, drinking and smoking, some sleeping, some just sitting in silence. Aside from the main body, Taymir al Bad lay on a couch fidgeting nervously.

In the second hall, Daud was presented with the awesome sight of forty-one corpses all laid out in a row in varying states of decomposition. By the head of each corpse were neatly laid the garments of the deceased fellow, and beyond that, all the equipage of his camel: straps and blankets, bags and ropes. At the foot of each was a pile of gold bars, gleaming even in the gloom as the treasure stole all meagre light to itself. Atop all but one of the forty one stacks of bullion, like some guardian spirit, sat the ghosts of the camel drivers – Daud's camel drivers. He recognised them immedi-

ately and understood their sad defiance. Wordless, he communicated heart
to heart with each in turn. And in turn these faithful shades informed
Daud how nightly they plagued their murderers, those miscreants of the
first room, by invading their dreams. The stronger-spirited of the camel-
drivers made spectral appearances to the more susceptible of the brigands.
The brigands had become sleepless and confused, and had been unable, so
far, to disperse the stolen goods. The camel drivers' charge had been to
deliver their cargo, and they were not giving it up without a fight. Only the
forty-first pile of gold, with its rotting corpse, had no ghostly guardian.

This loyal guarding was no longer necessary, thought Daud. Death
had relieved the cameleers of their responsibilities. He tried to communicate his feelings to them, but they were adamant in their wish to fulfil
their duties before making their departure final. That their passing away
was not complete was not really surprising. The prayers for the dead had
not been said for them. They had broken camp, the camels loaded, the fires
doused, but the caravan had not moved on.

Daud retreated to the first room where a visitor arrived to see Taymir
al-Bad. Although unable to hear their conversation, Daud understood
clearly what passed between them:

'Salaam aleykum!'

'Wa aleyka salaam!'

'Greetings of peace to you, o great warrior, and servant of the saga-
cious one.'

'Likewise, o noble Abdul Qahhar, and what brings you all they way out
here?'

'Oh, just passing, just passing. You know how it is, training the hunting
dogs…, you get about quite a bit.'

'Can we bring you coffee, something to eat perhaps.'

'So very kind. Perhaps later, it's still barely gone breakfast time.'

'But surely there is something we can offer you?'

'No really, you are too kind. But I was wondering, how did you manage
with the Arwadi's caravan? It is rumoured that he escaped. Is that true?'

'No, no, he is in there with the rest of them, come and see.'

'Why, yes, I'd very much like to.'

Daud followed the host and his guest, back into the charnel house of
caravaneers, and was surprised at what he now saw. From the shoulders of
Abdul Qahhar emerged a horrible wraith-like creature, the form of an

enormous and greedy jinn. The ghostly caravaneers cowered behind their piles of gold at this terrible apparition. Abdul Qahhar saw them, and their rotting corpses, but conned immediately that one pile was unguarded. They returned to the first room.

'So, now you have seen, you can report, ok?' said Taymir.

'Yes. Forty one corpses, what could be clearer. Now, I had another reason to visit you, I have a message from our true benefactor. He wants to reward you. Let's go outside where none of this rabble can hear, they will only be envious, and who knows where that may lead, eh?'

'Yes, certainly. They are thieves, not men. And envy among thieves is more dangerous even than jealousy between lovers.'

Taymir was relieved that it had all gone so well, and happily stepped out into the daylight with Abdul Qahhar. Daud kept his distance as they ascended the steps to what is called the Tower of the King's Daughter. All the while, Abdul Qahhar spoke softly into the ear of Taymir al Bad telling of the robes of honour and the pearl-skinned concubines with almond eyes awaiting him as reward for his unstinting service to Omo Sharleen. Taymir was relieved. The kind words and silken tongue of Abdul Qahhar were a hypnotic balm after the long months of fretting over the missing Daud, and he felt as if he was walking on air. Together they gazed out over the hills to the distant Mediterranean, feeling the wind swell the atmosphere as dark clouds gathered. Abdul Qahhar put his arm across Taymir's shoulder, an avuncular gesture, friendly, as if gently ushering him on. Daud indeed thought he saw Taymir's feet step out over the precipice, as a strong gust lifted his clothes, and the bandit leader flew gently, silently, to meet the rock below. The jinn upon the hunter's back shrank into the form of a black birdlike thing and swept down to snatch the soul of Taymir just as the force of impact with the ground shook it free of its mortal housing. There was, after all, no point in letting such a devoted servant go to waste.

The shock of what Daud witnessed broke whatever spell had allowed him these strange insights. He found himself back sitting on the hillside, perhaps a mile away. He needed to take stock. Daud had been privy to all that had taken place, yet it seemed a veil had existed between the jinn and himself. The caravaneers had been visible both to him and the jinn, yet the jinn had been unable to see him. Daud was not yet aware of the strength of protection afforded him by his Damascus Drum.

Remembering the caravaneers, standing sentinel over the stolen cargo, Daud felt saddened. He took up the Drum, and began tapping it slowly. In his mind's eye he saw again the mournful souls of his employees, and a wave of loving compassion filled his heart. He began to recite the prayers for the dead, prayers which he didn't even know he knew. Then he blew the bright essence of his recitation across the valleys to leaven their hearts and illumine their souls in their dark and lonely outpost.

The response from the castle was almost instantaneous. From within the distant towers and walls, a crowd of black birds took wing in raucous flight, heading north pursued by a huge eagle. As peace returned, forty doves flew up from the central bastion, rose high and disappeared from view in the brightness of the sun. Then heavy clouds closed in from the west, the wind became stronger, the sky darkened and with it came the spitter spatter of rain on dry earth. The first of the autumn storms had arrived.

TWENTY

An Egyptian interlude

S THE early morning sun warmed the pale stones of Seydnaya and bright-eyed sisters in dark wool balaclavas flung open the convent's windows to the freshness of the day, as carpenters stoked fires under tar-pits and sharpened their chisels and adzes in the shipyards of Arwad, as Touma and his fellow merchants in the souks of Damascus sipped coffee and greeted each other at their shop doors – while all the people in the holy lands between the Arabian Peninsula and the Eastern Mediterranean, from the heights of Anatolia to the valleys of the Nile, from the flood plains of Mesopotamia to the desert shores of Yemen, shook the sleep from their eyes and let in this single light – within that same awakening dawn the assassin Abdul Qahhar ran through the hilly desert at an easy trot, surrounded by his pack of slender hunting dogs. Like steam from a distant train, their breath hung in a trailing cloud over the rocky ground as they made their way between boulders, down ravines, and rising up escarpments; never stopping, speeding up or slowing down, but moving at a steady pace in the cool air.

Abdul Qahhar had picked up the spoor of a lion and was giving his young hounds a practice run, to familiarise them with the scent of this beast, now so rarely seen in Asia. On this occasion he had no intention of letting the hunt become a kill. The dogs needed time to get to know the ways of such a quarry, to discover their own strengths and weaknesses in the face of this adversary. Mostly, they had to learn the discipline of following the lead of Abdul Qahhar, their top dog. Anyway, the spoor was old, and a challenge even for such an experienced tracker as he. There was no danger of a confrontation that day.

The same early morning sun greeted the inhabitants of the ancient city of Hama. Hama lies upon the Orontes River (the 'rebel river', so-called because it flows away from south to north, in geographical opposition to the noble Tigris or magnanimous Euphrates). Here the great workhorses of hydrotechnology called *norias* were being unchained by their guardians. The slow creaking timbers of these fifty-foot high waterwheels rang a gentle reveille as they turned to their task of replenishing the thirsty fields.

Following Orontes' sweet waters south, the sleepy town of Homs awaited the arrival of the first travellers of the day. Upstream beyond Homs on a high hill sat a wild-looking country man surveying the land below and the hills beyond. Not far off grazed his goats, now increased to around forty in number in the months since we left him deep in prayer upon another North Syrian hilltop. Circling around were three smallish Canaan dogs, acquired during his wanderings to help protect his growing herd. From time to time Daud shaded his eyes and pointed to something down below, speaking as if to a companion, although no one else was present to view.

Daud had been sitting there since before dawn. Although it was a chilly night, he was warm within his fleece-lined cloak. While he kept vigil, the sky had shed its own glittering black cape, revealing deep purple, blue then paler raiment, until gradually the landscape dawned within the veil of the still-hidden sun.

Below the hill was a small stream. Further on, perhaps a mile away, was the Orontes, which here divided around a large island on which stood a walled city. To Daud's right, a couple of miles upstream, the river spread shallow over a rocky ford, beyond which a scrubby forest extended.

With daylight Daud could make out shapes and movement on the plain below. The scene was remarkably different from the empty landscape upon which the sun had set the previous evening. He held the Drum close to his chest and asked questions aloud. It had become a habit during this period of retreat. He was neither expecting, nor was he surprised when out of nowhere came the voice of his erstwhile companion and guide, Shams:

'It's the Egyptians, here to battle with the Hittites from the north. But you don't have to see this if you don't want to. It all happened so long ago.'

'No, I don't mind, but you'll have to explain.'

'Then understand. We are not the first to sit up here, and we won't be the last. This land hasn't always been such a sleepy backwater. Why, there was a time when great events took place right here, events which shaped the world at the time – and men's minds are shaped by the world they live in. But now, there's not even a castle ruin to remind you, like at Qalat al Hosn. The spirit of the world moves on, and few people remember the battle of Kadesh, when the great Pharaoh Ramesses II was stopped in his tracks and very nearly wiped off the face of the earth...' Shams paused in his narration and sighed the lofty sigh of a wise old billy goat. 'Yes, events which shaped the world. But did they *change* it? Did they change *minds*, I wonder? Who knows...? Perhaps ever so little...'

The sky was lightening to a dull yellow. It was easy now to make out the encampment below, a vast army of tents and lines of tethered horses and pack animals. Then the sun appeared, but in the western sky. They seemed to be stepping backwards in chunks of time for it was now just before sunset. A distant clattering of cooking vessels, jingling of harnesses, and barking of orders reached Daud's ears. Smoke from dozens of camp fires drifted as a ghostly haze over the army.

'That's the camp of one of Ramesses' four army divisions. Look how relaxed they are. They think the enemy has retreated to Aleppo, when actually the Hittites are on the other side of Kadesh city, out of sight,' said Shams.

'But I don't understand, how does it go backwards? I mean, time – how can we see this stuff from the past ?'

'It doesn't go backwards. We're simply looking at the logical layering of events. Time happens in depth, as well as forwards and backwards. In fact, the forwards and backwards only happen because you take a point of view within it.' Shams paused, as if rearranging his thoughts for a mortal man's understanding, and then continued; 'Time occurs wherever there is a where, and someone to stand in the place of that where. It's really no different from a book. We can open it up and look into it where we choose, and when we do, then there we are as well! If it's our own book, and we don't like the plot, we can rewrite it. After all, a book is only a book. It's the meaning of the story that matters.' Then his tone changed to excitement,

'Look over there, there's Ramesses' own camp, separate from the main body of the army. All those magnificent tents are for him and his nobles, and those splendid guards in fancy dress. Now see what's happening, some soldiers have captured a couple of enemy spies, and they're being brought before Ramesses.'

Daud looked, and instantly found himself present inside the Pharaoh's tent. His point of vision was situated on the right forearm of Ramesses himself, as if he was a jewel in a bracelet. It was a good view. Two rough-looking men, wrists bound, were flat on the ground before the Egyptian ruler. The prisoners, naked, bloodied and grimy, were each held down by a spearhead and a guard's sandalled foot upon his neck. Through interpreters they were explaining that, yes, the Hittite army had in fact not left the area, but was camped just on the other side of Kadesh, the walled island city. The Pharaoh gave orders to bring up the second army division right away.

Does time move on, or do we move through time? For Daud it was like peering through honey, everywhere a glistening bubble with a new scene. Now it was the following dawn.

'Look over there, see that dust rising? It's the Pharaoh's second army' said Shams.

A couple of miles to the south and beyond the river lay dense woods. Daud could see dust rising, but there was a strange silence. Then out of the trees and bushes lining the riverbank burst a mass of chariots carrying bowmen and lancers, drawn by horses bedecked for war. Behind them ran foot soldiers, and then supply wagons pulled by oxen and lastly the camp followers. They careered through the shallow water, fording the Orontes en masse, splashing over the stones, and up the near bank. They were midway between the river and the Pharaoh's first army when the Hittites struck from their right. Dozens of heavy Hittite chariots had crossed from the east and drove right into the centre of the Egyptians, scattering their smaller chariots which barely had time to turn. Arrows filled the sky with their dark hail. The Egyptians were in rout as they tried desperately to push on north to join up with the Pharaoh's first division. Chaos was added to chaos as the second Egyptian army reached the first camp with the Hittites pressing hard on their heels, their archers firing at will.

'Watch Ramesse,' said Shams.

Another viscous bubble of time floated into view. A tall, dark figure appeared, the Pharaoh, dressed in noble robes of gold and lapis lazuli and accompanied by a group of well-armed men. They mounted a fleet of light Egyptian chariots pulled by pairs of strong, disciplined horses. As arrows flew in every direction, the pharaoh and his guard held off the attack while others hastily removed his family members from the battle ground. Seeing that the Hittites, whose unwieldy vehicles had become bogged down in the fight, seemed more intent on plunder than victory, the Pharaoh turned his attention back to the battle. With his noblemen at his side he fought on untiringly until reinforcements arrived. Then the Hittite contingency, sated with blood and booty, retreated across the Orontes.

Daud plunged further through waves of time: Ramesses back in Egypt, signing a peace treaty leaving Kadesh in Hittite hands. The Pharaoh marrying a Hittite princess. Then, Daud heard sweet music playing upon a lute, whose complex harmonies and beguiling beauty absorbed him entirely.

'Look now,' said Shams.

The sun was well up. Where moments before armies engaged in reckless slaughter, now the land was empty except for a boy leading a few cows down to the river. The walled city of Kadesh had vanished, the cries of battle gone, and the luxurious music echoing in Daud's ears faded away. The only sound was the bleating of his goats as they munched the dry grass and leaves on the hillside.

TWENTY-ONE

Excursions into joined-up being

ENERABLE and terrible rises the citadel of Aleppo, encircled in skirts of stone, a despot enthroned upon an ancient mound. Below, in the corridors of the Great Souk, second only to the Grand Bazaar of Constantinople in its bounteous display, the merchants fuss and bus among the shunting crowds. Five thousand years of human habitation hang layered in its dusty atmosphere, every step and thought imprinted in the air, motes upon an invisible web, so that by the simple act of breathing, the traveller is infused with history from the very beginning.

Following the disturbing events at Qalat al Hosn, Daud continued his solitary way. He was happy that the faithful caravaneers could now pursue their journeying in the next world. But the matter of Abdul Qahhar worried him. Seeing that monstrous jinn made Daud realise that he had become the quarry of a hunter whose net reached beyond the mundane to subtle realms. Daud travelled north, thinking to disappear in the crowded streets of Aleppo, but after a time the cloak of urban anonymity began to smother him. He needed space. He wanted an horizon.

Daud quit the city and turned south. He spent weeks close by the banks of the Orontes, moving through Hama and Homs. Sometimes, in the dark hours before dawn, he had the uncomfortable feeling that someone or something was looking for him. It wasn't like being followed, but something was definitely out there, sniffing the air, trying to pick up a scent. Daud dared not name it, nor even think about it, lest the smell of his fear alert the pursuer. He knew he faced evil but felt impotent. He thumped the drum from time to time, but no response came from its dry skin. He felt abandoned.

Daud eventually came onto the trail of his lost caravan, south of Homs, near the road to Damascus. It was a lonely road this time round, without the companionship of his forty brave caravaneers. Then Shams had returned briefly, and together they witnessed the battle at Kadesh. Seeing such grand panorama reduced to a history lesson in the dust of time gave Daud a different perspective on his problems, and he became less preoccupied with his own mortal fate. The weather became colder, snow fell on the high ground and ice-laden winds poured down from the steppes and deserts of Persia and Anatolia. Clear skies, deep blue above the frozen mountain tops, gave welcome relief to his troubled mind as he followed his herd. He still felt the sense of a pressing engagement with destiny, but he worried less.

One afternoon Daud arrived at a glade of trees surrounding a small frozen pool. A steep cliff rose above, at the foot of which was a cave. The place seemed strangely familiar. But the goats were nervous and the dogs growled as they paced the area. The dogs insisted on herding the goats away up a winding track, and the animals did not stop fretting until all were settled on a wide rock spur high atop the cliff. Daud was not going to argue, neither with goat nor dog, even if it meant sleeping under the stars. He cooked up some chick peas and peppers which he ate with yoghurt and unleavened bread, then fed the dogs with a porridge of the leftovers.

That night the drought in Daud's soul ended. Shams appeared to him in a waking dream. Not the friendly but irreverent, disdainful yet familiar presence of old, but a different Shams altogether. A Shams in battledress, so to speak, with the authority of a general before combat. His outward appearance had not changed, yet he seemed bigger, and his shaggy face emanated a deep sense of comradeship, the warmth of which filled Daud with renewed confidence and inner strength. Daud had the backing he needed. He sat up, attentive.

'Ready for battle are we, then?' Happily, Shams' manner of speech was as informal as ever.

'Well, yes, and no…' Daud was unsure what to think.

' "Between yes and no, heads separate themselves from their bodies, and spirits take flight…" That is what the Great Sheikh said, when he was only a child.' Shams' face took on a look of distant, yet profound recollection, a kind of returning to base. Barely a moment, then he was present again, 'A proper place to start, certainly, but you can't remain there. We must move beyond perplexity.'

'But what can I do, Shams? Abdul Qahhar is one thing, and bad enough at that, but that jinn is something else altogether. I couldn't deal with that anymore than I could kill a lion with my bare hands.'

'You can't kill him; yet, he too must meet his maker, or he will definitely be the end of you. And I don't just mean your body. Remember how he took the soul of Taymir al Bad?'

'Yes, but I am powerless against such a monster.'

'No *yes buts,* boy. You are not powerless, you are *nothing!*' Shams roared the last three words. Daud quailed, even as a small quail quails.

'And that *nothing* is your only protection.' Shams continued, 'Be nothing, and by that be everything. But to really be nothing, you have to be brave. It's time you learnt to rely on something other than this *Daud* that you think you are. What is Daud? Come on, tell me?… See, you can't. You thought it was your body, then you thought it was your mind. That's over. Now it's time to dive in and see.'

There was a pause, then for a split second Daud imagined he saw Shams' goaty hoof stretch out to take his hand. He sensed the earth disappearing beneath him, and then he was falling out of himself into a different place. It was like dissolving into the gentle foam which follows the roll of surf upon the ocean's shore. But this was no earthly event. What Daud now experienced was beyond any consideration of time and space as he knew it.

In the world of shadows that he had just left, Daud had always believed that each moment of existence proceeded from the previous moment, that one event caused the next, and so on, in an unbreakable chain of consequence. In this new world of light, it was different. Each thing appeared unique and yet connected as infinite reflections in a single mirror. Like sisters from the same womb, it was the essential inheritance that held sway, not the apparent lineage of cause and effect. The event of each moment was its own perfect *raison d'être*.

Then everything changed. All the conditions by which Daud differen-
tiated himself in the world, it all disappeared, and he joined up. Joined up
what? Daud asked himself this question later, after he came to. Or rather,
after he returned. For it was on the one hand like arriving back at the place
where one started having turned around on the spot; and on the other
hand like returning from a journey that had lasted an unimaginable length
of time, in a place of truly inconceivable dimension. The more he tried to
fathom what had just occurred, the less it was possible until his mind
collapsed under the inadequacy of his thought. His heart had opened so
wide that its perimeter had simply disappeared. He had become 'l'homme
sans frontières', and he was just left crying out with a rather large and loud
'aaaaaaaaaahhhhh!!!!' of relief, as Jonah might have on being expressed
from the whale's belly.

'So, now you see,' said Shams, and paused, 'or not?'

At that moment Daud knew he had nothing to fear from the jinn.
What he had seen, he had seen, and nothing could ever take that away.
Even if he couldn't explain. Even if he couldn't remember in any conventional sense what it was, a certainty remained that went beyond the
annihilation of all he had previously thought. It was an imagined annihilation, as it had been an imagined Daud. *That* Daud he never was and
never had been. He was moving in different circles now. This was joining
up.

Daud looked at Shams. And he saw that Shams knew exactly what had
happened. Daud also knew that this appearance of Shams had come out of
that magnificent and inexpressible non-place, as had this appearance
called 'Daud'. He realised that, like Shams, he was simply a place, in which
appeared whatever it was he now couldn't find a word for. God. Existence.
Reality. No-thing. His mind fumbled, tumbled over itself; whatever word
he gave it was both true and not true at the same time, and yet there had to
be a word for it. He wasn't it, yet at the same time, when he forgot himself,
he was so in it that he knew there was no difference. So, for now, it was It.

Shams looked back and smiled, the most ancient, kindest and grandest
grandfather Billy goat of them all and Daud felt like a small baby.

'Don't worry,' said Shams, 'you won't forget it. And even when you
forget, it'll still be there. It will never leave you. But you can leave it, so
beware! Hold it close, nurture it, remember it, learn to love it. Then it will

remember you. Call on it and it will help you and it will grow in you and make itself known in you, as who you really are.'

'But how do I remember it?'

'Just keep on being nothing, that should leave it plenty of room.'

Daud was exhausted but exhilarated. He fell asleep on the cliff-top, under the stars, and dreamed a dream. First he was back in Krak de Chevaliers, in the dark hall of dead caravaneers. Then he was travelling into the past, to the very conception of his adversary. He saw how Abdul Qahhar had acquired the jinn just when his drunken father had planted his seed into his mother's womb. At that moment she had turned her face away from her husband, wishing with all her heart it was another in her embrace. And in that look aside, a great jinn of pride had entered into her vision and attached itself to the child-to-be, giving it the powers of the hunter, to follow tracks invisible to others, to see great distances with the jinn's eagle eye, to dissemble his own traces to less than a shadow, and to possess the strength and confidence to face lions and kill them. Years later, in return, Abdul Qahhar learned to kill men with impunity while the great jinn fed upon their corpse-fleeing souls. If only his mother had envisioned the best picture of human potential, with its noblest attributes, how different her child's life might have been.

The dark hall of the castle became even darker. Daud sensed the shade of the jinn deep in a corner, sucking to itself what little light there was, growing darker and heavier. Daud felt it pressing up against him, pushing him down, a great weight crushing his chest. He could no longer breathe properly nor cry out; he was being pulled into that darkness and began to lose consciousness. Then he remembered. And he called to It. Not with words, he was beyond that, nor with sounds, but with his being. He was calling to what he knew was there in himself, something so much bigger, so much more powerful and real than any jinn or feverish nightmare. And in that call Daud felt himself reinforced, as a small lagoon is replenished by the tidal inundations of the ocean, pouring over the levee of his small heart.

Then a cry came out from deep inside him, a cry which, had he heard it as others did, might have terrified him as it did them. Some heard an unearthly call, fit to raise the dead. Some heard the howl of a banshee wind from the desert. But for one hunter lying by his campfire among his dogs it was the roar of a lion like no lion he had ever heard.

The jinn instantly released his hold upon the soul of our hero. It had heard the cry as a command that must be obeyed, from the One to whom all will return one day. And the jinn understood. It had been living on borrowed time, and now was the reckoning. Immediately the jinn prostrated before Daud who was wide awake, his own cry ringing in his ears. Then the veil of sleep descended upon his inner eye, and although he never saw the jinn, he knew its attack had been defeated.

The lion's roar woke Abdul Qahhar out of a nightmare from the darkest underworld of unresolved lives and unrequited actions. He had dreamt himself surrounded by a phalanx of ghouls representing all the victims of his murderous life. They were pointing at their wounds, accusing him and cursing him. He broke away, trying to escape. But the ghouls were always there, right on his tracks, calling his name. They closed on him and for the first time in his life, Abdul Qahhar was afraid. Then the great roar from across the mountains penetrated his sleep, and the image of a lion replaced the hideous forms of his nightmare.

Abdul Qahhar awoke with his heart pounding. The cool pre-dawn air cleared his mind and he focused on the business in hand. 'So, the beast is still about.' he said to himself. 'And what a beast it must be!'

In training his salukis throughout the summer, Abdul Qahhar had covered much the same ground as Daud, as if in parallel pursuit. He had followed tracks, losing and finding and losing again the spoor of that elusive old lion. He had become convinced it had left the area, but now it had announced itself through that mighty roar like a warrior spoiling for a fight. Abdul Qahhar was ready to take up the challenge. The excitement of the chase was upon him and quickly erased the disturbing memories of the night. He looked out from his hillside camp beneath an overhanging rock, but his accustomed eagle-eyed sight, one of the gifts of his association with the jinn, was no longer with him. He merely experienced the normal view of objects gradually diminishing into an oblivion of blurs, smudges and indeterminate shapes. 'Strange.' he thought, and for a moment his mind lit upon the fading reveries of the night. 'Maybe I'm just getting old.' But he quickly dismissed this thought, along with the sense of self-doubt which the discovery of his failing vision had provoked.

The hunter gathered his salukis round him. He did not feed them – that would come later – but talked to them soothingly, encouraging them. They were not the usual hound for hunting lion, too light, lacking in the

necessary aggression. They were more suited for chasing down gazelle. Abdul Qahhar liked their speed and agility, and being meticulously trained to obey his commands, they were a great help in cornering the prey while he readied himself for the lion's charge.

Abdul Qahhar was a desert man. A Zaghawa from the western borderlands of Sudan, he always hunted alone. Others now resorted to modern devices, the rifle and the musket, to bring down their prey from a safe distance. They hunted in rowdy packs with as much subtlety as a platoon of drunken janissaries, and as often as not someone received a mauling. Abdul Qahhar relied solely on his dogs and a single, seven foot spear, upon which he would invite the animal to impale itself.

The salukis trotted off with Abdul Qahhar in the lead. They soon picked up the scent. It was fresh, for the animal had passed that way the previous evening. The trail drew them further into the hills to the south. Soon, however, the dogs took the lead; somewhere Abdul Qahhar had lost the scent, and they continued ahead while he followed. 'Strange...' he thought again, and doubt further shadowed his eyes. He ran faster, aiming to outstrip this unwanted visitor, but it remained, lurking in the back of his mind.

The lion roared again. They were close now. An unaccustomed chill rose from the loins of Abdul Qahhar. It was fear. His chest tightened and his breath became short; he rallied, gripping his spear and running harder than ever. The dogs were two hundred yards ahead as they approached a wooded area below a cliff.

Daud had heard the lion roar, and peered down from his camp on the overhanging rock. Below, in the clearing between the cave and the pool, lay the lion, chewing on the remains of a goat. This unfortunate victim had escaped the protective net of the Canaan sheepdogs in the brief period of mayhem following Daud's own mighty roar, and had run straight into the lion's den. Beyond the trees Daud could see a pack of hounds, followed by a hunter, making their way swiftly towards the cliff.

Daud watched the lion lift its head then rise on its forelegs, holding to itself the dead goat. The first dogs appeared through the trees. The lion dropped the carcass and began to snarl, pacing back and forth, as the pack gathered around in a semi-circle. The salukis approached, first from one side, and then the other. The lion swished its tail and roared, making a short rush at the dogs on his left, who skittered back into the undergrowth. At the same time dogs moved in from the right. The old lion turned and swiped the air with its paw, clipping a hound and sending it tumbling in the dirt, where it lay yelping. The dogs backed off a little. The lion stood its ground, gurning and thrashing the air. The impasse was short lived. Seconds later Abdul Qahhar broke through the trees directly opposite the lion, stopping dead within range of his quarry. The lion pulled back, concentrating all its strength prior to charging.

The hunter barely had time to butt his spear in the earth when the lion leapt. Abdul Qahhar had miscalculated. The spear was angled too high to strike the animal's chest, and instead the tip of flattened steel pierced its throat, slicing through all but the neck bone itself. Abdul Qahhar was caught wrong-footed, and instead of vaulting nimbly to his left, he tripped, spun round, and received the weight of the lion's right claw across his back. The lion did not die immediately, but spent its fury upon Abdul Qahhar, opening his flesh to the bone from neck to buttocks in four parallel furrows, before its own life melted into the frozen earth, and its breath fled upon the icy wind of morning.

TWENTY-TWO

A cave story

 AUD witnessed the scene below the cliff without any particular emotion. Only when he heard Abdul Qahhar's sobbing did he begin to appreciate what had taken place. He ran down and hauled the dead lion off the hunter's back. It looked very bad. The lion's claws had ripped deep gashes, and the hunter was bleeding freely, though no arteries had been cut.

Abdul Qahhar was barely conscious and too shocked to speak, but his face said it all. It would have been easy for Daud to finish him off there and then, a quick snick of the knife across the assassin's bared throat. Even easier to let nature take its course and let him bleed to death, which would happen soon enough. But Daud felt compelled to act. He took from a small goatskin pouch beneath his cloak some salt, a sharp needle and a fine thread of angora goat hair. Having washed the wounds as best he could with water from beneath the frozen surface of the pool, he proceeded to sew up the four bloody furrows which split the hunter's back. It was not a particularly neat job, it must be said, but it was firm, and it staunched the flow of blood. He took off his cloak to wrap his now-unconcious patient against the cold and dragged him into the cave, where he lit a fire. He then moved his own camp down from the cliff top, and laid Abdul Qahhar upon a bed of dry grass and goat skins.

Daud went out to look for herbs to make a poultice. He didn't know which herbs he should use, but he knew he needed to ease the shock which was causing so much pain and preventing the life from flowing in Abdul Qahhar. He also needed heat, and then something to counter the infection which would undoubtedly come from the lion's mauling. Daud scrambled up the goat path, trying not to think, while at the same time asking to be shown. Suddenly, one of his goats jumped off to the side of the track, reached up and snapped the top leaves off a bush growing in the rock face. It then returned to the track and dropped the sprig. Daud picked it up. It had a strong, astringent aroma. The goat climbed on and performed the same action with a different plant, which Daud picked up – the crushed leaves had a soft, sweet, calming scent. A third time the goat pulled up a whole plant and left it for Daud. Its smell was acrid and its taste bitter. The goat then went back to grazing normally.

With these three gifts Daud returned to the cave. He stripped the leaves, broke up the stalks and made an infusion with which he bathed the wounds of the unconscious Abdul Qahhar. He was worried that the hunter was beyond help. Already it seemed some infection had appeared, for his whole back had swollen and the stitched-up wounds formed four long welts of raw flesh, dark purple in colour. He covered him up again and stoked the fire, then towards evening he had another look. It was bad. The wounds had begun to suppurate, and Abdul Qahhar's whole body was burning with fever. Daud bathed the wounds again with the herb water, and then applied a mixture of the same herbs, mashed together and pasted directly on his back. Abdul Qahhar remained unconscious throughout the night and all the next day. On the third day Daud reapplied the poultice, while Abdul Qahhar lay there with barely a movement. His breathing was irregular and weak. The fever burned on. What little life remained was hanging by a slender thread within his ravaged body.

Daud tended to Abdul Qahhar through a whole week, at the end of which his patient began to have periods of consciousness. His eyes would flicker briefly, as if reluctantly clocking back on to life. Daud would then attempt to give him warm water and weak broths carefully spooned into his mouth. Feeding was extremely difficult as Daud had not dared move Abdul Qahhar from his prone position for fear of disturbing the wounds. It was a case of holding his head sideways and pouring gently the liquid between his lips, in the hope that some nourishment would be taken in, and at the very least stave off dehydration. The rest of the time Abdul Qahhar slept fitfully. It was hardly sleep, for a battle raged in his mind as well as in his body, expressed in delirious outbursts, the horrible causes of which Daud did not even try to imagine.

In the third week the wounded hunter began to take milk and yoghurt, and the periods of wakefulness lengthened. Mostly Abdul Qahhar would stare vacantly like a newly born baby, not a real seeing, just a barely distinguishing of inner from outer worlds. The condition of his back began to show improvement. The swelling reduced, and with it the amount of pus. The danger of gangrene receded. As he changed the poultice, Daud also removed stitches where the wound had healed properly. This was a painful business, and perhaps risky, but Daud was reluctant to leave the threads in for longer than necessary.

It was a hard winter, but the cave extended deep into the hillside. It had a water source and the herd could shelter if the snow came too deep outside. There was no shortage of firewood in the immediate area. The salukis had fled when they had seen their master fall beneath the lion, and so Daud had only the three Canaan dogs to feed. He butchered the lion and air-dried the meat in the cave, rationing it out to them with milk and scraps. The goats foraged for themselves up and down the tracks in the cliff face, and kept Daud in good supply of milk. He made occasional trips to a small market at a crossroads half a day's walk north, where he exchanged yoghurt and cheese for dry goods like flour and salt, as well as pulses, vegetables and occasionally pomegranates or lemons.

Whatever battles were going on inside Abdul Qahhar, in caring for him, Daud was experiencing a re-awakening of his own. It had been years since Daud had felt so strongly connected to the world around him, not since his childhood perhaps, when nourished to his depths upon the sea air, he had played among the rocks and waves of his island home. Again he felt the wind, the sun, the rain, fresh with the light of its own creation. He became simply a witness, the place where the vision of life occurred. But there were moments of intimacy too, when the beauty of this vision collected in a single face, informing him that it was all there for him alone, the whole creation was a lover's gift to his heart.

This newfound sense of belonging made it easier for Daud to deal with the person in his care, to dress his wounds each day, to feed him, and to wash and change him after the inevitable bodily messes. The same motherly affection with which he tended for his goats he now applied to caring for Abdul Qahhar. And bit by bit, the hunter began to respond. The deliria visited less frequently, and with their demise so the fevers abated. In time his vacant stare gave way, first to fearful looks, and then recognition and acceptance, and occasional signs of gratitude. One day Daud came back from collecting wood and herbs to find Abdul Qahhar crying. He had tried to raise himself in order to lie sideways, but the effort and the pain involved had defeated him.

'It's hopeless, why did you bother with me? Can't you see I'm useless? You should have just slit my throat. I would have in your place. Or at least you could have left me to die. Why did you save me? For what?' Abdul Qahhar's voice was hoarse and stertorous, barely more than a whisper.

Daud was heartened to hear him speak at last, even if only to be reprimanded.

'Wonderful, wonderful, you're really getting better at last.'

'Better for what? What kind of a life can I lead now? All I know is killing, and that I cannot do any more. Except myself. Yes, I should kill myself. It's the only way.'

'Now, now, let's not hear any more of that kind of talk, it doesn't help the healing. Look on the bright side. All the stitches are out now. Very soon you'll be sitting up. You know, there is life possible even without the powers that jinn gave you.'

Abdul Qahhar looked dumbfounded. He had always suspected there was more to his abilities. He was not unaware of people's murmurings, but had preferred to think his powers were his own. He knew something was up that morning when his long-sight had left him and he could no more see the spirit-beings of the natural world. Now it dawned on him. He had been duping himself all his life. He silently accepted the cup of broth which Daud offered and sipped it slowly.

Over the next few weeks, without revealing his own identity, Daud discreetly let drop that he had been shown certain things of Abdul Qahhar's past. For his part, Abdul Qahhar did not question this. It was well known that shepherds and goatherds, living alone in the wild places of the earth, were not so different from hunters. They were often natural visionaries and in communication with the unseen spirits of desert and rock, mountain and stream.

As Abdul Qahhar's health improved, his remorse deepened. Sporadic nightmares and ghastly visitations from the souls of those he had dispatched without mercy from this world came to haunt him. During these deliria, Daud could hear him begging forgiveness from those he had unjustly murdered. An endless multitude came before the now defenceless former executioner to extract confession and recompense. Women, children, old and young, still the plaintiffs came and Daud realised how important it was that no case be overlooked and nothing be covered up in this period of reconciliation if true justice was to be served and the defendant was ever to find rest in this world or peace in the next.

Whenever Abdul Qahhar emerged from one of these trials he would relate the details to Daud, describing the circumstances which had led to each of his killings, and in this way Daud gained a unique insight into Omo Sharleen's criminal activities. Abdul Qahhar revealed who was in whose pocket, and for what. The web of corruption spread throughout the Sultan's eastern domain, from Beirut to Jerusalem, from Baghdad to Damascus and beyond. Its activities centred around a well-organised band of brigands composed of army deserters, escaped slaves and other desperadoes. They were informed by a network of spies, compromised officials mostly, who knew which caravans to plunder, and where and when they would be most vulnerable. Daud even heard the tale of his own caravan's ambush, and the subsequent doubts surrounding his death, and the need to find and liquidate him. Abdul Qahhar also described the events which followed his dispatching of Taymir al-Bad from the Tower of the King's Daughter at Krak de Chevaliers.

'The gold was packed upon camels and taken to a ruined church to the south of Qalat al Hosn where it was buried. Then all the bandits moved down to one of our hideouts in the Bekaa Valley where they thought they were to be rewarded. A huge feast was prepared, which was, of course, poisoned. Now I alone know the whereabouts of the gold.'

'Well, actually, you're not the only one,' thought Daud. He knew exactly to which church Abdul Qahhar referred, for he had sheltered there a number of times during his wanderings.

And so the former assassin underwent a long period of purgation, contrition and expiation. As for Abdul Qahhar finding rest in this world, it would only come with difficulty. The wounds on his back did heal, but in such a way that he was unable to bend. Daud was no plastic surgeon, and when he had sewn him up, he really had done a good job. The tightness of the resulting scar tissue meant that Abdul Qahhar was only able either to stand upright or lie prostrate. Except for being able to turn and bow his head, which he did most abjectly much of the time, there was little alternative posture available to him between these two extremes. Even to kneel sitting on his heels caused such pain to his lower back and rear end that he could only take that position briefly before having to fall forward on his face. Eventually he learnt how to lie on his back, and this gave him the most relief. But he had lost forever the ability to lope these desert hills like a wolf, soft pressing the earth beneath the pads of his bare feet, gliding silent and invisible towards his prey. Walking, when Abdul Qahhar was finally able, was a slow, hesitant march, as soldiers do behind the coffins of their fallen comrades.

Daud, for his part, had plenty to occupy himself with during the short but harsh Syrian winter. First he set about curing the hide of the lion. It was not so very different from dealing with goatskins. He stretched the skin over a rough frame made from brushwood branches, and carefully scraped off any bits of blood and fat. He then washed it thoroughly before stretching it over the frame again to dry. Next he rubbed salt over the entire surface of the skin, and left it rolled up on a ledge in the cave for a couple of days before salting it again. Later he soaked the hide once more and then hanging it over a smooth log he set about fleshing it with his knife, removing all the fat and membrane loosened by the soaking. He had acquired an old olive barrel on one of his expeditions to get supplies, and in this he made a solution of hot water, vinegar and bark from the sumac tree, into which he submerged the hide to tan for most of the winter. When Daud pulled it out a few months later, the tanning had done its work, and after washing and squeezing and pulling and kneading it for days, the result was a soft and pliant pelt that would serve its wearer a lifetime of winter storms.

The lion's cave was certainly a lucky find for a man who likes to keep busy during the short days and long winter nights. Daud was able to stable the goats, bring them fodder when the weather was too bad, and milk them well into the winter. He turned most of the milk into delicious *darfiye* cheese, the kind that comes all sewn up like a ball inside a goatskin, where it matures slowly into a hard crumbly pungent delicacy. The goats were happy in the warm darkness, and provided Daud and his patient with a seemingly endless supply of nourishment. And what, you may ask, about the smell? It is a well known fact that the odour, not to say ordure, of goats can be pungent. Well, the cave stretched far back and into the hillside, and had other smaller access tunnels which opened high in the cliff face, allowing a free flow of ventilation, removing smoke and smells. This, and the fact that Daud was fastidious in maintaining a well-swept manor, meant that human and capricorn were able to exist side by side in a state of relative olfactory harmony.

Winter wore itself out, and the spirit of the new year came first to freshen the air, to pour life into the waters, then quicken the seeds in the earth. Abdul Qahhar's inner trial was complete, the fires of his deeds had been cooled and punishment received and accepted. There was left only the need to forgive himself. For that he needed to make a vow, a vow which he would keep for the remainder of his mortal life, at whatever the cost, to preserve all life, including his own. Abdul Qahhar renounced his past life and all its connections, and vowed never to hunt nor to kill another living thing which moved on two legs or four, or flew or swam. Well, that didn't leave him much, thought Daud, so he gave the poor fellow the lion skin and a couple of pregnant she-goats, which he accepted humbly.

The night before Abdul Qahhar's departure, Daud had a dream in which was revealed the true name of his guest. No longer was Abdul Qahhar suitable, a name of such violent compulsion. Henceforth the newly-shriven assassin was to be known as Abdul Gafur, the servant of the Most Forgiving. Daud brought him this good news in the dawn. They embraced each other, a little stiffly under the circumstances, but with good heart. Then with his pair of goats in tow, and the time-softened skin of the noble lion upon his back, Abdul Gafur shuffled off upon his solitary way.

A few days later, an errant donkey appeared at the goatherd's little settlement beneath the cliff to drink from the pool. It was just what Daud needed to transport his burgeoning supply of mature darfiye cheese, all wrapped up in the salted skins of the goats he had eaten during the winter, cheeses which filled every ledge within the cave. The time had come to travel, man and drum, dogs, goats, donkey and cheeses to market in Damascus.

TWENTY-THREE

A veil is removed

AUD stood by the river bank and watched the sun setting beyond distant mountains. He had taken his flock south by a roundabout route, wandering among the black tents of the Bedouin by the edge of the desert, skirting the towns and the known roads. He slept nights blanketed beneath sapphire skies, grazed his goats in the empty ruins of proud Zenobia's Palmyra, kept distant companionship with herds of gazelle and oryx and returned the circling gaze of steppe buzzards and black kites, until he reached the area known as the Meadow Lakes, about fifteen miles east of Damascus. It was a marshy land teeming with ducks and water life. Here he had rested his flock awhile to let them feed up before pushing on into the city.

The following day was market day, Saturday, and Daud was keen to divest himself of his surplus stock, and the abundance of cheese. He reached Zeinab, a busy, bustling village surrounding the tomb of its eponymous saint, the daughter of Ali and Fatima, and granddaughter of the Prophet Mohammed. The twilight was short, and the moon had not yet risen. He had met people on the way, wanderers like himself, renunciates like Abdul Gafur, who spoke of a comet which could be seen in the evening sky. Heavy matters were in the offing, they said, and the comet was the herald of these events. For weeks the weather had been cool and cloudy, but tonight was clear. He searched the sky to the north-west and soon found a bright smudge against the yellowing-blue horizon. Justice will come from the north-west, they had said. This talk of 'heavy matters' sounded ominous, but any fool knew they meant the Caliph Sultan in Constantinople.

Daud contemplated the cosmic visitor, now falling into the northern horizon, and wondered whether he would ever attain such finesse of patience and perfect timing. One of the travellers had said the comet had last visited the skies of our earth around the time of Noah, whenever that was, but certainly too long ago to bear thinking about.

In Zeinab, Daud's senses were assaulted by the glister and glamour of the stalls in the village, with their overblown religious iconography and tourist knick-knacks. Everywhere hung the protecting hand of Fatima fashioned in silver or clay and prayer beads made of brightly coloured glass. Tables were stacked with little sandstone tablets which served as a marker for the direction of prayer – the *mihrab* – for the predominantly Farsi-speaking pilgrims and followers of Ali. Sweetmeats and pastries, chicken and lamb roasting on skewers, flat bread piled high, all savorous aromas before Daud's nostrils – he was back in town all right. He moved quickly through the busy main street and on out of Zeinab into the relaxed peace of the descending night. Here he regained the open road, leaving behind the sounds of barking dogs and mothers calling children home, the smell of wood smoke and home cooking. The failing light revealed glimpses of well-watered glades of walnut trees and poplars, orchards of pomegranates, pistachios and blossoming almond trees, and gardens filled with budding rose beds for Damascus rosewater. Beyond were fields of young wheat and barley, stretching right up to the city gates.

The first person Daud met when he entered Damascus near the Bab as-Salaam was Refik.

'Qays! Long time no see. Where've you been?'

'Oh, here and there, you know, with the goats.' Daud gestured with a tilt of his head to the massed flock behind him.

Refik looked puzzled for a moment, then laughed. 'Ah. Like Uways al Karani.' Refik was referring to the legendary camelherd of the Yemen, who was inspired directly by God.

Daud blushed, ashamed at this comparison. 'No, definitely not like Uways. More like another lost sheep trying to find his way back home.'

His friend smiled. 'Yes, we're all looking for the way, aren't we. It's just that… well, sometimes I think maybe you know more than you say. Like when you told that story in the cafe that day, the one about the flutes, what was that all about, eh?'

For a moment, Daud thought that perhaps he should try and explain how it was with the Drum. But before he could speak, the Drum, which was slung on his back, twisted sharply and detached itself upon the road with a deep boom and a jangle of its little chains. Within the 'boom' Daud heard a resounding 'No!' in Shams' unmistakeable tones. He picked up the Drum and reattached the chord which had mysteriously untied itself.

'Say,' said Refik, 'Are you able to leave the goats for a while?'

'Sure, the dogs will look after them. Why?'

'There's a gathering tonight at the tomb of the Great Sheykh. A *zikr*. I'll be playing the violin, you could bring your drum.'

Daud had heard of *zikr* but had never had the opportunity to take part up until then. Should he take up the invitation, he wondered. As if encouraging him, the Drum gently pushed him from behind.

He smiled. 'Yes, why not.'

Night had fallen over the ancient city by the time Daud and Refik reached the mosque of the Great Sheykh Ibn Arabi on the slopes of Mt Kassioun. Crossing the courtyard, they joined the throng who had just completed the sunset prayers, and crowded down the pink stone steps to the room in the hill where the Sheykh was buried.

The white-robed door keeper ushered them through to the space beyond the tomb. People were sitting in lines three or four deep, either side of the room facing the centre. The place was rapidly filling up, but they squeezed in and sat down.

All manner of people were present: street sweepers and marketeers, young boys and bearded ancients; dervishes of every description, from ragged-clothed Kalendar *fakirs* with unkempt hair, to solemn Rifa'i, and neatly-dressed Mevlevis sombre as tombstones in their tall felt caps. There were merchants and businessmen wearing fezzes. Even a few off-duty Turkish soldiers had joined at the periphery of the room.

The evening began with enthusiastic *salawat* as the congregation sang the liturgy asking for blessings upon the Prophet. There followed a hymn to the Great Sheykh himself, and hymns in praise of love. At first there seemed little apparent order, but gradually, as the night unfolded, Daud discerned a subtle balance to the proceedings, in the way that a musical composition comprises a number of distinct forms which together make up an integrated whole. Different members of the gathering would begin singing, or repeating a particular Divine Name. This would run a short course, building in intensity as everyone joined in, then gradually subsiding and giving way to another expression arising from a different part of the chamber. There was great spontaneity and evident enjoyment in calling out the Names, and everyone seemed to know what to sing and when.

At one point, a dervish in a tall felt hat like a pillar of stone stood up and began to turn on the spot in the centre of the room. Rotating anticlockwise, he unfolded his arms, stretching them out at his sides, his right hand upturned heavenwards ('to receive *rahma* – the divine mercy,' whispered Refik) the left turned down, ('dispensing the mercy into the earth'), his right foot stepping around the pivot of his left, the young man turned as if in self-circumambulation. The wide skirt of the dervish blossomed out as he spun faster and faster. Then Daud noticed that the man's feet were no longer touching the floor. In fact the dervish was beginning to rise ever so slowly. Daud couldn't believe his eyes and was about to cry out 'Look!', when there was a loud knock of wood on wood. One of the dervishes, an old white-beard, had rapped his walking stick hard upon the floor, and brought the young spinning top back to earth. The dervish tottered ready to fall, but some of his companions caught him, wrapped a cloak around him, and led him away.

Throughout the ceremony, a couple of white-clad attendants moved among the gathering, enthusiastically hurling bread rolls to all around them and scattering sweets at random. This largesse was accepted eagerly, especially by the contingent of street urchins present, for it carried *baraka*, blessings, from the Great Sheykh.

Daud began to tap the Damascus Drum gently in time with the slow stepping pace of the recitations. He had heard of these ceremonies. People said they were meant to induce a trance, but now he saw that this was not at all what was intended. On the contrary, people appeared more awake and aware as the evening progressed. And yet something definitely changed in his inner state. He felt he was floating on water where he sat, as if held in a gentle transubstantial balance. He kept his eyes open, observed, and listened. He recalled his experience of 'joining up' on the night he had faced the jinn, when he had remembered and been remembered by this deeper well inside him, which he knew to be his real origin and place of returning. This was the same. But different. For a start, many were present, but there was only one sound, only one voice, and in a strange and inexplicable way, at times only one body. He looked again. The praise singers and their prayers were as reeds in a stream, waving and bending in the movement of the current flowing through them, their song and their sighing a keening wind which searched among them as a lover for their beloved, their faces radiant within the light overflowing the well-spring of their original nature.

Shams appeared in the face of the Drum, and words arrived as thought in the mirror of Daud's heart. 'They think that in this *zikr* they are remembering God, but it's not like that. We cannot even remember ourselves, unless we are remembered by that which is our essential being, remembering in the place we call ourselves. Then, tell me, who is remembering whom?'

As the chant died down, there rang out the pure bell voice of a young boy singing one of the Great Sheykh's poems to love. The chamber became as silent as the desert. Daud looked around and was overcome with affection for these people whom he had not even met. It was a sense of connection reaching back beyond bodily forms and the garments of souls to a place of ancient possibilities, a place of true closeness shadowed forth in the light of a single spirit.

Daud now saw a room of true originals. To his left sat an old man of most refined demeanour, tall, with a white turban, and a snowy beard which fell in loose curls to the middle of his chest. Leaning against the far wall were three gentlemen, their heads covered in simple white cloth, whose faces became brighter as the evening proceeded. With their long white beards, they could have been Patriarchs from the time of Abraham. Two men with woollen scarves tied over their heads in the fashion of these parts, stood eyes closed in silence next to each other throughout. Some among the gathering looked and acted as if the sober bonds of reason held their souls too lightly. As the evening came to a close, one poor fellow, overcome by some interior emotion, became agitated and had to be gently restrained. He began to weep, and friends calmed him with kind words and prayers blown over him. Even this did not disturb the joy which the *zikr* brought Daud. It had the same atmosphere of conviviality, he thought, as he might have enjoyed drinking with a party of good friends, except here the wine had never inhabited grape skin or oaken cask, and no hangover was in the offing.

They emerged into the freshness of the black night. Light rain began to fall. Daud and Refik joined some other musician friends in a small eating place nearby, where they ate a late supper of soup and bread. There was little conversation and the party soon dispersed, each keen to preserve the sweet state of the evening until they reached their beds. There beyond the veil of sleep, gifts of help and knowledge might be bestowed. Or at least they might rest in the proximity of that ancient place.

Daud checked his goats, which he had left in a stock yard nearby, then made his way to his old lodging in Touma's khan. The khan was busy, even though it was late in the evening. The air was heavy with spice smells as piles of freshly ground cumin and coriander were being weighed and packed, and retail sellers haggled with the merchants making their last sales before the next day's market. Touma wasn't there, so he let himself in and went to bed.

TWENTY-FOUR

Spinning webs

UNLIGHT was shining through a small grill high in the wall above Daud's head. The light formed a beam which spread through the dust of the room and came to rest upon a pile of sacks in the opposite corner. The light was almost tangible, made visible by the tiniest motes and shaped by the hole in the wall. Lying there, he felt comfortable, warm and safe. He gazed at the sacks with the beautiful emptiness of mind which comes when both body and soul are well rested. Then he saw that the beam had moved and was now illuminating some grey material which had been stuffed in behind the pile of brown hempen sacks.

Daud was curious, and he crawled across the room for a closer look. It was some kind of clothing. Without thinking, he pulled on it, but the weight of the sacks was holding it fast. He pulled harder. All of a sudden out it came, causing him to fall over backwards, and the large, grey piece of clothing flew up in the air and landed on top of him. As he disentangled himself, he saw it was a burqa. Not new, although its cloth was of excellent, but by no means ostentatious quality. Women's clothing. Why was it hidden in a spice merchant's warehouse, a place where only men ever came? Or did they? Did Touma have a secret life? Was Touma having a clandestine affair and was this dress some sordid souvenir?

As Daud stood there half-naked in the morning light, it dawned on him that this was not any woman's burqa, or if it was, she must have been some big lady. At first he refused to believe what his mind was telling him. Could it really be? It was too confusing and besides, it complicated everything. It just didn't feel right. So, his friend was a transvestite. He didn't know whether to laugh or cry. Daud was so taken by surprise at this thought that he did not hear the footsteps outside until the door opened and Touma himself crossed the threshold, smiling at seeing his old friend again. Touma's smile turned to a startled gasp when he saw the burqa in Daud's hands. Daud himself continued to stand there open-mouthed. It was Touma who spoke first:

'Well, the secret's out now, I suppose. What are you going to do, have me arrested or what?'

'Come on now, it's not that bad. I hear that in certain parts of Hindustan and in some circles in Arabia it's now quite accepted.'

'Please, don't add your mockery to my shame, for the sake of our friendship. But hear me out. You probably won't believe me, but at least give me a chance to explain.'

'Nothing to explain, old boy.' Daud was no stranger to the variations and tastes of men – his time in Beirut had removed any prejudices in that department.

Touma looked at him quizzically.

'No, it's important that you hear me out – since you're in it up to your neck anyway. It wouldn't have been safe to tell you before, there was too much at stake. But since you have proven yourself in the field so well in the past months, and now my secret is out anyway, we'll have to take you on board. If you want to come along, that is. There's no compulsion in this.'

Now it was Daud's turn to look puzzled. He leant back on his cot, the grey burqa neatly folded on his knees. 'Okay, what's the story?'

'This may take a while. You get dressed, and I'll order some coffee.'

A few minutes later the two old friends were seated cross-legged on the bed sipping coffee and nibbling *sanbusak*, little half-moon pastries filled with soft cheese, which came still warm from a nearby bakery.

TOUMA'S STORY

'First of all,' began Touma, 'I wasn't born in Damascus. In fact, I'm not
Syrian at all, really. My mother's family was Greek, my father's family had
been Christian also, but his grandfather converted after he was
conscripted into the Janissary Corps and he entered the Sultan's service
in Constantinople. That was in the days when there were still Janissaries,
of course. Great-grandfather distinguished himself here and there in
skirmishes in the Balkans and was taken into the Palace Guard. Even after
the Janissaries were destroyed, because of his loyalty and service, he
continued in the Palace, and my grandfather and father after him. Our
family was highly regarded and given land along the Bosphorus, but
mostly my father lived in the Palace. I grew up in the household of the
Sultan and I was schooled alongside the young princes. We were like
brothers in one big family. Before I too went into the army I made an oath
to serve my princes in whatever way they chose.

'When the present Sultan took the throne, it was a time of revolt here
in Syria. Local officials were holding back taxes, there were bandits everywhere and the roads weren't safe – well, you know that yourself, Daud.
Even the beys and pashas were not responding to orders coming from
Constantinople, except to complain of course, and give excuses as to why
they couldn't forward the taxes due. The Sultan needed to have someone
here he could trust, someone who wasn't known to the local officials, who
would give him a true picture of events. And so I became his eyes and ears
in Damascus – and in Beirut, and Hatay and Jerusalem. Wherever he
needed to hear what was going down in the bazaar or the port, what the
real state of a certain regional governor's finances were, there was I, seeing
and hearing. I would send reports to the Sublime Porte in coded messages
through secret channels. You know, half the traders in Damascus are
spying for somebody else's government. Even the Franks are at it. That's
how I first came across Omo Sharleen. He had tried to put the squeeze on
one of my trading contacts when a shipment spoiled, and my chap came
to me because he couldn't deliver on time. In fact, I had sold him the
shipment knowing it was rotten, to see what rats it might bring to light.
And what a nest it opened up. The dirty work was all being done through
the minions of Abdul Qabid of course. Omo Sharleen made sure he never
had direct contact with his victims. Anyway, I compensated my agent, and

then followed the money. It lead to Abdul Qabid, and then back to Omo Sharleen.'

At the mention of Omo Sharleen and Abdul Qabid, Daud sat up. 'Just where is this going?' he wondered.

'At first I thought Sharleen must be just another small time Beyruti mobster, with his patch of turf, like so many on the coast from Haifa to Hatay. You know the sort – some smuggling, a little extortion, and girls of course. But then I discovered that this fellow had got into the big time socially, so to speak. Those who were in his pocket one day, were firmly under his thumb by the end of the week, and from then on were rolled around like the beads on that fat amber *tesbih* he is always playing with. There was no one I could trust. Everyone here has a personal agenda, they're all in it for their own gain, from the Governor's secretary to the guy selling *sahlep* in the Souk Hamidiyeh.'

Touma was describing the state of affairs throughout the empire. The old order had prevailed in Syria ever since the time of the Ottoman Sultan, Selim I. In conquering Damascus Selim had completed the prophecy foretelling that the tomb of the Great Sheykh Muhyiddin Ibn 'Arabi would be found and restored when the *'sin'* (that is, the letter 's'- س – of Selim) would enter the *'shin'* (the letter 'sh' – ش – of Sham, Damascus). The empire had reached its zenith during the reign of Selim's son, Suleyman the Magnificent, whose armies besieged Vienna, Nice and Malta, and conquered Baghdad, Budapest and Tunis. Then a small worm entered the picture. It came in the form of a bribe – the first bribe paid to a Palace official – to the Grand Vizier Rustem Pasha. Although the order remained strong for many centuries, the rot had begun and the empire corrupted bit by bit. Now the foundations were beginning to crumble.

'The Vali of Damascus rules in name alone, and only in his palace at that. His own intelligence network, the local *Mukhaberat*, are completely compromised. I informed my Padishah who ordered me to infiltrate Sharleen's group. This I have done, but at what a cost. Do you have any idea what it is like being a spy, trusting no one, creating false friendships, double-crossing innocents in order to prove your *bona fides* in the dark worlds of crime and corruption?'

Daud gave him a questioning look.

'You, Daud, were the only exception I made. Don't think I wasn't tempted – there is nothing I wouldn't do for my Sultan. But when you appeared out of the mountains looking for all the world like one of those shaggy little kid goats of yours, I couldn't believe you were any kind of threat. And you had that Drum. That's something powerful, isn't it? I heard it last night at the *zikr*. Something powerful, that's for sure. Yes, I was there, incognito. You wouldn't have recognised me in a dervish hat and a false beard. You remember when that young Mevlevi began to spin round and round, and lifted off the floor? Who do you think it was who banged his stick to bring him back to earth? Such poor self control! The real dervish needs to have his feet planted firmly on the ground. Only then can he be the instrument of Divine Mercy, bringing grace down here where it is needed, not to use it as an escape route from this world of trial, like some thief up a rope. *Ayip!*' Touma used the Turkish word to signify shameful and tactless behaviour.

'Anyway, by the time you came along I was getting to the root of things. It seems that Sharleen has been planning for years to take over the country, all of it from the Franks' Canal at Suez in the south, through Jerusalem and Damascus, right up to Antioch and Alexandretta. He has been recruiting bandits and mercenaries from all over the place, Somalis, Sudanese, you name it, and with the loot from plundering caravans he has been buying up petty governors and police across the three *pashaliks* of Akko, Aleppo and Damascus. Your caravan would have paid for a large shipment of guns and ammunition which he has been arranging through dealers in Germany and Britain. Of course, even if initially Sharleen managed to take control of Syria, he could never hold it. The country would be in chaos for years. Imagine it: the Druzes, the Kurds, the Jews, the Bedouin and every kind of Christian, all fighting for their own bit like tribes again, it would be a blood bath. And then the Franks would probably move in just like they did in Egypt. In the meantime, I have been doing my bit for the Sultan, putting our people in place, gathering evidence, carefully building up a counter-insurgency network so when the time is right we can take out all the key players.

'The problem is that since you survived Taymir al Bad's attack, and then got rid of Al Haywani and Abdul Qabid, and Abdul Qahhar went AWOL, Omo Sharleen has begun to suspect that you are actively working against him. Now he is beginning to cover his tracks.'

Touma paused and let out a laugh. 'He's always suspected someone was on his trail, and now he's convinced that it's you. So, we need to move fast or else he'll put the whole plan underground before we can act.'

Daud interrupted him. 'But why on earth does Sharleen think I'm involved? I've been trying to keep out of the way. And as for their deaths, it's not what you think – they were nothing to do with me.'

Touma gave Daud an indulgent look, and continued. 'After Haywani died, I didn't think you had anything to do with it. And I even managed to persuade Sharleen of this. It was so typical of Haywani, to go after that girl like that on such a hot day. His death was entirely plausible, and what with the police chief's testimony there was no reason to think that it really was anything other than an accident of nature. Then Abdul Qabid turned up inside the body of a shark in the fish market in Beirut when he was supposed to be in Tartous, and that surprised us all. But again, he had upset the Arwadis, and we, Sharleen's mob that is, have never had any influence over those islanders. The Arwadis are a law unto themselves; they hold their independence higher than mere imperial loyalties, so Sharleen has never dared mess with them. And now we hear of the conversion of that Sudanese half-jinn Abdul Qahhar at the hands of a mysterious goatherd whom he calls 'the Lion of the Desert'. The coincidences are as thick as blood in the sun. What's really upset Sharleen is that Abdul Qahhar, or Abdul Gafur as he now calls himself, is refusing to say where your gold is. This Abdul Gafur character insists that it be returned to its rightful owner, and he is roaming the northern wastes at this very moment trying to track you down.'

'But what about the woman in the Grey Burqa that Haywani and Abdul Qahhar mentioned? She must be pretty good to cover her tracks even from Abdul Qahhar.' asked Daud. 'Surely she's the one to worry about now?'

Then, as they say, the *piastre* dropped. Daud looked at the folds of grey cloth in his lap, and then at Touma, and chuckled. Touma gave him a sheepish look, and gradually he too saw the joke. The two friends began to laugh together unrestrainedly until tears were rolling down both their faces.

'But seriously,' said Daud, after they'd recovered, 'What's to stop you arresting Sharleen now? His organisation must be pretty shaky after all its recent losses.'

'The trouble is people are too afraid to talk. The more important the witness, the more they have to protect. We need more evidence. There are still a lot of loose ends to tie up if we want to net all the big fish.'

'Oh? Maybe I can be of some help here,' said Daud, who then proceeded to reveal to Touma all the secrets which Abdul Qahhar had confessed during his weeks of delirium and subsequent remorse. Daud recounted with a tallyman's accuracy the details, names, times, places etc., surrounding all the crimes and circumstances stretching back years which the penitent hunter and head-gatherer had confessed to him during the long winter months spent together in that mountain cave. He added to this everything Gülbahar had gleaned in her pillow talk with Haywani.

As the information poured out, Touma leaned further and further forward, his face slowly changing expression, from initial scepticism, to wide-eyed disbelief until eventually he sat back with the smug confidence of the police inspector who sees the last crucial pieces of evidence falling into place. Then he took Daud's hands in his own and kissed him on both cheeks.

'There will be medals in this for you, and gold, land, women, whatever you want, it's yours for the asking. The Sultan doesn't let your kind of bravery go unrewarded, I can assure you.'

'Not necessary, really. Prefer things just as they are. A quiet life, you know.' said Daud, suddenly feeling acutely embarrassed.

Touma rose slowly, rubbing his hands together. His eyes took on a far away look and when he spoke again it was in a tone of steely resolution. 'Well then, there we have it. I think it's time to put Operation Hamam into action.'

'?'

'You know. The Steam Bath. We are going to remove all the stains, scrape off all the dirt, wash away all the filth. But it's going to require a lot of very hot water and some hefty brushes.'

So, while Inspector Touma hurried off to see a large number of men about an equally large number of dogs, Daud retrieved his own dogs, goats, donkey and his cheeses, and went to market.

TWENTY-FIVE

Operation Hamam

HE sky above Damascus glowed grey, dull as unpolished steel. Its heaviness lingered over heads on which no sun shone; fezzed heads, turbaned heads, heads in tall black priests' hats or satin yarmulkes; hooded, burqa-ed, yashmak-ed and kalpak-ed, veiled in deceit and covered in forgiveness, all were obliged beneath the Saturnine affliction of this sky.

Daud leaned over the bridge by the Bab as-Salaama – the Gate of Peace and Safety – and looked down upon the fast-moving waters. The spring snowmelt rushed on its way to the Meadow Lakes. Everything was in flux; even the Barada was excited. From a broken culvert opening high in the river's retaining wall a pigeon appeared, perching briefly on the lip of the clay pipe before flying up. A second pigeon followed close behind, and the pair took off in the direction of Salihiye.

From the area just beyond the Citadel, in the north east corner of the Old City, came the sound of an explosion. A small puff of white was followed by a large cloud of black smoke which rose up, its darker pall adding a morbid density to the already-obscure sky. Red flames licked out beneath the smoke, and cries and screams were heard. Then gunfire, the popping of pistols, rifles cracking. The noise was concentrated in the same quarter the smoke and fire had appeared. Elsewhere the city was strangely quiet.

The calm was short-lived. From the merchants area, around Midhat Pasha Street, and over to Bab-as-Sharqi – the Eastern Gate – came a humming sound. The hum became a burble then rose to a tumult of uncontrolled, abusive shouting. It was the sound of a mob. Operation Hamam had kicked off.

If the pigeons had been real travellers, and not simply urban tumblers of minarets and aerial amblers of bell towers and the skies over Kassioun; if they had been curious missionaries and sought distances and adventure, they might have witnessed similar goings on across the mountains in Beirut, in all the coastal cities from Alexandretta to Haifa, and inland within the walls of Aleppo, Jerusalem and Ramala. Wherever the deadly tentacles of Omo Sharleen had spread, to whatever their choking extent, the net of wily Inspector Touma was now cast and closing. The struggle was in full flow.

Today Daud was an unadventurous pigeon. He too headed off towards Salihiye, which so far remained undisturbed. He sat in a small coffee house where the talk was all of the 'occurrences'. It seemed that an altercation between some Druzes and some Arabs had escalated to a brawl and then into a full scale riot. Someone had exploded a bomb, right by the Citadel, and the Turkish garrison had started shooting. At anything and nothing in particular, as frightened soldiers do. Next, an argument in the Souk Hamidiyeh between two merchants of differing faiths lifted the lid off a simmering pot of contention which then boiled up, spilt over the whole area, and blistered on tongues and hearts and hands from street to street across the city. Blood was flowing. Lives were changing places.

Daud was not interested in the details. It might have been some story teller's tale, with no direct bearing on reality at all. It wasn't that it was someone else's war. But rather, that what was happening was a cover, a smokescreen for something quite real and vital that did indeed involve him, but not in any way he could define. He felt detached. Wherever he looked, people appeared somehow diminished, like players on a distant stage. Terrible events were in process, certainly, but to him they were strangely irrelevant, as so many mundane repetitive human actions; man waking, eating, working, sleeping, making love and killing. It had become a shadow play. The performances of the actors had become disconnected from the meaning of the drama, to the point that they no longer knew what they were acting. They had forgotten the reality and meanings which their lives had been intended to convey and had assumed the characters of their veils. Daud sipped his coffee and the Damascus Drum twisted and fell against his knee. He took it up and began to tap it. As if answering a summons, the conversation faded and heads turned his way. Then he began to tell a tale…

'There was a time, a time ago, beyond the well-watered groves of Iraq, and far across the deserts of Persia, in the land of Hind where lions still roam and striped tigers steal through the jungle, where the mountains rise higher than man can breathe. There lived a man…

'This fellow, a prince by birth, through no fault other than his stubborn refusal to bend his proud neck and accept his own mortality, to live and work according to the gifts of his own inheritance, had become a brigand. It began with small things, petty violence and bullying of his siblings and associates, lying and deceiving his parents, thieving whenever the opportunity arose.

'As the years passed his dishonesty grew, and with it his evil reputation. His family shunned him, and so too did the community in which he had been born. His behaviour became so vile that finally he was forced to go and live in a neighbouring state. There, in exile, he further developed his perverse talents. Not content with using physical force and threats to get what he wanted, he now cajoled others, greedy, weak-minded and fearful people, to use violence on his behalf. Thus he became the leader of a small band of outlaws. They established a hideaway in the thick mountain forest and preyed on the villages and towns below.

'News of their deeds eventually reached the ears of the Maharajah and he ordered that the gang be brought in, dead or alive. For many months the troopers chased these villains over high mountains and through the trackless jungle without success. In the end it was the carelessness of the cook which betrayed the elusive brigand and his band. This disgruntled and dissolute chef of hearth and pot had become bored with endless barbecues of game birds and venison. He longed to vary the menu with hot spices and sweet delights, with fresh vegetables and green herbs, rich butter and cream from the village markets. And for too long there had been no liquor to stimulate the appetite, just hashish and hand-twisted cheroots of badly-cured tobacco that kept going out. 'O for a glass of moonshine whisky, drunk at midnight with the chokidar and the rickshaw drivers' was his constant complaint as he turned yet another haunch of venison on the spit.

'One day the cook could bear it no longer. He abandoned the austere safety of their mountain lair and snuck down to the town to purchase a few little luxuries. But he was not a lucky cook. His abandoned wife just happened to be in the market that day, begging food for her six fatherless children. She recognised the fugitive on sight in spite of his ragged clothes and bushy beard. She flew into a rage, screaming and scolding him for a wicked ne'er do well, grabbing him by the ear, and revealing his identity before everyone. The villagers responded to her vivid hue and cry by jumping on him and handing him over to the law. The Maharajah's soldiers had little difficulty in getting him to divulge the whereabouts of the bandit hideout. The gang were surrounded, and being by now quite hungry, surrendered without a fight.

'The chief was brought before the Maharajah, and forcefully prostrated by the guards. His fearful shame was matched by the surprise of the sovereign who recognised the prisoner as no other than the younger brother of the Maharajah who ruled the adjoining state, the brother who had been exiled long ago. The outlaw who had been born a prince understood that death was near, and wept in fear of what was in store for him. He immediately confessed his many crimes, and pleaded for mercy on behalf of the fellows he had led astray. And his own shame caused him to beg that his family be spared the ignominy of a public execution.

'The Maharajah ordered the prisoner's removal from the grandeur and light of the palace to await his fate in a dark and fetid place underground, there to dwell in harsh chains among the rats and cockroaches, to wail and gnash his teeth and contemplate his immanent departure from this life.

'The Maharajah, meanwhile, was in a dreadful quandary. He too was loathe to besmirch the dignity of the ruling class by shedding royal blood. The public beheading of this distant cousin would be most inauspicious. Then the Maharajah's personal physician, a medical practitioner and a renowned yogi, made a suggestion:

' "It is established that the plaintiff is guilty," said the doctor, "but he has shown remorse and accepts execution as his fate. So, we must arrange his death in a manner which while satisfying the requirements of law, also has due consideration to Your Majesty's sensibilities regarding shedding royal blood, and that of a relative to boot. I believe I have an acceptable solution."

'And so, the following morning, after the prisoner had suffered a sleepless night alone with the fears and agonies of uncertainty preceding his dispatch to the next world, he was informed that the Maharajah had consented to a private execution, namely, his being bled to death within the confines of the prison. He was assured that it would be a painless death, which would come over him gradually like sleep. Far from reassuring him, this information made him worry even more. However, the struggle of his mind against the inevitable gradually subsided. When at the appointed hour the gaoler's key unlocked the iron door of his cell, the brigand was docile. He meekly submitted to the blindfold and was led lamb-like up into a quiet room in the palace. There he was lifted onto a table and each of his limbs was tied down so that his feet and hands hung over each corner.

"Now, you will suffer no pain," said the King's physician, "just a little scratch on your wrists and ankles, and afterwards you'll just slowly drift away. Don't worry, it will soon be over."

'At the corners of the table the doctor-yogi placed a brass urn with a small tap at the bottom, and below each tap he put a marble basin. At a given moment, the doctor took a blade and scratched gently at a point near the veins on the brigand's wrists and ankles, not so as to break the skin, but with enough pressure to make the condemned man believe his veins had been opened. He twitched involuntarily at each imagined cut. At the same time an assistant turned each of the four taps of the four urns ever so slightly. The sound of the water gently trickling down into the marble basins confirmed to his imagination that his life was now slowly draining away. Bit by bit he believed he was drifting into death. The attending surgeon-executioner and his associates gradually lowered their voices. Then the flow of water was reduced to a slowly diminishing drip…drip…… drip………drip……… and then… silence.'

Here Daud stopped beating the Drum and allowed the audience time to absorb the moment of death. He concluded:

'The prisoner had reached the end. His body, at the suggestion of his imagination, became detached from the animating power of his soul, and gave up the ghost. His breath fled, and his heart stopped. No blood had been spilt. The requirements of custom and law had been satisfied.'

In the hush which followed, Daud slipped unnoticed out of the cafe. The heavy skies had darkened further. The hidden sun had passed beyond the great hill of Kassioun and night's shadow covered the city like a vast black bedouin tent in which no stars shone.

For the next few weeks Syria and Palestine lay under a dark cloud. The rioting between religious factions that Daud had witnessed in Damascus erupted simultaneously throughout the land. Within this fog of hysteria Touma's secret army went about its murky business. No one looked for motives when the body of a tax inspector in Hama was found spiked upon the frame of a *noria*, appearing and disappearing, grotesque and dripping, as the the great waterwheel continually rotated the long-drowned corpse. No one asked questions when a judge, a prostitute, a gangster and a police-man were found beaten to death in the garden of the judge's villa near Tripoli. There were no surprises, either, when the harbour master in Sidon, an Imam in Ramala, a Rabbi in Acre and a Priest in Nablus were found in their beds with their throats cut. And that is just to mention only a few of the more prominent victims of the purge. Numberless petty officials were rounded up and marched north into Anatolia. The few who escaped Touma's cull were mostly Bedouin, whose allegiance to the world of the sown was as insubstantial as a mirage. They melted back into the desert at the first sign of trouble where they maintained their time-honoured traditions of blood-feuds and raiding among themselves.

Touma himself had led the raid on Omo Sharleen's fortress palace in the rugged pine-clad hills above Beirut. An altercation outside the trades-man's gate between the butcher delivering a load of meat, and the figure clad in a grey burqa who claimed the meat was tainted, preceded a series of explosions which began in the kitchen itself. This should have engulfed the building in fire. However, in one of those strange sympathetic coincidences that ever impress upon the mind of man our intrinsic binding with mother earth, at that same moment a small earthquake, centred near Sharleen Villas, rocked Lebanon. Omo's *repos* was a hastily-erected example of orient-meets-occidental glitz, all marble, gold and crystal combined in extreme bad taste by an over-enthusiastic Italian architectural student who believed he was the herald of a new renaissance. Sadly for his client, the Italian failed to take into account the geological instability of the region and did not provide the necessary underpinning of this colossal structure. Chez Sharleen fell apart like a cardboard wedding cake, extinguishing the nascent fires from Inspector Touma's explosive devices. When some weeks later the ruins were excavated, the remains of Omo Sharleen's body was discovered in a marble hamam, each limb pinioned by four fallen marble pillars. It seemed he had not died immediately, but his inevitable detachment from this world had been brought about by a combination of thirst, starvation and the depredations of rats.

Abdul Gafur, former assassin and hunter extraordinaire, had been sighted wandering the desert fringes of Northern Syria in his search for Daud the Arwadi. There were rumours that in the end he self-combusted, a fitting demise, some people said, for one who had made allegiance with those beings of fiery nature, the jinni. But this was not true, for he had already died once under the paw of that great lion whose skin now mantled his shuffling form, and many times again in those months of painful recovery and self-discovery in the cave, suffering the hell-fire of regret and self-recrimination. Abdul Gafur lived out his days according to his vow of non-violence, and according to his name he returned to his Lord in the fullness of his time, forgiving and forgiven. And, it was believed, he took to his grave the secret of the Arwadi's gold. Stories of the goatherd's hidden treasure later gave rise to some of the early archaeological expeditions in the region between Qamishli and Harran, but that, as they say, is another story altogether.

Drums sound and the army marches on. What then for the reluctant warrior? Meeting up a few weeks later, Daud heard from Touma the good news that all of Syria had been freed from the grip of Omo Sharleen's evil ways. Daud was now at liberty to resume his former activities. But he no longer felt inclined to the life of a merchant; not as he had been before. He was not ready to retrieve his gold, although he knew he could do so anytime he wished. During his long winter retreat, in between nursing his erstwhile assassin, he had removed the treasure to a much safer place than the crypt of an abandoned church. For the present Daud was content to live a simple life, in which his goats would keep him busy and provide for his worldly needs. And, of course, there was the Damascus Drum. But his heart too held a secret which something told him would be uncovered one day.

TWENTY-SIX

A goat comes home

 A'ID bin Adam placed the last stone upon the earthen mound. Burying his wife of nearly sixty years had not been easy. Rarely during his long life had he felt real sadness, but since Maryam's soul had departed after a short but intense bout of pneumonia, the simple unity of his vision appeared fractured.

He had sat with her until the end, holding her hand as her breath slowed, then stuttered and gulped one last time. Her old frame had shuddered slightly as her soul shook free, then everything became very still.

His sadness came briefly and intensely, as he remembered the joy Maryam had given him, day in and day out, during the long years of their companionship. Throughout their marriage Sa'id would bring her flowers in season, picked from the green pastures on the slopes of Mt Kassioun. She would set them in a small bowl in that part of their little house where the morning sun would light up the low table on which they took their meals. He remembered Maryam's face and the flowers together. Something in the colour of her cheeks and eyes, and her hair which changed from dark to light over the years, always seemed to shine brighter in the company of flowers.

From the outset their love pierced the surface of things, and in time they plunged its unknown depths together. It was a quiet love, and unfussy, like the meadow flowers; a love of moments and glances. But beneath flowed an ocean whose currents ran deep and which knew no shore. No children came, but so many goats… so much milk.

Now, as Sa'id leaned upon the stone on which he would eventually chisel his wife's name, the weight of his sadness lifted. He remembered the joy again, not as something past and passing, but in the presence which remained.

Yet, in spite of this, Sa'id wept. He wept for his own separation. He wept and wept, until eventually the turbulent waters of his heart swept him from the reef of his own loss into the endless seas of love's longing, and there he drowned a while. When he re-emerged his vision was whole again; nothing was missing as he looked out over the smoking city of Damascus: nor as he surveyed his immense herd of goats nestling and nuzzling for spring flowers in the shade of the dry stone walls, among the rocks and thorn bushes, and in the greening grass of the meadow slope; nor as he gazed again at the mound of soft earth and stones before him, and he breathed in deep the sweet perfume of Maryam's presence. Everything was in its place again.

His gaze returned to the goats, the only things moving in the stillness. 'I'll have to sell some of you now,' Sa'id spoke his thoughts aloud. 'I couldn't possibly milk all you lot on my own.'

It was a year since his old billy goat Shams had disappeared. When he had discovered the bell and its frayed collar he had felt a little sad. But that is the way of goats, always pushing out the boundaries of their world. Shams was simply going on his last pilgrimage, and Sa'id wouldn't deny him that.

He sat all day by the grave looking down over the green slopes of Mt Kassioun. Late in the afternoon a wind came in from the desert, clearing the smoke from the city and driving the clouds back over the mountains. In the crisp spring sunlight, far below where the houses of Salihiye stopped and the open land began, a man emerged with a small herd of goats, some dogs and a donkey. They were heading his way up the steep hillside.

It was some time before the herdsman and his animals reached the place where Sa'id was sitting. As the man approached, Sa'id noticed the large goatskin drum slung over his shoulder, and his heart suddenly began to beat faster.

'Shams!' cried Sa'id, getting to his feet as quickly as his age would allow.

The drum (for this is no other than the Damascus Drum) then detached itself from its moorings and rolled the last few yards to present itself at Sa'id's feet. The goatherd, who was none other than the newly-released-from-threats Daud, saw there was something in this encounter which he needed to know.

Sa'id picked up the Drum and held it to his chest. Then he remembered the visitor.

'I'm so sorry. You see, it's an old friend. I mean... oh never mind, it's difficult to explain.'

Sa'id was surprised and ashamed at his own behaviour. He had not even greeted the stranger; he had completely forgotten his manners and addressed an old skin drum instead.

'Please, forgive me. Let me greet you again with peace.'

'And peace be with you, and the mercy of God and His blessings,' Daud responded, reversing the accustomed etiquette where the one arriving greets first, the incumbent then replying.

Sa'id continued: 'You must be thirsty from your climb. And I have bread. There is room in my house if you wish to stay, for the nights are still chilly and there will be rain by morning. My name is Sa'id bin Adam. My wife died last night and I have just buried her here. I would be grateful of your company tonight; perhaps we can say the prayers together.'

'I really don't want to be any trouble, I was just trying to get out of the city. The roads are full of soldiers and there's trouble everywhere. I was looking for a direct way. But...' then Daud looked at the Drum, which Sa'id was still clasping to his chest. 'You know... you knew Shams?'

'Yes, he was my lead goat. He was old but such a beauty, a true sultan. Then one day, whoosh, he just ups and offs. I can't blame him really, every goat must have his day.'

As if in agreement the Drum emitted a long drawn-out deflating sound.

Sa'id laughed. 'Well, Shams,' he addressed the Drum again, 'You haven't changed so much, have you?'

He handed the Drum back to Daud who looked a little sheepish. 'He behaves like that sometimes. But perhaps you know. It's difficult to explain...'

'No need to. Really,' said Sa'id. 'Come on, let's bring in the animals, and we'll make some supper.'

Daud didn't know what it was about Sa'id, but from the outset he felt completely at home in his presence, as if he had known him all his life. Sa'id was old enough to be his father. Grandfather, even. And felt as familiar. At first he thought it might just be something about the shared experience of goatherds, but then he remembered he was only an accidental goatherd, a year into his apprenticeship, and he still had a universe to learn in respect of goat husbandry. Daud had been lucky so far, and he'd had Shams to keep him out of trouble (Although it seemed Shams as often as not was responsible for getting him into trouble in the first place.)

The two men ate a light supper of spinach and chick peas, a little bread and some of Daud's *darfiye* cheese with olives. Later they lit oil lamps and went out to the nearby spring to perform their ablutions. Crossing the field to the graveside of Maryam, they spread out a couple of old goatskins and knelt down. Above, the spring sky was darkening. A new moon faded gently into the horizon, chasing the sun into night. Sa'id produced an old Qu'ran bound in rough goatskin, and Daud held the lamps as the old herdsman read aloud from its well-fingered pages the Chapter of *Ya Sin*, for the departed one's soul. Then Sa'id took out his rosary of ninety-nine beads and began to pronounce quietly certain Names of God, over and over, interspersed with the occasional hymn or prayer, just as they had done in the *zikr* at the tomb of the Great Sheikh. Daud joined in where he knew the liturgy, otherwise he sat in silence. After perhaps an hour, Daud's knees began to give up. He shifted into a cross-legged position. Another hour passed. Daud found himself drifting, daydreaming at first, looking over the slope down onto the city of Damascus, wondering where his path would lead him next. Then he began to doze fitfully. Meanwhile Sa'id was still sitting upright, gently murmuring in prayer, sometimes nodding his head in time to the repeated phrase, sometimes quiet and still. It was as if the old man inhabited a kind of inner comfort zone in which the hours of sitting on the damp hard ground did not impinge. By midnight Daud was fast asleep, curled up in his cloak next to Sa'id. He woke in the dark before dawn to see Sa'id still in attentive devotion, and sat with him as morning's light once more flooded the mountainside. A pair of ring doves rose from the roof of Sa'id's little house and flew into the sky, before alighting in a thicket higher up the mountain. Then the rain came and Sa'id and Daud went inside and slept a few hours.

In the following days, Daud joined Sa'id in helping with the goats. His own flock easily assimilated within Sa'id's large herd, and with help from nearby farms the milking was accomplished correctly. No mention was made of how long Daud would stay, or when he would leave. He just found himself fitting into each day as it arrived on the mountain, and Sa'id accepted this as if it had always been so. For Daud it was a relief after the strange life he had been leading of late. For Sa'id it was a comfort after the loss of his dear Maryam to have the company of someone of a similarly contemplative nature, who didn't require much in the way of social maintenance.

Which isn't to say they didn't converse. On the contrary, there were evenings, as the two men became better acquainted, when conversation flowed between them as a vigorous stream on matters as diverse as one might find in the most fashionable coffee houses in Damascus. Occasionally frivolous, often passionate, always informative. Sa'id, for all his hermitic seclusion atop Kassioun, seemed well up on all the latest gossip and goings on in the metropolis below: which army officer's daughter was becoming betrothed to which Sheykh's son, which merchant had been banished to the desert regions for giving short weight, which banker had made a killing in the Egyptian grain futures market. He was not at all surprised by the details of Daud's own adventures, and even added little snippets of his own to the story: how, for instance, Inspector Touma, an Ottoman aristocrat, had been able to pass himself off as a merchant and raise such a close network of spies and agents; how he had been able to keep secret his identity as Grey Burqa Man; and exactly what Touma's position was in the Mevlevi dervish order. Daud realised that his old friend, while appearing to have such a significant role in the management of events on the world's stage, was one of many players in life's concert. There were some whose involvement had been just as crucial in bringing the heavy matters of recent days to a satisfactory conclusion, and others who by keeping an eye on things in the market place, so to speak, were instrumental in maintaining and protecting the order.

'Life is like that,' said Sa'id, during one of their evening conversations. 'And people too. Some appear in positions of power. You know, they are like the finger-plectrum, striking down on the strings of the *kanun*. The strings jump, and according to the arrangement the sound is either harmonious music or a cacophony; the strings appear powerless as they are played, but from these strings a song is heard; others are less obvious but perhaps more knowledgeable, the hand holding the plectrum, knowing when to strike, while in the background sits the composer writing his black dots, and the conductor keeping the right time. Then there are those who hear the music and dance between the lines. And when one song finishes, another begins.

'Maryam moves on, and the next day here you are, bringing Shams. Some of my neighbours think it nice that you came to look after an old man in his mourning, and I don't disillusion them. But one day either you or I shall move on too, and nothing can change that. It's what we witness, what we really are aware of in each of these events, which counts, not who appears doing this or doing that. It's knowing what vibrates in you when you hear the music, and knowing there is a light that illuminates what we see. And following the sweet scent of existence back to its source.'

One day when the two goatherds sat out on the mountain, their large flock spread between them for half a mile grazing among the rocks and grass, Daud tapped idly on the Drum. It had been ages since he had delved into inner spaces, and his tapping was hesitant, like knocking on the door of an old but unpredictable friend, half-hoping he won't be in, a bit afraid that further out-of-control adventures and emotional discomfort might come on the heels of such an encounter.

Shams didn't need much encouragement. The vision fairly flew off the face of the Drum. Glowing red, shaggy and flamelike, it was a glorious rendition of Shams the Goat which now appeared to Daud, who immediately fell backwards off his rock, flabbergasted.

'What are you doing still here? Have you forgotten Seydnaya? Your payment for my efforts? Efforts which cost me my life!' Shams was nothing if not passionate. It was tupping time after all, and although he no longer had the means, nor in his elevated station, the personal inclination to descend to matters carnal, as an ancestor he still had responsibilities.

Of course. It dawned on Daud in a flash: ten percent of the offspring from Shams' long night of love among the she-goats of the convent of Seydnaya. It was time to collect his dues.

'And there is still a chance to cover all those little darlings again, if you're quick. Ask Sa'id – maybe he will fix you up with one of my sons.' Shams added proudly.

And so it was that early the next day, Daud set out once again for the lofty desert mountain of Seydnaya, accompanied by a strong young billy goat called Baibars, a true and lusty heir of Shams of Kassioun.

TWENTY-SEVEN

Mother Superior fainted

AKLA rolled up her sleeves and set to work. It was Easter time again, and she had a huge feast to prepare, after which she would take her yearly break and visit her family. All the guest rooms of the mountain fortress which is the convent of Our Lady of Seydnaya were full, and many pilgrims had been farmed out among the local population. They came from far and wide, Christians and Muslims alike, to celebrate this rememoration of the spirit's resurrection in life, to venerate the holy icon called '*Shaghoura*', the 'Famous', and to consume vast amounts of food at the Easter feast. Takla's task now was to ensure that all the dishes were in the best possible taste as befitted such an occasion.

In the vast ship of the kitchen under full sail, she was the keel: the silent, stabilising force that underpinned and steadied her crew in the swirling stream of their activities; the compass point holding lightly but unswervingly the direction upon which all their efforts were fixed. Easter bread baked by the oven-load, young kid goats and lambs roasted on the spit, eggs by the dozens, as well as a spread of vegetable dishes cooked in olive oil, cheese and yoghurt; rice puddings flavoured with mastic, almond ones scented with rosewater, sweet pastries of walnuts, dried apricots, and the raisins for which Seydnaya was famous. They had stuffed trays of pale green peppers with rice; they had folded dozens of pastries filled with crumbly goat cheese, mint and parsley, to be deep fried in olive oil; chickens had been slaughtered and hung, then plucked, drawn and boned. The meat would be pounded and made into a special 'koubeh' with fine bulgur and pistachios, and the bones would become stock for the soup. Takla had organised the making of a huge cauldron of pumpkin soup, flavoured with ginger and nutmeg brought all the way from Hindustan. A frill of novices encircled the large kitchen table. They chopped emerald green mounds of parsley and dill, wept upon a hill of sliced onions, sweated over a huge stone mortar filled with chick peas, and parted by hand whole seas of rice, lentils and dried fava beans as they washed out the small stones before cooking.

Then, as battle closed, Takla became the Captain. She was everywhere, the tireless commander stirring her comrades to continued efforts, tasting this and sniffing that, commenting and complimenting, '… more lemon… less salt… more oil, definitely more oil…', demonstrating the exact size of fine dice of tomato, pepper and cucumber for the salad, or the slimness of slice of onion for the aubergine dish she was about to cook, castigating with a frown the novice who thought to do it her own way rather than its way, the way the dish itself required.

Takla was paying special attention to the preparation of this aubergine dish. It was the first time it had been cooked in the convent. Purple aubergines, long and slender as young girls' slippers, lay before her on the chopping board. They were the gift of a wealthy Cairene who had come to reverence Seydnaya's sacred icon of the Virgin and Child. The Cairene had brought a large basket of the best of the aubergine crop from his Nile delta estates. He had also brought a recipe from his cook, a famous Palace chef from Bolu in Anatolia, whom he had won in a game of *tavla* from the Khedive of Egypt himself.

Takla could barely read the Arabic script, let alone comprehend the syntactical contortions of the Ottoman tongue, so the Cairene himself, a large jolly fellow with a huge belly and a commanding brow, descended into the heat of the kitchen to supervise. It caused quite a fuss as the Cairene also brought his nargileh with him. He sat in a corner by the door, a position which caught the breeze and mercifully extracted most of the smoke of the sweet, pungent Yenidje tobacco. From this vantage point he would give instructions, waving in gesture with the amber-lipped mouthpiece of the hubble bubble from which he took intermittent puffs. His other hand rested on a delicate silver-topped ebony walking stick which he would lift occasionally and prod the air to point or emphasise.

'The onions must be cut very thin, so they cook easily and don't crunch. And red onions, mind you, sweeter you see. Cut the onion in half, vertically down from top to bottom. Then slice from the edge in the same way, top to bottom.' His voice was strong and gentle, his Arabic mellifluous and measured, which made it easy for Takla, who had only learnt to speak the local village dialect as a child.

Takla relayed the instructions to the young novices, firmly pointing out that a sharp knife was essential, and patience; 'Haste makes waste, and waste makes want, and want makes strife between a good man and his wife,' she cooed, tempering the over-enthusiasm of some of her younger helpers. 'The recipe doesn't call for Ladies' Fingers, just onions and aubergines.'

The onions were put to cook in a large, shallow-edged iron pan with olive oil; a lot of olive oil. The Cairene looked to make sure there was enough. 'Drench them, drown them!' he said.

'And wooden spoons only, onions don't get on well with metal spoons,' said Takla, as a novice reached for a long-handled iron spoon. She looked at the Cairene who nodded and smiled.

'Now, bring me an aubergine and a knife.'

Takla brought the items and a small wooden chopping board which she offered to the Cairene.

'We don't want to argue, do we? So put the knife down there,' he said, nodding to a shelf next to him. She did as indicated. The Cairene took the board and vegetable from her hands, and then picked up the knife.

'First, cut stripes along the length of the aubergine like this,' and he took the blade and carefully peeled a narrow strip of skin from the tip to the base, repeating all around the vegetable. 'And we make this one wider, where the onions will sit.' He then made a shallow V in this stripe and scooped out a little of the flesh. 'Keep the flesh, we'll mix it with the onions later. And don't remove the stalk from the end, just trim the woody bit back so they will fit easily in the pan.'

The whole basket of aubergines was prepared in this way, while the onions cooked gently to a soft, pinky-golden and oily mass. The striped and sculpted aubergines were salted lightly and left to drain, while Takla

served the Cairene his morning coffee with a couple of salty cheese
sanbusak. The little pastries left crumbs and sesame seeds in his moustache
and all over his topcoat, which he carefully brushed into the palm of his
hand and put outside on a window ledge for the house sparrows. He
returned and puffed awhile on his nargileh, which Takla rekindled with a
piece of glowing charcoal taken from the fire beneath the kitchen range.

'Now the aubergines. More oil. Lots of oil.' And into another pan
Takla poured about an inch deep of the sweetest olive oil, another gift to
the convent which had come from Jerusalem. After the aubergines had
been washed of their salt, drained and dried, they were placed in the oil.
'Not too hot, or the skin will crisp, but they must cook as well as take up
the oil.' Again the Cairene came and leant over the stove to supervise. He
took a metal spoon and gently ladled the hot oil over the purple pods
which had shrunk a little now, both from the salting, and the heat. 'Just
keep them cooking steadily a while till they are golden. Don't fry them,
cook them,' and he turned them over gently on their sides, and then on
their tummies, and again on their backs. 'Let them relax properly in the
oil. Let them enjoy it.'

The aubergines cooked slowly in batches until the whole basket was
done. Meanwhile the stuffing was prepared. Pine kernels were gently fried
to a pale gold, and put aside. Tiny 'bird' currants which had been soaked a
few hours were added to the nuts. The cooked onions were taken from the
oil, and mixed in a large bowl with the pine kernels and the currants.
Cinnamon was added to the mix, as well as salt and sugar, handfuls of
finely chopped parsley, fragrant dill and some lemon juice.

'Now the diamonds,' said the Cairene. 'Please, bring me a tomato…
thank you… now look,' he took the knife and cut diamond shapes an inch
long out of the skin of a large ripe tomato. 'You will need two diamonds for
each aubergine. Chop up the rest of the tomato, fry it with the aubergine
pulp and add it to the onion mix.'

The aubergines, now limp and saturated with oil, were carefully placed
in iron trays like so many plump bathers resting prostrate after hours in the
steamy hamam. The filling was laid upon the scooped out length of the
flaccid vegetables, and piled up until all the aubergines were well stuffed.
Then the Cairene came and positioned two tomato diamonds on top of
one of the filled aubergines, as an example, dividing it into three. The green
of the herbs, the dark of the currants and purple skin, the red of the toma-

toes, the pale gold and cream of the oil-soaked flesh and the pine nuts, each became a purse bursting with sapphires and rubies, gold and amethysts, emeralds and mother-of-pearl.

'And now into the oven.'

Four round trays were slid into the big wood-fired clay oven where they baked slowly for an hour or so, until the marriage of ingredients was fully consummated. Then, under the Cairene's instructions Takla took a knife and held it just above one of the aubergines, letting the point slip under its own weight down into the firmer flesh of the neck where the stalk emanates. It went as easily as into soft butter, confirming that the cooking process was complete, and the trays were carried down to the cellar to cool. Later they would be presented on platters, remoistened with all the cooking juices and decorated with sprigs of parsley and dill.

The feast that Easter Sunday would be remembered for years to come. It established the standard by which all other feasts at the convent were measured, at least during the life of this Mother Superior. The soup was a congratulation itself to the efforts of Takla and her brigade, and laid out the palate for all the savouries and dainties which followed. As each dish was tasted, a series of hums and umms and aaahs of delight provided a gentle background chorus to the clatter of dishes and silver and brass cups from which the dignitaries and guests ate and drank.

The finest of Seydnaya's vintages, their tannins softened and flavours matured for a generation like the hearts of old hermits lost in still contemplation deep in the cellars of the convent, were broached for the occasion. Their intoxicating spirit bathed the wearied and fast-shriven souls of the pilgrims in the open waters of forgiveness and compassion, for themselves and each other. With the wine came fine conversation, fragrant yet heady with subtle points and delicate nuances. But when the aubergines were presented with their gentle, musky scents of cinnamon and dill, the meltingly sweet onions, and the buttery flesh of the vegetable itself, then a reverent silence descended upon the assembly. Mother Superior, who up to this point had been duly impressed by her kitchen's efforts and pleased that her convent's hospitality had acquitted itself with honour, took a piece of aubergine and lifted it to her lips. As the honeyed smoke perfume of the spiced dish reached her nostrils, entered her lungs and dissipated in her being, inexplicably she began to weep softly. Then, as she swallowed, almost drank, the portion, she promptly fainted. The

Cairene, who as if prepared for this had a place of honour at her right, caught her discreetly before she fell completely from her seat, thus saving her from injury and further embarrassment.

But embarrassment was the furthest thing from Mother Superior's mind. In the instant of fainting she had been transported, not to some dizzy transcendent spiritual height, but to a moment in her distant youth when she had known the taste of love, briefly, exquisitely, and ecstatically. A mortal sin according to her religion, and an impossibility because of her lover's own circumstances; she had preserved the moment in that corner of her heart where it crystallised in a bitter-sweet, yet unrecalled memory. It had remained there, obediently silent as she steered the course of her life into another vigorous current, the quest for spiritual satisfaction. Now, as the memory stirred, in a moment of untypical candour, flouting the accustomed order and dispensing with the formality which the dignity of her office demanded on such an occasion, she called the servant Takla up to her table. Then she embraced and congratulated her cook before the whole congregation. Takla looked at the Cairene and was about to speak, but he put a finger to his moustachioed lips and smiled conspiratorially. From that day forward that Easter feast became known as the Feast of Mother Superior's Fainting, and the dish of aubergines, although known elsewhere by a similar but different sobriquet, was always referred to as Fainting Mother Superiors.

It had been a very full year for Takla. First the pregnancy, and then mother-hood on top of running the kitchen. But caring for Yahya was a joy and the growing bond of love between them fulfilled all her emotional needs. When hungry, Yahya cried with full voice. But he needed little more than the warmth of his mother's or any of the novices' embrace and access to a full breast of milk to restore him to his accustomed state of bliss.

Takla had not forgotten the event that had brought all this about. In fact, she would often relive the instant of that meeting in her mind. While Daud's recollections bestowed upon the encounter transcendent, even cosmic significance, her memories were more practical. In the heat of the kitchen, thinking of her lover in spite of his absence was like a reassuring hug. When she dreamt of him, although he looked angelic, he was also a man.

On the morning after the great feast, Takla set out early from the kitchen door for her home village. She could not help but think of the last time she had made this journey, and for a moment wondered if perhaps she might encounter another brave gallant along the way. But Takla quickly dispensed with the thought. She was, after all, a woman now and a mother, not some frivolous novice. Mother Superior had allowed Takla to take a donkey with her on this trip, and a milking goat in order to feed Yahya, so her journey was easier, if slower, as the goat insisted on grazing the verge at every opportunity. But she was in no hurry. After the efforts preparing the Easter feast, this trip was for her a well-earned holiday. Released from the gravity of her daily routine, Takla again felt uplifted by this freedom. But this time, as she took in the austere beauty of her surroundings, she found her focus in the intimate facing of Yahya. Only as they reached the hidden pool beneath the cave, and stopped a while to rest at midday, did a deeper emotion stir within her, recalling that original opening to love. Yahya, having sucked greedily upon his mother's breast, was soon sleep. Perhaps he too felt some cellular resonance, some undefined recollection of an arrival, like the salmon which intuitively returns from the sea to the source of its own birth.

TWENTY-EIGHT

Sons of Shams

 HILE Takla and Yahya were resting in the shade of the cliff by the pool, Daud and the billy goat Baibars crested the rise before the convent of Seydnaya. On the way from Damascus Daud had met a steady stream of visitors returning after the Easter celebrations. They seemed in unnaturally good spirits, and from brief exchanges with the pilgrims, he gathered that the Easter feast truly had been an affair to remember. Apparently the dishes had come from Paradise, borne on angels' wings, and laden with indescribable delights prepared from recipes dictated by Gabriel himself.

Daud also gleaned that the Mother Superior had fainted when a rich Cairene had asked for the hand of the cook as his second wife; that the Cairene had offered the convent a huge dowry (but the proposal had been turned down as the cook's religion prohibited polygamy); and that this same noble Egyptian had made a generous donation to the convent in spite of the disappointment to his heart. Then, strangest of all, the convent's great herd of goats had been bleating continually since first light, the noise of which only increased the excitement of the pilgrims. Religious fervour, over-active imagination, the divine scents of love and food and ancient wine, it all seemed to have got a bit mixed up. Finally Mother Superior had put her foot down and declared the day one of silence, fasting and ablution.

Suddenly all the distracted visitors discovered they had pressing engagements elsewhere, and had upped and left.

As the dust of the departed settled, Mother Superior lifted the dictat
on silence and fasting (they had, after all, just come through the rigours of
Lent), and everyone set about giving the convent a thorough spring clean.
By the time Daud arrived before the convent gates, peace reigned once
more over this gentle community of devoted ladies. All that stirred the air
were sweet scents of lavender and honeybees' wax, and the sighs and hums
of black-clad nuns washing stone and polishing wood in the cloisters and
corridors of their desert retreat.

The herd of love-starved she-goats, which had been bellowing away all
morning, calmed down immediately as the first whiff of the mighty Baibars
blew in over the hill. And at the appearance of this proud son of Shams, the
convent's herd came over all coy. They drooped their eyes lugubriously and
crowded the fence of the paddock in anticipation as Daud and Baibars
passed by. The sight they presented was unequivocal. They might just as
well have hung up a sign saying 'Ready to be ravaged, if you must. And you
must!' Baibars, for his part, affected an air of aloofness.

The nun in charge of the goats met Daud below the steps of the
convent.

'Not a moment too soon,' she said. 'We had almost given up hope.
What with all the disturbances in the country recently, we really weren't
sure if you would come. Well, good news, all the goats gave birth to twins,
one male and one female, and twenty she-goats have been reserved for
you. All the males were slaughtered quite young, as you know males at a
certain age... and we are a community of ladies...' she laughed without
blushing, 'so if that billy goat is available,' she indicated Baibars, 'perhaps
we can continue the arrangement as before. Mother Superior says you are
welcome to stay here in the convent if you wish.'

While Daud was being shown to the guest quarters, Baibars was led
away from the stony confines of the nunnery to participate in extra-mural
activities with the convent's herd of she-goats.

Daud was pleased with the arrangement and enjoyed his brief stay. It
was a time of rest and meditation, a period of renewal. He took his meals
alone in the small courtyard outside his room. Simple convent fare in the
aftermath of the great feast, but with it always a flask of delicious red wine.
Every day he took a hike in the surrounding hills, but he also spent many

quiet hours within the labyrinth of the monastery.

His meanderings would often end in the kitchen watching the small brigade of novices busy themselves making bread, chopping vegetables, washing salads and ladling yoghurt, all the daily activities of a communal kitchen. It was a comfortable place, and he felt at home there, sitting by the back door. In the morning the high walls of the castle convent shaded him so that sometimes he shivered a little with the dark cypress which grew outside. Then the novices would bring him tea or coffee which always seemed to be brewing, with some sweet pastry or savoury piece, and he would sip and nibble away happily. Or if it was evening, they would bring him a glass of wine and a dish of olives and some goats cheese, and as he drank, his gaze would be drawn towards the rocky hills to the north.

What was it about this place, Daud wondered one morning. Why did he feel so content here, and especially in this kitchen? Daud looked around at the young novices and for the first time in his life found himself experiencing real fatherly feelings. It was not what he had felt years ago as a young man, when he had beheld in wonder and excitement his own image reproduced in his children. The initial connection he had felt with these little squawking things had gradually faded, perhaps because of the constant presence of their mother and a gaggle of female relations. But also his regular and lengthy absences had prevented normal familial relationships developing. What he felt now was something else. Did he unconsciously sense in the kitchen's atmosphere the imprint of an absent cook and her child, impressing his heart with such affection?

Baibars' paternal instincts, on the other hand, were much more down to earth. While not quite matching his sire's fatally inspired performance, he nonetheless disposed of the task in an efficient and resolute manner. By the third day, all two hundred-odd she-goats had been well and truly served. A somewhat dishevelled Baibars returned to Daud, bringing in tow the selected icosahedral herd which would accompany them back to Damascus.

Daud was invited to continue the ten per cent arrangement the following year. Thus the annual tupping became a fixed point in Daud's and the convent's calendar. Each year with the coming of Easter, Daud would head north with an increasing number of billy goats, spend a few days of quiet retreat, and return with his decan of the previous year's offspring. His path and Takla's never crossed, but the perfume of each other's presence continued to meet and mingle in the kitchen, veiled in warm flavours of coffee, wood smoke and freshly baked bread. And in that subtle union there grew a deepening relationship, free of the mundane frictions and abrasions which so often accompany constant physical companionship. The companionship of the spirit endures, no matter the distance between the lovers' forms, so that on her return, Takla too enjoyed this curious intimacy. She too did not suspect the underlying cause, but put her feelings down to a half-awakened memory returning with the presence of its original happening.

But here was a difference, for Takla had learned not only what it was to be *in love* – the complete surrender of her will, the abandonment of self and the inability to resist the face of her beloved – but also she had come some way in learning *to love*. She had a natural aptitude for love's ways, and the discrimination which love endows informed her actions. She loved her child, and this love expanded to all the necessary actions of serving that object: to Yahya's feeding and protecting, to educating with scolds as well as kisses, and now to teaching him the names of things. And, necessarily, because her nature was not selfish, this abundance of affection and diligent care overflowed into her daily work, enriching her cooking with its colours and tastes.

Takla had fully embraced her role of cook for the convent. With the increased funds accruing from the burgeoning goat meat and milk products industry, Mother Superior correspondingly increased the kitchen budget to allow the cook to develop her growing talents for the benefit of all. Takla now kept up a regular correspondence with the Cairene, whose Bolu chef had the knack of releasing his latest recipes just in time for some big feast or other. So what had once been an average provincial kitchen providing simple but wholesome fare to travellers, pilgrims and the local poor, now established a reputation for the fineness and imagination of its cooking. Seydnaya became a must on the itinerary of pilgrims journeying between Rome and Jerusalem, and for not a few enlightened *hajjis* between Mecca and wherever. As well as sharing his cook's recipes, the Cairene would also in season send crates of fresh produce from his estates: the youngest and fattest vegetables, plump geese and ducks, quails and partridge, Nile perch live in tanks, casks of meaty black olives and boxes of sugared chestnuts from the slopes between Bursa and the Marmara Sea. Once, even, he had white peaches packed in snow shipped all the way from

Adrianople. These gifts would be sorted away by the excited novices while
Takla stood by shuffling through sheets of recipes written in Arabic, trying
to work out the best way to prepare these exotic ingredients.

Takla continued to raise the child as if her own, and no one thought it
odd that when Yahya first spoke, it was with the word 'mama' addressed to
the one designated his foster mother. Yahya's second word was 'goat'. It
might just as well have been his first word, for from that moment on,
whenever he saw these woolly creatures he was in raptures. And when he
heard them bleat he clapped his hands and shrieked and gurgled with
delight. Nothing was more certain to stop any untoward crying or bad
temper, and enable Takla to get on with her work, than have one of the
novices take him down to the goats. There his distress would dissolve and
he would stare wide-eyed and cooing at the hairy flock. By the time Yahya
was four years old and running wild in the corridors of the convent like a
little kid goat himself, he could make his way down to paddocks on his
own; and it was only with the promise of being able to go out with his
grandfather's own little flock that he could be parted from his precious
herd each year to go with his mama to visit her family.

Daud too was learning about love, and the service of love. In the past
he had experienced love like a great flame in his heart. It had burnt him up
so much at times he cried just with the pain of his separation; then it had
left him empty and frustrated, causing him to cry again inwardly in
longing. Now, worn out by the poisoned sweetness of its seductions and
cruel truths of its caprice, he began to see that there was a real difference
between what he thought .was love, and the beautiful movement of love
itself, that invisible ocean which surrounded him, and where, in rare
moments of unselfconsciousness he was drawn into its timeless ebb and
flow. Even the memories of that beauty in the desert, he realised, when
conjuring them out of his own hurting soul, were his own creations,
distorted echoes of a spirit long fled. For she was that silver-lipped beauty
of his sleeping hours, whose message her beauteous form embodied,
whom when he followed she disappeared into that dark night beyond the
stars. Had that wondrous girl appeared before him now he would have
been ashamed. Was she the messenger, or the invitation? or if she was
simply the envelope, what was the profound and meaningful epistle of her
interior being? She could even be, perhaps, the declaration of love. But she
was not love itself, no matter how much it seemed to pour from her image.

But truly she was not other than love. Love – that was all around him, ineffable yet inescapable, like air. And yet… there was something in her atmosphere, like an encircling scent, like the disappearing distant footfall, which led him on, to want to dive beyond the stars of his own heaven. What exactly was it that this love wanted? If she was the hook and he the fish, who had cast this line? And what was this ocean of tribulation in which he found himself drowning?

Daud's salvation in those days lay in his companionship with that noble goatherd of Kassioun, Sa'id bin Adam. Sa'id, who was not a simple man, was endowed with a singular character. His pure heart shone bright like unalloyed metal. As gold among the elements of men. Under Sa'id's guidance, Daud took on more and more of the day to day ministrations of the herd. He organised a small cooperative among local farmers and herdsmen to pool their labour and produce, and arranged joint transport, sales and marketing down in Damascus. There were half a dozen markets in various parts of the city, and with Daud's energetic administration, the farmers of Kassioun gained a reputation for high quality produce at reasonable prices. No one had to spend more than one day each week away from their farms, and each was assured of having their product freshly marketed.

With his income from Seydnaya, over the next few years Daud's own position as a herdsman increased like the proverbial grains upon the squares of the chequered board, so in that second year, his twenty head of goats became forty, the next it became eighty, and so on. Each year he looked forward to visiting the convent, and he always returned revivified from his short retreat.

By the sixth year the convent's herd had swelled into the thousands, and Daud's own share was more than five hundred goats. Servicing them, as well as maintaining the large herd he managed jointly with Sa'id, was growing into a major operation. Daud had brought overland a dozen of his best stud billies to inseminate Seydnaya's expanding herds. His work now involved tramping the hills outwith the convent, delivering his tups to wherever the various herds were pastured and returning to the warmth of the convent only in the evenings. He felt it was time to rein in both his and the convent's ranching ambitions, and brought this matter up with the reverend Mother Superior.

'Ah Daud, how lovely to see you again.' said Mother Superior. She had always liked this man, for he was straightforward and appreciative, and his presence never upset the calm and concentrated tenor of the convent. His otherworldly countenance provoked only respectful awe, thereby sparing him the unwanted attentions of the young novices. After some small-talk, Daud began to explain his thoughts regarding the goats.

'I know it has been good to increase the herd, but we are reaching saturation point at Kassioun, and probably you are here too. We can only just manage what we have. We must think about sending more goats to slaughter. Prices in Damascus are good at present, but it might be better to send some over the mountains to Beirut, or even Jerusalem, where they'll fetch a higher price.'

Mother Superior liked to hear this kind of talk from Daud. She could see that underneath that shaggy goatherd exterior was a true business man, professional, measured, not greedy; aware of the necessity to turn a fair profit in order to maintain a buffer for thin times, but knowing the natural limit of growth for a particular project. These talks never failed to confirm in her mind that, for the convent, things were going as they should. While in no way could she have been considered dictatorial, she was not afraid to exercise authority to maintain direction in her community. She preferred to pray, to watch and wait, and then make decisions based on what inspired her with the greatest feeling of wholeness in any situation.

'As I have always said, risk is nourishment,' said Mother Superior. 'We are not wanting here. The larders are full, the donations generous, and you're right, we do have too many goats. We can only keep so many for milk and some extra for meat, so take the surplus to market in Beirut or Damascus, wherever you think best. You can either leave the money with our sisters in Mount Carmel, or bring it here. In the meantime, I have another proposition for you...' And here she outlined the story of the foundling Yahya.

'So, you see, the lad is six years old. Up until now he has only enjoyed the company of women, apart from when Takla – she's his foster mother, and also our cook – takes him home at Easter. Yahya just lives for the goats, spends his whole time taking them out to pasture and back. But he's getting to an age now when he needs to spend time in the company of his own sex. He needs a father, and he needs to be able to learn his trade properly. Would it be out of the question for you to take him on as an apprentice?'

There was no question of it being out of the question. The Damascus

Drum, which accompanied Daud on all his journeys, had mostly remained silent since he had joined Sa'id. It now came to life, booting him firmly in the ribs.

'AAAAAAAGH… of course, it would be no trouble, and we could really use the extra help. But tell me, what of his religion? Is he baptised? Or is he a Muslim? What would you want for him in that respect?'

Mother Superior paused for a moment in her train of thought and took a long deep breath. 'We are all people of the Book,' she said pragmatically, 'and we both aim to serve the same One we call God. Are our aims so different? Our religion is one of love, and love is that deepest feeling inside and beyond each of us. It is what speaks to us when all the words have failed, and it informs when the mind is perplexed. It is what moves us on even when life seems impossible. Isn't that really what we serve when we say we serve God? Love is not something which can be taught, not something created and corruptible. Yes, here we have rules, and the bishops have their dogmas, but they are just the fences for cattle, to stop them trampling the flowers in the garden. So, that is the religion Yahya was born with, the only religion he has in his heart. The boy will be yours to educate as you see fit as a father. You know a father's love should be like God's love, full of patience, caring, and merciful; but mercy covers everything, and for love's sake, when guidance and wisdom necessitates, that mercy may appear as punishment. He is like you, you'll see. He won't be any trouble.'

Daud found himself listening with that same ear into which his Drum had so often poured its wisdoms. 'Perhaps our religions are not so different after all,' said Daud, 'Our aim is one of surrender and submission, to that same One whom you follow in love's stream. And in our surrender is our education, the unlinking of the soul from our little ways and tying ourselves to Its way. Perhaps our religions are closer than we think. Perhaps too our God is closer to us than we think.'

And so it was arranged that twelve months later, when Daud returned for the next tupping, he would take charge, *in loco parentis*, of young Yahya.

TWENTY-NINE

The pain of love

SAAC before the knife of Abraham, the intimate one of God. Joseph thrown into the well and then sold into Egypt. Moses adrift in the bulrushes. What strange tests life sets in the name of love. A mother brings a son into the world against all odds, and having cast him out upon a sea of snow, he is returned to her with the coming of the dawn. Then, having fed and loved and spoiled and chastened him to boyhood, once more she is required to launch him into the company of strangers. But is not the tearing pain of separation also the turning of Providence's plate to be filled anew from the source, a constant reunion, a continual rebirth? Takla's breast was sore from the squeezing of life's imperatives. This new thing was much harder than giving birth. That had been just a physical event, its beginning and end measurable in a short space of time, and its result the joyful disclosure of a long hidden treasure. Now that treasure was being withdrawn from her sight, and with it went her joy. She felt her heart had been ripped open and her soul exposed, raw and vulnerable. That young vessel in which she had invested her love, that store of all her hopes and endeavours was about to embark into a mist of uncertainty. It was a new experience which she imagined must compare with a sudden, unexpected and unwanted death. And like this conjured death, a seemingly impenetrable veil had fallen between Takla and her son.

Mother Superior had been sensitive to the situation. She had begun the conversation lightly by discussing Yahya's love of goats, bringing it round to the visit of the shepherd with the drum who came each year from Mount Kassioun with his billy goats for the tupping. From there she let it drift into talk of how Yahya was growing up, and how independent he seemed, wandering all day in the hills, sometimes even staying out at night with his dogs and the flocks. Takla was proud of how fearlessly her young son had taken to his life as a herder. When Mother Superior addressed the matter of his education, mentioning that perhaps he should now be sent to join the monks high up on Mount Kallamoun behind Seydnaya or in the caves of nearby Maaloula, only then had Takla protested.

'Please, no, he would dry up like a raisin in there,' she said. 'He needs the open air. He needs to be able to roam under the stars whenever he wants.'

'Yes. But he is a bright boy. He will benefit from an education.'

'I can teach him to read and write,' said Takla. 'Any of the nuns could, for that matter.'

'It's not just that. The only human beings he ever sees are women, except for when he visits your father. The lad really needs to spend more time with men.'

'But those monks aren't really men, are they?' Takla had her suspicions about the dark-cloaked denizens of the monasteries which crowded the valleys and mountains of the Holy Land. All those books and incense and closed windows. And those scraggy ascetics with long grey beards living in caves and surviving on nettle soup with barely a rag to cover their nakedness. It seemed dull and stuffy, queer even, and not at all the sort of environment she could imagine her son growing and being happy in.

Mother Superior neither agreed nor disagreed, merely saying 'The monks are as much men as the nuns here are women, no more no less,' and left it at that.

'Well what about this then…' and here, as if the thought had just struck her, Mother Superior broached the idea of Yahya going off to live with the goatherd from Mt Kassioun. Takla, for whom convent life had provided a great security during her seven years of motherhood, now felt her world was being pulled out from beneath her, and she was flying into space with nothing to hold onto.

'Of course, he would come back every year for the tupping, and he could still go with you to visit your parents if you wish.'

Takla controlled a strong urge to break down and tell Mother Superior everything. What good would it have done? It wouldn't change the fact that Yahya still had no father. And it was true, the boy really did need to spend some time with men. He needed to learn men things if he was going to survive, and from what she had heard about Daud, he seemed a trust-worthy person, and a kind and thoughtful one, a 'proper man' according to the nuns who entertained him in the kitchen during her absences. Mother Superior wouldn't have suggested it if he wasn't suitable. She knew it was kind of Mother Superior to be having this discussion at all. So, she bit her bottom lip, and did not burst out crying until after she had left Mother Superior's office and made her way to the shrine room of the Shaghoura.

Before the holy icon of the Virgin and Child painted by St Luke, Takla wept a river from her poor broken heart, and her tears wet the stones of the darkened chapel floor until they glistened at her feet. It seemed her sorrow had pulled down the heavens and all the golden stars of the dark blue ceiling were crying with her in the reflected candlelight. Between the tears she begged the saintly mother Mary to intercede on her behalf for light from God to mend her heart and give her the strength to bear this separation. Only when her tears were spent and her eyes were dry did she leave the little chapel and make her way outside of the convent. Takla stood on a hill looking over to where Yahya was leading a large flock of goats to pasture opposite. She watched her little boy about his work, skipping from rock to rock, gaining a high vantage point and sitting to watch them as they grazed slowly, then rising again to call and cajole the ragged beasts on round the hillside until they were one and all lost from her sight.

Then the thought entered her breast: 'If Yahya goes away, won't it be just like that? He has gone with the flock to the other side of the mountain. Then later he will return. Until that time, he is just out of sight on another slope. He is still my son. I love him just the same whether he is in view, or out of sight, neither more nor less.' The sense of intimacy which came with this thought fell like a moist and cooling breath upon her troubled head, cleansing her of the interior dryness which came after her tears. Takla made her mind up from that moment to let love and hope, and not sadness and fear, determine the memory of her son in his absence.

When Easter passed and the day of parting came, it was Takla who was first to leave. She had talked to Yahya in the preceding weeks about their impending separation, and she had been surprised at his reaction. He grew silent a while, carefully looking at the implications of this new situation within the parameters of his child's knowledge, and then said,

'Will he be my father?'

'Well, sort of. Not exactly, but it will be like that.'

'Can I call him 'papa' like I call you 'mama'?'

'I don't know. Perhaps. You'll have to ask him.'

'Oh, I hope so... Does he really have thousands of goats?'

'That's what Mother Superior says. He saved our herd, and now look at it. I imagine he really does have thousands of goats.'

'Good. Then I can help him look after them.'

And that was all Yahya had to say on the matter. Except that he grew more and more excited as the day approached. He was looking forward to his new life as much as Takla unadmittedly was dreading it. She had intended to stay to meet her son's new guardian, but a message had come with one of the Easter pilgrim's that her mother was very ill, and so she had bade farewell to Yahya in Reverend Mother's study, handing him back, so to speak, to the one who had lent him to her. The tears were lighter this time, for they were the tears of a heart brave in the certainty of love, not of a soul oppressed with emotions. When later in the day Takla reached the pool by the cave, she lingered a while, drinking in not one but the two memories which came alive for her in the atmosphere of the place. The reverberations of union informed her own feelings of love, strengthening her resolve, and she hurried on to her ailing mother.

Meanwhile, Yahya the goat boy stood before Mother Superior and the famous Daud. Yahya had heard many stories of this man from the nuns and novices, not all of them true, but all complimentary, and these stories had created in his imagination a quite impossibly heroic image for Daud to live up to. An image, which if the truth be told, rather frightened the young would-be goatherd. Yahya looked closely at his new master.

'Did you really walk all the way across the desert from India with Shams the Billy Goat?'

Daud laughed, 'No, of course not. I just came over the mountains from the north. It's not far, a week maybe, we can go that way together one day.'

Yahya was relieved. 'And did you fight lions single-handed and kill them with your knife?'

Again Daud laughed. 'No, not at all. I wouldn't be here today if I had tried to take on a lion all by myself. My dogs keep all the lions away from me and my goats.'

Again Yahya was relieved. 'Is it true that the jinn keep away from you because of the smell of the goats?'

'Well, there may be something in that.'

'Will you be my papa?'

This last question almost wrong-footed Daud, until he realised that it was an invitation of acceptance. 'Of course, if you will be my boy.'

'Yes please.'

'Then that's settled.'

'And will you marry my mama?'

Daud laughed out loud. He knew the story of the foundling, but he didn't want to hurt the boy's feelings, so he played along.

'Well, that really depends on whether she would want to marry me. But first things first. We've got a lot of goats to take to market. Come along and let me introduce you to the chaps.' Daud meant the crew of billy goats he had brought with him for this season's tupping. As man and boy walked away across the forecourt, Mother Superior could hear their excited conversation drifting up to her where she watched from her balcony.

'Well there's Baibars, he's a cool customer, likes to think of himself as superior to all the rest, and the most handsome with his long floppy ears. He's certainly the tallest billy goat I've ever had, but he's no match for Saladin when it comes to staying power. Saladin can serve a hundred every two days for a fortnight and they all get pregnant. Then there's Zengin, a bit sly but the girls love him …'

A week later the huge herd moved off with much raising of dust, yelping of dogs and a very excited Yahya running hither and thither, saving the stragglers from every imaginary danger on the secure and well-trodden road to Damascus.

The evening of the same day a small figure cloaked in a black wool blanket entered the convent by the kitchen door and collapsed on the bed in the room nearby. Early next morning Takla went to speak to Mother Superior. She asked her permission to leave the convent once again, this time for an indefinite period to look after her father. While Takla's father had always been the one with all the aches and pains, her mother had maintained the best of health throughout her life. Then suddenly during Holy Week she had been taken ill with some stomach ailment which brought with it a fever. The fever burned without abating and it seemed only death could cool it. Just two days after Takla had arrived at her parent's home, her mother's now frail body gave up its spirit. Takla spent the remainder of her break organising the funeral mass and burial, and trying to comfort her father who was completely heartbroken and virtually inconsolable. Her parents had never spent a night apart in all the years of their long marriage. This wasn't unusual in a small farming community, but it made life after bereavement even harder to bear. So now Takla was asking permission to return for as long as necessary. Mother Superior gave her blessing, and a little money from the convent's funds to tide them over for the present.

'But we will miss you, Takla. You know your place is waiting here for you whenever you are able to return.' She embraced her little cook warmly before Takla once more set off in the dawn. This time she didn't linger by the pool, although its warm scents eased her heart as she passed. Takla's life had changed a lot in the past few months. She was no longer a child, she hadn't been for some time. Now she was beginning to feel different altogether. The gathering of responsibilities, which had begun with her work in the kitchen, then the joys of looking after her child, and now in the same week her son's departure, her mother's death and her poor distraught father to care for in his grief, left her no time to mourn the passing of her own childhood. Takla was a practical girl, and she was moving on in herself. She no longer had any idea where the road ahead was leading, but that didn't seem important now. What was certain was that there was a road, her road, and wherever it led, she would follow.

THIRTY

The man in the eye

T WAS a month since Takla had left Seydnaya. The afternoon heat in the little mudbrick farmhouse was stifling,
and as she lay resting in the main room of the house, she
daydreamed of her child. Takla playing with Yahya, at the
pool by the cave. Yahya laughing and making her laugh too. Then she
drifted into sleep, and dreamed a scene of rocky mountains with herds of
goats covering the slopes. She saw in the distance a bearded man dressed

in an old camel hair blanket and carrying a staff. Takla tried to see who this man was, but the great herd of goats lay between them. She strained to see. Suddenly the distance between them folded up, and she was face to face with him. It was the face of her son, with his happy, guileless smile and his eyes full of love.

He recognised her and she tried to speak to him, but her body wrapped her like a prison, holding her down, a heavy lid upon her chest. The face faded to whorls in the walnut of the bedside table and the flocks of goats became the tumbled tresses of her own hair upon the pillow. Awake now, the warmth of the experience lingered and she felt close again in spite of the separation.

She thought it strange that she had dreamed of her son as a mature man. Then she realised whom she had really seen. Those eyes that gazed back so adoringly were the eyes that had brought her to love in the first place. She had seen Yahya in his father's eyes, in his father's face. The fact that her baby might grow in the image of her lover had never occurred to her. Only now, distanced as she was from little Yahya had the original image resurfaced, as a mirror to her more recent love.

Takla went outside and splashed her face with water from a bucket by the well. The sun was low and a light breeze was blowing from the south, rustling the leaves on the terebinth trees which grew along the roadside. The hamlet, for it was not really a village, just a place where one road met another and a stream ran through, comprised a few humble cottages backed by small orchards of plums and apricots, figs and olives, with plots of vegetables in the flat areas nearest the stream. There was a communal threshing floor and odd yards and buildings for animals and storage of crops. Beyond, some small fields showed green lines of new barley and wheat breaking the pale soil. The fields gave onto rough grass and scrub, then bare hills where goats grazed and tortoises paced slowly among the rocks. She felt the breeze cool on her wet face, refreshing her mind from sleep, but the images remained strong and affected her in different ways. The memory of her son calmed her, made her feel secure and happy, useful and grateful as a mother. But the recollection of her lover's face was disturbing. It returned her to that strange and brief meeting, to its passion and its light, in a way that it had not done before. Back then in the joyful aftermath of her union and during the ensuing pregnancy, Takla had felt wholly fulfilled and without need of anything beyond what each day provided. It was a matter of perspective. Now the memory of the event was claiming its real place in her past, and a different kind of desire made its presence felt in her. For the first time since she had made love to that wild man at the pool by the cave, she found herself wanting to be with him again. And the more she felt this want, the more there grew in her a resolve to find him. But how? She didn't even know his name or where he was from. Up until this moment she had barely let herself believe that he had actually existed in the flesh. She had kept her pregnancy and the birth so secret that at times it was as if she believed her own deception.

'No matter,' thought Takla, as she recalled her son's face, 'I will recognise his father when I see him. And when I find him, what then?' This question did not bother her at all. 'When I find him, I'll know.' It was as simple as that. She was still a practical girl and knew not to worry about problems for which the solution was not immediately apparent. Time would take care of it as it always had done. Now she had made the intention, and resolved to carry it out, there was nothing more she could do. The immediate task was to take care of her father.

Gradually, with Takla's support and companionship, her father's spirits lifted and he began to work his fields and tend his goats as before. Throughout the summer Takla lived the village life again. Not as a girl this time, but as a woman: milking the goats, making cheese and yoghurt, weeding and pruning in the vegetable plot and orchard, setting chillies and apricots to dry in the yard, and threading strings of little bamya to hang near the hearth for winter soups. She ground the barley and spelt from her father's fields, baking it into bread in the clay oven outside the house, washing and mending clothes, cooking and cleaning, and followed the stream up into the hills to gather herbs and collect fallen firewood for winter. All the things she had helped her mother to do, now she did again as mother to her father for whom old age brought a new kind of dependency.

When the first cold winds of late autumn came whispering down from the north, Takla's father began making arrangements to leave. With his neighbours he began to speak of the time when he would be gone, as if he were emigrating to a different land. To Takla, he was like a bird preparing for the long flight south as winter approaches. He pecked around his old nest in a disinterested way, poking here and there with his stick, stroking the walls affectionately as if to say, 'Well, it's done its job, the brood has grown and flown, no need to remain here any longer.'

One day he came in from his fields and said to Takla: 'Well, now that's done, we're ready to go.'

'What's done? Ready to go where?' she said

'Oh, never mind, I'm tired now. We'll talk in the morning.'

Of course, when morning came, and the large heron flew the length of the little stream and disappeared south over the nearest hill, the time for talking had passed. The unspoken words revealed that Takla's father had passed on into the next life. On the previous day he had arranged the transfer of the fields of his small farm to a younger male cousin living nearby who had a large family to provide for. The house, kitchen garden and orchard, and the goats were to remain Takla's, but it was expected that she would go and join the cousin's family anyway.

The body of her father, eyes closed, washed and wrapped in his best garments, was lain upon a flat board inside their house. By mid-morning the mourners had arrived, old women from neighbouring hamlets with nothing better to do than disturb the peace of the dead with their raucous cries in return for a few pennies, as custom demanded. Her cousins dug a grave next to her mother's at the foot of a rocky knoll near the house. Then the priest came and together they carried the bier up to the grave. The funeral was without ceremony. Amid the wails of the professional mourners, and a few prayers from the priest, the corpse was lain in the hole, the earth filled in and large stones heaped over the grave. After the burial everyone gathered outside Takla's house to share food and wine and praise the life of the one departed. Later Takla would pay for a mass to be said by one of the priests at Seydnaya.

By mid-afternoon Takla found herself alone at last. She went and sat by her parents' graves, the one showing new shoots of grass and forget-me-nots, the other still a dark wound of barely-closed earth and stones. She shut her eyes and spoke her heart, telling them all she could never say in life. She spoke of her son, of what they had always known anyway, that he was their grandchild. She spoke of the child's father, her lover of an instant, and how she would find him one day.

Suddenly she felt their presences so close, almost tangible, without the veil of mortal form. Then a gust of wind blew strongly but briefly, and the connection began to fade. She knew then that her father's death had released her from her mother's vow. She opened her eyes. Before her the two small graves appeared as a bridal bed and in her mind's eye she saw her parents' spirits reunited, departing forever the fog of worldly trial and separations.

Takla had always worn lightly the fact that she was bonded to the convent by her mother's vow. It had never been a burden as such, and Mother Superior had always treated her more as a daughter than as a servant. The strange thing was, at the instant that she was freed of this obligation, she felt no desire other than to return to the place that felt like home. So, having entrusted her house and orchard into her cousin's care, and with the few possessions her parents had left packed up on her father's donkey, she led her small herd of six she-goats and their six little kids over the mountains back to Seydnaya. She had made up her mind. She was going to ask Mother Superior to let her train to become a nun.

Takla had no intention of secluding herself forever within the convent – she had, after all, only just rediscovered that desire which had resulted in motherhood. Maybe she simply wasn't ready to leave home yet. She knew she had more to learn, and not just about cooking; and as for that other desire, she saw no contradiction there. It was as though her life was running on a number of parallel tracks, and she was quite capable of entertaining multiple possibilities. As Takla had no idea what the future might bring, she didn't want to limit its outcome.

Yet, she had lost her lover, her child was gone, and now she was an orphan. In spite of having lived so long apart from her parents, the cutting of these mortal ties was yet another painful event which only time would assuage. In her grief she longed for the fostering care of the convent, and the kind counsel of her Mother Superior.

Mother Superior looked up from her desk and over her pince-nez at little Takla who was sitting patiently in the window alcove.

'So, you want to become a bride of Christ do you? Our little Takla… whoever would have thought it. To be united to the Word, eh? Well, I suppose you have had ample opportunity to think about it. But I thought you were so happy looking after the kitchen, and bringing up little Yahya? Well, there's no reason why we shouldn't give it every consideration. But you will have to remain in the kitchen of course, we shall not let a talent like yours be wasted. And you will have to fit in a lot more now besides:

prayers, meditation, study, chapel, all that sort of thing. Are you sure this is what you want?'

'Yes.' Takla smiled back, nodding. At that moment she was completely certain.

In fact, thought Mother Superior, there was no reason at all why the girl couldn't have taken the vows right then and there. Takla's commitment to the life in the convent was total, her compliance to the regime innate and unresisting, it was as if she had been born to it. But Mother Superior still had some concerns. Not about Takla's veracity, but something told her there was a lot more to Takla than even she in her God-given wisdom could surmise. It was about a possibility, and hence a necessity. She had always felt Takla had been lent to her, unlike the other nuns, who spent their lives being shaped by the order of the convent under her direction. It was as though Takla had her own direction, that she was following a path already firmly established within her own being. But Takla seemed to have no difficulty in adapting to any situation. She certainly had no trouble conforming to the rule of the convent, and that was how Mother Superior saw it now. 'Well,' she thought, 'it just happens that today Takla wants to be a nun, so we'll comply with her request, for the time being, and see what happens.'

And that is how Mother Superior took charge of Takla's spiritual education. She could have left it to other experienced nuns, but she wanted to see for herself how Takla would respond to the disciplines and exercises of the order. She also felt drawn to her in a way which may have stemmed from the knowledge she shared, unbeknown to Takla, regarding the true parentage of the child.

Whereas Takla had only recently discovered Yahya's resemblance to her lover, Mother Superior had become increasingly aware of the child's likeness to Daud when he returned for the annual tupping. And more. As in a pool at times one sees through the surface reflections to the depths within, so too did Mother Superior observe in Yahya the manner of his foster mother in the qualities of his soul. And all this even had Mother Superior not looked out from her balcony upon the mysterious beauty of that natal night and observed Takla's comings and goings below in the snow.

The nuns and novices teased Takla about Yahya, saying that lovers grow to look like each other. Mother Superior just smiled to herself and

waited 'til the next Easter. But when it came she knew she couldn't interfere. She sent Takla off home as usual, and encouraged Daud to stay for
as long as possible, but the coincidence never occurred. She had really
hoped that they would meet when Daud came to take Yahya away with
him, but even then the day had configured in an unexpected fashion.
Some strange destiny was being worked out here that she could only
observe from a distance.

And so Takla began learning the contemplative way under the supervision
of Mother Superior. They started with meditation.

'Meditation is the easiest thing in the world. It is simply doing nothing.
Not sleeping, not dreaming, not thinking, just doing nothing. Rather, it is
doing 'not doing'. Perhaps it is not even that, but just the not doing without
being in the doing of the not doing. It's seeing what's there when we turn
off the 'me'. You could say it is just being. But meditation is not without an
object, nor without a subject. And that subject and object is not you, but
neither are you other than it.'

Mother Superior paused, expecting to see the usual signs of puzzlement from the novice, but she saw only the face of a child eager to hear the
next bit of the story.

'Now, you need to set some direction, some intention for your meditation. Imagine you are setting out from Beirut to Haifa in a boat, and you
need a northerly wind... ah! but of course, you have never seen the sea,
have you? OK, what about this? You have a camel and you want to cross the
desert. You point the camel in the direction you want to go, you shout *hat!*
hat! and whack it with your riding crop and you set off. But if you don't
know where you are going, you'll be neither here nor there. Or worse,
you'll be like those who go round and round in circles, imagining they are
travelling just because they are following the sun, but actually they don't
get anywhere at all. No, you need to know where you are going, you need
to set your course.'

Mother Superior paused again and peered closely at Takla who was all
wide-eyed and rapt attention. She continued:

'So, you set an intention. Now, of course you don't know the end of
your journey yet, but you do know that there is a destination, and so you
can make that your goal, even if it is not specified in any way. And your

intention, depending on its strength, and its purity, will carry you to your goal, because that intention is like a gift to you from the goal itself. Your wish to follow this way comes from the way itself, from what lies at the end of your journey. The strength that the intention has in you comes from the quality of the response it finds, whether it is free and unconditioned, or if it comes with reservation. And it will stay pure if you do not add anything to it from your self. The intention carries its own inner guide.'

Mother Superior looked at Takla, who looked back smiling, showing neither comprehension nor incomprehension of what she had just said.

'Is it like when I close my eyes, and try to see God, but then I realise that only God sees God, and I have to sit back and just be like the eye through which it happens?'

Mother Superior stifled a gasp, and said, 'Yes, exactly. Carry on just like that. Think of an arrow in flight, it will always reach its aim. You just have to watch it, and never doubt it will hit the target. And remember, it is love which gives the arrow flight. The target wants to be hit, and your intention is the arrow.'

'Sometimes I just fall asleep, you know.'

'Yes, that happens too. Nothing to worry about. It isn't meditation, but sometimes it lets other things happen that have to happen.'

'And sometimes I look to see what God sees in me, and it's like I'm looking into an endless space, and I think I'm falling and I always wake up to myself.'

'Yes, that's fine too. But let yourself fall, and still be the eye. One day, if God wills, you'll fall right into yourself, and then you'll see what God sees. Only, you'll see it by God, not by yourself.'

Mother Superior was surprised by what she had said. It was not the sort of conversation she had ever had with any of her nuns, let alone a would-be novice. Yet it came so naturally, as though Takla's words fitted spaces in her knowing heart that had waited patiently for years to be filled. It was like talking to the daughter she would never have.

And so their discussions continued. 'Thoughts,' Mother Superior said, 'will take you away from your intention. They are like conversations you overhear in the market, they will distract you from the job in hand, buying your groceries. These people in the market, they never stop chatting, whether you pay them any attention or not. But your business is with the shopkeeper. Go and get the best price for the best produce. That's your job.

Stay awake, be aware, don't be satisfied with anything but the best, pay the price and don't accept short weight.'

Another time they discussed contemplation. 'Sit quietly. Take a word, an image, some question you have, whatever, and let that be the object of your contemplation. You just state it, and when your mind wanders, return to it again as you might look again at any object. Don't create imaginations about it. Let it speak. Don't invent it. You know, when I was a young nun in Jerusalem, we had a Mother Superior – in our contemplations she always wanted us to imagine the horrible things they say they did to Jesus. One nun got so carried away by the idea of stigmata that she started bleeding from all the wrong places and ended up giving up the ghost. Better to choose a beautiful image, then the results will be beautiful too.'

'I think I know what you mean,' said Takla. 'Sometimes, when I miss Yahya, I just say his name to myself, very quietly, just once, and then it's as if he is right here with me, and sometimes I even see him, not like a memory, but like he is really here and I could reach out and touch him, only I think it's happening inside me, not outside. If I try to touch him, he disappears.'

'You can make contact, only not with this…' Mother Superior reached over and tapped the back of Takla's hand, 'unless the vision is exterior. And it's very difficult to make an exterior vision, and not usually necessary. Except for the Big Ones, of course, like Solomon.' Mother Superior was an advanced person, without a doubt, and an adept in the protocols of the imaginal worlds, but she knew that certain gifts were not in everyone's portion.

'It's all in the breath,' Mother Superior said, 'that's the key,' and gave no further explanation. Takla pondered this last comment, and stored it away for future reference.

'You need to know the place where real vision happens. You need to explore your heart. That is your real home, the place where things are not separated, where you are not divided from the world. But you have to learn the nature of this heart. From this point of view, here in this rough and crude world, your heartland is a very delicate place, a fragile place. It is like a bird that flies away if startled. It is like a child that will not speak if it is frightened. It is a lover who will not be persuaded by reason, but only by the essential knowledge that comes with love, that it is made of the same substance as its beloved. Actually, it is not a fragile place at all, but a place of unimaginable strength, the safest refuge. That is why it seems so difficult to find, and to maintain. Staying in it requires such a letting go of the strengths and forces of this world, its forms and attractions, its weights and gravities. For most of us it is only when we die that we surrender enough of what we imagine is our real life to be able to see that much, much bigger life we inhabit in the heart. But we can approach the heart by practising death before our death actually catches us. We have to be ready. And to be ready we need preparation.'

Takla again looked at Mother Superior with that look of concentrated receptivity. As the old nun spoke, Takla found herself not so much listening to the words themselves, but experiencing the energy rolling in waves from the being of the person sitting opposite. Later, she reflected that it was like watching ripples in a pond from the splash of a fish's tail, sweeping shimmerings of light over the surface of the water, but at the time she found herself immersed in the presence of meanings to the point of drowning, yet arriving at such a clarity and stillness in her own being, as one might discover in the heart of a great explosion.

Time passed and many other things were discussed, mulled over, dissected, their subtle meanings extracted, absorbed and reconstructed, in short the whole noble sentiment of the spiritual life brought to view, magnified by taste and returned enhanced by the descent of self-knowledge. In fact, Takla had little time to spare for all the prayer and meditation that Mother Superior had mentioned, and certainly fasting and silence figured not at all in her new regime. Whatever time she could spare from the kitchen, she spent with Mother Superior.

Before long it was accepted that Takla was *de facto* Mother Superior's personal assistant. As their dearly beloved lady was now elderly, not to say venerable, it came as no surprise to the community that she should need the assistance of one young and strong like Takla to help take the weight of some of the old nun's necessary activities. Takla looked after all her personal needs, cleaning her room, bringing her tea, washing her clothes. But most of all they talked. Talk flowed like a stream between the seas of their hearts, and Takla's heart grew like the small bird grew when it flew high above the world, nestling among the feathers of an eagle, its vision widening beyond its known boundaries in an infinite sky. And in the growing receptivity of Takla's expanded soul were planted the seeds of mysteries and beauties unimaginable.

THIRTY-ONE

The goatherds of Mount Kassioun

AHYA pushed away the stones and brushwood from the mouth of the cave where they had sheltered the previous night and name-checked the goats one by one as they skipped out onto the rocky face of Mount Kassioun.

'Teal, Duck, Lark, Finch, Crake, Snipe, Gull, Tit, Shrike, Swift, Kite, Coot, Grebe...' Yahya took a deep breath before continuing, 'Sparrow, Pochard, Babbler, Ibis, Serin, Hoopoe, Wheatear, Warbler, Courser, Sand-grouse, Wagtail, Bulbul, Robin, ugh!,' another breath, 'Sunbird, Bunting, Buzzard, Heron, Eagle, Wryneck, Stonechat, Bluethroat, Chiffchaff, Plover, Kestrel,' and so it went on, 'Cormorant, Gallinule, Harrier, Bee-eater, King-fisher...'

One of the first lessons Daud had set his young charge was to learn the names of the goats in his herd. There was a trick to it, Daud said, as each one was named after a bird with which it shared certain characteristics. All Yahya had to do was match them up. Take the swift, for instance, fleet and fancy free, it never seems to land. Carving the air as an Indian dancer, this name was given to a particular goat which, once let out to pasture, rarely remained still long enough for its four hooves to touch the ground at the same time, leaping here and there, rootling about the bushes to snatch a tasty shoot or bud as a swift might take an insect on the wing.

Or the gallinule – just a simple common moorhen really, a shy creature which dwells in ponds and marshes, but fiercely courageous in defence of its young. The gallinule's long feet make its head jerk when it walks and white feathers peek out from beneath its rather dull brown wings and tail. So, a small goat, cautious yet independent, no great beauty with its clodhopper feet but with sudden attractive flashes of white below its tail and forelegs. And nervous, it disappears under bushes and forages away, popping up after ages somewhere quite else.

Well, it wasn't so easy as all that, as Yahya soon discovered, for many of the goats had the same first name, with the addition of a second name, often a flower or plant, or a kind of rock, to distinguish it. Sometimes a colour or a mood or a quality of the goat's behaviour, or a simple physical attribute such as 'big' or 'little' or 'dark' etc, was added as well. And then there was the place where it had been born: by which stream, near which rock, under which tree. There were by now literally thousands of goats under Daud and Sa'id's care, each with its own name and its own character and qualities. As for the birds, not only had Yahya never come across many of them before, but at Seydnaya they had all just been 'bird': small bird, brown bird, big black noisy bird. He knew eagles, of course, they were the ones that stole the kid goats away; and the doves which nested in the eaves of the convent or on rocky mountain ledges, going *huu huu* like nuns at prayer. And then to cap it all, at least half of the goats were at first glance just one colour, dark brown. In time he was able to distinguish the reddish-hued, the darker shaded, the pepper-black with white splashes hidden underneath. The remaining goats were white, but gradually he learnt to discriminate faint shades of strawberry and flecked cinnamon from dust and spatters of mud.

The billy goats were easy, as there were relatively few. They were all named after heroes, generals of armies or great lovers. Daud would introduce each one with a description of the various feats of this or that champion of antiquity, describing the battles, the history and the geography of the lands they conquered or defended, and in this way young Yahya began to build up a world picture, peopled by magnificent characters who had lives of supreme adventure, performed brave exploits, and inevitably risked all for the sake of their beloved ladies, their closest companions and the people they led. But remembering the endless stream of she-goats, each with a bird's name, a flower's name, a physical attribute and a behavioural characteristic posed a formidable task. It required Yahya to look closely and pay attention to the details. And it taught him to question. What did 'coy' mean? Why was that particular goat referred to as 'hard-bitten'. Why was one capacious and another capricious?

Yahya's education extended to everything in his new world: he learned the paths among the hills, as well as the rocks, trees and slopes which defined their passage and often recalled some significant event. And streams, which ones should be avoided in the spring because of sudden torrents, and which flowed wide, providing easy watering places. Where did they lead? Did they join the Barada, or did they flow east behind Mount Kassioun to meet the Maraba which poured down from beyond the distant heights of the Jebel Kallamoun?

In time the topography of this new world revealed itself as a map, the names and the physical definitions inscribed in Yahya's memory. So he grew not just to distinguish one goat from another, to recognise birds and flowers, and the pathways between pastures, but he knew how to read the signs for danger and where to find places of refuge; he could see the future pattern of the weather in the shape and movement of clouds, and was able to find his way in the dark from the celestial map of night. Slowly too Yahya learned how to read the names of people, just as he had the directory of the herd. He learned to tell their real names from the added attributes of accident, habit or history. He knew too not to describe people by their lacks, but always to determine them by their essential humanity, that which he shared with them.

'Knowing by letting things announce their identity to you.' was how Daud explained it. 'It's like knowing something by taste, rather than being told about it or thinking about it or having an opinion.'

Then, when Yahya's mind had become capable of holding all these names in order, to be picked and chosen at will like items on a shelf; when this inward filing of qualities and information could be called upon to respond instantly to the stimulation, not just of the outward forms of things, but by their inner lights; when the stories had been committed to memory, the histories and geographies soundly established as source for their conversations, only then did Daud teach him to write the letters of the alphabet.

Again it began as an oral exposition: first sounding the original letter, ﺍ – 'ha' – , an explosion of air expelled from deep down within his being.

Then elongating with the sound 'ā', written as ١ – 'alef' – , the descended in-breath resuscitating as it rises through the chest, narrowing through the gorge of the throat to be formed like the clay of Adam, with the gutturals, palatals, dentals and labials until the final open 'ū', و – 'waw' – is sung from the concentrated lips and the breath is freed into the vast expanse of the air.

Together they would inscribe in the sand the shapes of the letters, joining them to form the sacred print of words, which shortly afterwards they would efface with a switch of grass so none could degrade them underfoot.

'Words,' said Daud, 'are the inspired creations of our souls. And just as we are the words of God, and our lives the stories that God tells, so too these words in the sand reflect their creator and must be given true value'. And when this had been absorbed, Uncle Sa'id showed Yahya the letters in the old order, the *huruf al'abjad*, one at a time, each with its numbered value – *alef* is one, *ba* is two, *jim* is three, *dal* is four and so on down to *ghain* which is a thousand. 'Each word has its own number as well. Take *hadi* for instance.' (Here Sa'id used the Arabic word meaning 'guide'.) 'It is made up of four letters, *ha, alef, dal* and *ya*,' and he inscribed them carefully in the sand. 'If you count the value of each letter, they add up to twenty. And if you remember it like this, saying *hadi* twenty times, you will bring this quality of guidance into focus. Then, God willing, you won't lose your way in life.'

Daud's time on the mountain with Sa'id bin Adam had also been a time of education. He too had learnt about goats, but that had come quite naturally. Mainly he had acquired the knowledge of putting one foot after the other. At first he had just followed Sa'id around, accompanying him, helping in the daily chores of a herders' life. Although he did not notice anything at first, as the years passed Daud realised that Sa'id had a subtle influence on the people he met. People would stop by at their farm on Kassioun, casually it seemed, spend a few minutes with the old man, and then return from where they'd come. Not just farmers and herdsmen, but city people too, ladies from the villages and people from the desert. Old sheykhs would come to converse with Sa'id. The local imam would bend his ear over a cup of tea. Priests and rabbis too would make their way out across the stony fields to him among the goats, perhaps bringing a loaf of bread or some dried fruit, and they would sit on their haunches beneath the mountain pines and pass the time of day. A judge, a military man, a shopkeeper, a merchant, street vendors and beggars, an Algerian sheykh and an English lady, there was no particular pattern to those who sought him out.

Sa'id did not seek their company, but his sense of good form meant he was unable to refuse the demands made upon his time. He always treated his visitors with patience, listening to their stories, asking them questions to clarify certain points, but never appearing to give advice, and certainly not telling them what to do, or not to do. He was simply a mirror in which they could see their state. Although Sa'id had acquired a reputation as a sage, it was not for wise words and eloquent phrases that people came, but for the kindness he showed them, the gentle counsel of his forgiving heart and the renewed strength they found in themselves after spending time in his company.

Sa'id was getting old. Since Maryam's death he had tended his herd each day much as before, but only because he had not received any indication from his interior to the contrary. He was simply following his days until the end. That year, as the weather grew colder and winter set in, and the first dusting of snow settled on the slopes of the distant mountains, Sa'id took ill. For a few weeks he thought it was nothing more than usual the aches and pains of old age, and he carried on, if a little slower than before, walking out with his goats each day. Then one early February morning he woke up feeling better than he had for a long time, the weight of his years had lifted, and the pains in his joints eased. He pulled himself up out of his bed, performed his ablutions in the water which Daud had heated up for him, prayed, and then went outside. Sa'id felt a lightness and a spring in his step, and he looked forward to the day which had dawned crisp and cloudless blue.

Daud was supervising milking, and Yahya was already away leading part of the herd further up onto the north slopes of Kassioun. As Sa'id approached his companion, Daud looked up. 'Something's different,' he thought, and then Sa'id collapsed into his friend's arms. Daud recognised the signs. He carried the old goatherd back inside and put him to bed. Sa'id's breathing was short and shallow, but it deepened as his body regained some warmth from the bedclothes. Daud fed him some hot milk with honey. He had a light fever so Daud piled some soft angora skins on his bed, stoked the fire in the hearth, and left him to sleep. By the evening Sa'id's fever had worsened and he wasn't able to eat anything. Daud sat with him through the night, dozing occasionally, and getting up from time to time to wipe his brow or make him comfortable, arranging cushions behind his head so he could breathe more easily. Sa'id was burning, and the bedclothes were damp.

The fever didn't break until late the next morning. Daud changed Sa'id's clothes and the bed, after which Sa'id slept deeply for a few hours. Daud stayed with him throughout most of the day. He rubbed lanolin and comfrey into his feet to ease the aches, and made him an infusion of yarrow to drink. The old man slept most of the time, just occasionally becoming conscious. He would thank Daud for caring for him, then his mind would drift, and he would start talking out loud as if to other people in the room. But there was no one else there. Sa'id was talking in a language which Daud had not heard before, and he seemed to be arguing mildly with whoever it was, as if unhappy about something. Then the arguing ceased, and he became calm, said something kindly to the mystery presences, and drifted off again. Sa'id slept well that night, but didn't take any food. The next day he was looking better, but was very weak. He asked Daud to wash him, which he did. He managed to eat a little bit of boiled egg and some broth, but barely enough for a small child. Throughout that day and the next Daud kept vigil at Sa'id's bedside. They didn't talk except to communicate a need, and Sa'id's needs were exhausted. By now Daud knew Sa'id was dying and that it was only a matter of time.

After sunset Daud went outside. The night was clear, the stars brilliant overhead. From the city far below him the sound of church bells floated up through the smoke of evening fires. He went back inside out of the cold and lit the oil lamps.

Suddenly Sa'id opened his eyes. He looked at Daud, but at the same time he was looking beyond him. For ages he seemed to be staring deep into the distance. When he finally spoke, his voice sounded bright. 'I can hear bells ringing,' he said. 'What day is it?'

'Wednesday eve.'

'Ah. The beginning of the Christians' fast. It's time. Everything is arranged. This farm, the goats, I know you will look after it well.'

Sa'id drifted off. A little later Yahya came in. He had been in the village with the yoghurt makers. More dairy produce was needed now as the Christians of Damascus would be foregoing meat for the forty days of Lent. He looked over at the old man lying asleep on the bed and asked,

'How is Uncle Sa'id?'

Daud had already explained to the young lad as best he could that the old goatherd's body was worn out and the spirit was preparing to leave. Yahya had grown close to Sa'id in the short time they had shared together. Whereas Daud could be quite strict and would not hesitate to reprimand when necessary, Sa'id had always been the indulgent grandfather to the boy. If he wanted to correct some fault in Yahya's behaviour he would always wait and bring to his attention a similar behaviour in one of the goats, pointing out how wonderful human beings were, who didn't have to imitate the impetuous ways of goats, but could choose to act with grace and dignity, even in the face of hardship and adversity. So while one pruned the sapling's wayward shoots, the other encouraged the height of his potential.

'He's sleeping now, but I don't think he's with us for long,' said Daud quietly.

Yahya frowned, not wanting to accept this kind of parting. Suddenly it all seemed so final. He felt a knot in his stomach as if his little world was all tied up there, tight and confused. No matter how hard he tried he couldn't arrange his thoughts to make any sense of what he felt.

'Come here.' Daud beckoned and the child came and curled up in the crook of his arm. He reached out and picked up the Damascus Drum. 'Now don't worry, Uncle Sa'id will still be here, you just won't be able to see him so easily. In fact he'll be more here than he is now, tied up in that bag of flesh and bones. Like Shams here…' and he tapped the Drum.

Yahya sat bolt upright. 'You can't make Uncle Sa'id into a Drum!' he shouted.

'Hello.' It was Sa'id. 'Did someone call my name?' His eyes were open and looking at Yahya, smiling.

'Don't let Daud make a drum out of you. Tell him he can't, Uncle Sa'id.' Yahya ran over to the bed, tears streaming down his face.

For a moment Sa'id looked puzzled, then the smile returned. It was a faint smile, the gentlest ripple, but behind it carried an ocean of kindness. With an effort he lifted his hand and stroked the boy's cheek before letting his arm fall again to his side. Then Sa'id looked Yahya in the eye and said, 'No, of course he won't. But, never, never think that I will leave you. Even when you don't see me, I am here.' He lifted his hand and pointed his finger at Yahya, level with his chest. And then, more softly, 'I am here.'

His hand fell. Sa'id's eyes were looking now beyond anything in this world.

Yahya gasped, 'No.' Then, although Sa'id's lips didn't move, the boy clearly heard the words 'I am here' echoing through him, loosening the knot in his stomach, shaking him like a fleece in the wind until all the tightness had gone.

Daud reached over and closed Sa'id's eyes. The two, man and boy, stayed with Sa'id through the remainder of the night. Daud felt no need to pray. He was content to sit quietly in the presence of his friend of seven years, as earthly ties dissolved, and a gateway opened upon the endless realm of the spirit. Yahya quickly fell asleep, and dreamed he was walking the grassy hills of Kassioun in spring sunshine, before him great herds of goats. And although he could never actually see him, he felt his Uncle Sa'id's hand in his, and heard his voice driving on the goats, and heard the click of his staff on the rocks, and knew he would always be there with him.

Daud fell asleep just before dawn. He too dreamt of Sa'id, only this time the old man's body was no longer wracked and worn, not the sloughed shell that lay in hollow silence on the bed, but a body luminous with the essence of life and vigour. Together they walked outside. Below lay Damascus, and above them the stars shone more brilliantly and seemed closer than ever could be possible.

Daud woke and went outside. For as far as he could see the earth was covered with a soft mantle of freshly fallen snow.

THIRTY-TWO

A forty day feast

 ORTY days after the spirit of Sa'id bin Adam had been promoted into the World of Remaining, Daud, as is the custom, organised a day of rememoration for his departed friend. In all the seven years he had served the venerable goatherd, he had not fully appreciated the true circumference of Sa'id bin Adam's circle of friends, a company in which Sa'id had been a central figure. In the days preceding the event it became obvious that something very unusual was afoot. People began to arrive, in ones and twos and dribs and drabs, lodging with friends or relatives in the area. Then came small groups, who set up camps in the neighbourhood, arranged field kitchens, built storage huts, even diverting streams to store water for drinking, ablutions, etc. Droves of sheep were brought up to the mountain and kept in hastily-built pens. Trains of donkeys were led in from the hinterland, their panniers piled high with firewood and charcoal. Domed clay ovens for baking bread and for roasting savoury dishes mushroomed overnight and were briskly fired.

More and more they came: whole tribal groups from out of the deserts of Arabia and further afield, in white robes and blue robes, from the sands and mountains of Africa, their heads swathed in cloth which veiled all but their dark eyes. They rode tall camels and were accompanied by women of confidence, with tattooed faces and shiny black tresses, adorned in colourful muslins sewn with gold coins, amber and turquoise. Dervishes turned up from nowhere in particular, upon their heads brown hats of felt, tall as tombstones, and coarse woollen gowns draped upon their backs. Green mantled and turbaned sheykhs were to be seen, fakirs in ragged patchwork cloaks with drums which they beat upon, and some carried swords with which they pierced their cheeks and stomachs and showed no pain. From the north came in black hats and sack cloths small bands of Christian monks, half-starved and wise to other worlds, and from Safed in the south sombre Rabbis led wild-looking youths with intense gazes, and beautiful unveiled women with cataracts of dark, tumbling curls, and silence and mischief in their eyes. Fire worshippers from the fish-rich shores of the Caspian fetched up, along with olive-skinned men and women from the mountains beyond Hind, shaven-headed in wine and yellow robes, fur-lined against the climate, telling beads uninterruptedly as they walked in their felt boots. And from the banks of Hind's great mother river came tall ascetics with matted hair, infinity in their eyes and nothing to hide their ash-covered skins but meagre strips of ochre cloth upon their loins, barefoot and oblivious to the weather. All these came, and more.

And from Damascus itself, on the day, arrived the sweet-sellers, the water carriers, the nut sellers, the tobacco men; along with the butchers, the bread makers, the mu'ezzins who called the faithful from the balconies of the minarets, the imams who led the prayers in the mosques below, the old ladies who cleaned the mosques when the men had gone, the round country girls who grew luscious green herbs and salads in the Meadow Lakes and sold their produce in the markets of the city, the plump women who looked after the hamams on women's days, and of course the children. It was as if the city had transported itself in miniature for the day, as if the Damascenes had said 'let's go up to Kassioun for a picnic, and anyone who happens along is welcome'.

Large fires were lit, spits set up, countless sheep were slaughtered (but, it has to be said, out of respect for the departed one, no goats were dispatched,), the butchers in rows quartered and chopped the meat, and women sat in circles moulding *koubeh* of cracked wheat and ground meat with such speed and finesse the eye was deceived into believing they were spinning tops in the palms of their hands. The smell of woodsmoke mixed with roasting meat and onions hung tastily in the air. Chefs vied with each other before their great brass cauldrons, turning rice with flat wooden paddles in the fat of the fat tailed sheep, twirling their extravagant moustaches and rubbing their round and trustworthy bellies as they cast into their pots mounds of pine nuts and currants, spreading gusts of cinnamon before adding gallons of well-prepared meat stock. The salad makers chopped in lines, the onion slicers wept as one, and the pudding makers liaised in harmony over vats of milk thickened with egg yolks and ground almonds and scented with rosewater. The event was progressing under a momentum which Daud, had he the powers of Solomon, would have been hard put to manage of his own accord. But, each time he rested his hand upon the Drum which hung inside the door of his house, he felt assured that all that should be done, would be done, and there was no need to worry because everything was being well taken care of. All Daud had to do was be present in his place, as the representative and heir of the noble and esteemed Sa'id bin Adam.

There were stirrings too during those days in the convent of Seydnaya. The forty day Lenten fast was about to reach its climax with the Easter Feast. Preparations were well underway and Takla was doubly excited, for not only had she a new dish to present, a fabulous buttery pilaf flavoured with safflower stamens, cardamoms and other spices cooked with chickens roasted whole, pine nuts, currants and tiny vegetables, but more importantly her little son would be coming home in a few days. Then, on the eve of Easter Day, Mother Superior called Takla to her room.

'Take a look outside and tell me what you see,' she said.

Takla went out onto the balcony, and far below by the convent steps she saw a train of donkeys, and some carts harnessed with bullocks.

'Don't be puzzled. We're taking our Easter Feast on the road this year. Tonight in fact, as soon as the Midnight Mass is over, so you better get a move on. All the novices are at your disposal to finish the preparations and to load whatever pots you need onto the wagons. You will have to wrap up warm and take something to sleep in. And don't worry about Yahya, he'll be joining us for the feast, I promise you. Off you go now.' And away scurried little Takla the cook, triply excited now at the prospect of unexpected adventure.

Much later, just after midnight, as the convent bells rang above Seydnaya, and joined the chimes which broke out over the hills north of Damascus, announcing the renewal of the Word into the world, a little convoy of donkeys and bullock carts carrying the nuns and their wonderful provisions, all bundled up under woollen blankets against the chills of April, wound its way through the shadows of the night-dark mountain road.

Takla, the farmer's daughter, the cook who would be a nun, the mother who would be a lover, was reunited with her son a little after sunrise on the outskirts of the encampment at Mount Kassioun. Yahya was so excited that he almost forgot the herd he was leading out to pasture. He called his dogs to keep the goats from straying and ran to meet her, jumping up onto the lead wagon where she sat, bleary-eyed with sleep and tears of joy. He embraced his mother, kissing her head and talking nineteen to the dozen, recounting in telegraphic starts and stops the brief headlines of his adventures so far, telling her all about Daud ('he told me all the names of all the goats and the animals and everything and is teaching me how to write') and Uncle Sa'id ('he's not dead, you know, he just doesn't have a body any more, and he's having a big party today'). Yahya was just about to start on a description of each of the Billy Goats, their lineage, and the history of their names and namesakes, when his mother put her finger on his lips and with a frown which slipped into a smile commanded his silence, ('Enough, enough. Aren't you going to greet Mother Superior?') And Yahya overcame his excitement enough to remember his manners and give proper greetings to the elderly nun, swaddled in white woollen cloth like an Egyptian mummy, who sat beside her. Takla then took a close look at her son, and her heart was satisfied. He had grown so much, and the words which poured out of him were fine words, rich with the seeds of knowledge of his new world, seeds planted in the fertile earth of his mother's earlier nurturing.

Yahya led the convent's little caravan through the encircling encampment to the home farm. The nuns unpacked and set up their kitchen in a clear area to the side of the house, and Yahya stabled their animals in a small lean-to barn nearby. Daud was at that moment away down the hill meeting new arrivals from Damascus. Mother Superior had told Takla something of Sa'id bin Adam during their night journey. The old nun had met him many times, but that is another story. Takla now went over to the tomb in order to pay her respects. She wanted to ask for his blessing, and to thank him for looking after Yahya. Takla knelt by the simple rock-covered mound, marked with two flat oval stones painted in green with the names of Sa'id bin Adam and his wife Maryam. She closed her eyes and opened her heart to the graces which flow freely at such gateways between worlds. The weariness of the journey lifted and the excitement of arrival evaporated, leaving her calm and relaxed.

This interior habit of prayer, the meadow of her contemplation, was wide and light. Having prayed for the souls of Sa'id and Maryam, and having requested their blessings and help, Takla was inspired to ask of the great unknown provider of being, that existence from which she was in no way separate, that some call God but is named by all the names, and yet remains beyond name; she prayed with all her heart to this original light, self-adumbrated now in the mirror of Takla's supplicating heart, that it cause the one whom she had loved those seven long years, the man by the mountain cave, to be returned to her, if such be her portion. Her prayer became a great cry from love itself, for love's true object. And the place of that calling – her soul, her heart, her breath – was magnified with that same love beyond the confines of its own imagined length and breadth to its imponderable and unfathomable source.

Her plea was accepted by the essential presence as a snow-fed stream rushing headlong over the hillside is welcomed into the deep magnanimity of the ocean through the intercession of a great river.

In her contemplation Takla became aware of herself kneeling by the tomb in the open air upon the hilltop of Mount Kassioun. She sensed the great gathering of tents all around, the smoking campfires, the little farm-house where her companion nuns were setting up tables and preparing food. She could feel the great city below, from where a presence of light spread towards her, filling her and leaving her in perfect ease. Then Takla heard footsteps approaching the grave from the Damascus side, stopping opposite her and kneeling down. For a while she continued to sit, unwill-ing yet to open her eyes. She wanted to be sure. The light, the ease she felt inside remained. Slowly she peeped out across the grave of Sa'id bin Adam. There was a man, his bowed head tied up in a rough turban of frayed blue wool. When he raised his head and looked into her eyes, she recognised Daud immediately for the man she loved, the man in the eye, the father of her child.

A rare thing that two should meet in such a way, like Rumi's lovers who could be both in Iraq and Khorasan, and also together in this same nook. Why should the great saint of Balkh and Konya write this if it were not possible? Daud, for his part, had knelt at the tomb, and was only aware of the person opposite, head bent and face hidden by her scarf, as a beautiful presence. He had addressed the owner of the tomb, and sought his blessing as had Takla, and had found himself immersed in the light presence of Sa'id bin Adam. Something, a breathly nudge perhaps from his old mentor, opened to him a strange and wonderful scent which evoked the memory of his beloved of the cave by the pool. He too looked. As their eyes met he recognised Takla for the object of his ardent desire, the jewel he had sought so long in his heart, at long last revealed.

And just as we did not intrude upon their earthly union, now with even greater tact we shall withdraw and allow a veil to fall upon this compact of hearts in the world of remaining. Together the lovers remained, joined in that same eternal nook a timeless while. Then the clouds of mortality descended lightly once again upon the two figures kneeling by the graves of Sa'id bin Adam and his wife Maryam. So much was under-stood. So much didn't need to be said.

Moses seeking fire found God upon the mountain in that burning form. If he had been seeking something else, then would not God have appeared to him in that? Daud and Takla found the true object of their seeking hidden in each other's forms. Eventually the veils of these forms will wear so thin, the gross matter fall as dust to reveal the gemstones of their true nature and what was a hint become a certainty and the longing return to its source, and as love needs a form, their hearts become capable of every form which shadows forth the beauty inexpressible.

'Will you?' The proposal, which was definitely a cry of betrothal, came not from either of our two lovers, but in a child's voice from across the field. Yahya too had been dreaming of this meeting and wasn't going to miss this opportunity to acquire a full set of parents.

'Will you? will you? will you?' Yahya was insisting now, not asking. Daud and Takla, caught by surprise, looked at Yahya, then looked back into each other's eyes, and answered together without hesitation. 'Yes.'

Takla then went to Mother Superior and formally requested permission to marry Daud the Arwadi. And Mother Superior, overjoyed as any mother would be, gave her unconditional approval. And so the Rememoration Feast of Sa'id bin Adam became also a feast of betrothal, and Takla's pilaf, expertly prepared under her supervision by her little band of companion novices, was duly named the Betrothal Pilaf.

When the time of the feast of the Rememoration came, everyone sat together in groups of twelve or thereabouts, the foreigners mixing with the local inhabitants, the Christians mixing with the Zoroastrians, the Jews with the Moslems, the tribes of the east with the tribes of the west. And where the language of the tongue was wanting, the language of the heart sufficed, enabling all to communicate perfectly.

As for the content of the feast, the variety and sumptuousness of the pilafs hailing from the sarays of Istanbul to the campfires of Khorasan, the subtle elegance of the desserts and ices, the vast array and perfect readiness of the joints of meats which surrendered unresisting to the carvers' knives and whose juices then ran savorous and freely, the well-cooked vegetables, the hot ones in butter, the cool ones in olive oil, which entered the mouth as firm but melted in an explosion of sweet herbs, the breads crisp and soft, sprinkled with nigella and sesame, fragrant and warm from the charcoal ovens, it would be too much to relate everything here. Suffice it to say that the recipe for Takla's pilaf was eagerly sought by itinerant chefs from as far away as pink Cathay; and the Cairene, knowing his reputation was on the line, had his Bolu chef do something with aubergines that amazed and confounded them all. Even his fiercest rival, the cook of an Algerian Bey, a man trained in the French cuisine who was not known for his appreciation of oriental fare, and who had produced a vainglorious excess of cream, fruit and meringues in the form of the Kasbah of Algiers, was heard to admit, 'I approve' on tasting the Bolu chef's simple but subtle creation. There was something for everyone, no one went hungry, and all were satisfied. The food was served by the young of Damascus, and from all their hands poured the blessings of Hatim al Tai the Generous.

As fingers and lips, moustaches and chins were licked and wiped with the last crusts of bread, and faces refreshed in bowls of water scented with rose and bergamot, Daud, as host and impartial friend of the departed, stood and gave a brief eulogy.

'How is it possible to speak with true justice of such a man?' he began. 'Sa'id bin Adam possessed that rarest of qualities which we poor humans can aspire to, the humility which comes from accepting completely one's true condition of poverty and neediness, so that he always remained ready to receive whatever life gave him at each moment. This was his real dignity and this is why we are gathered together here to praise his name and remember him. He was a mirror to us all, but a mirror which showed, not just our failings, but our true potential. He looked at us beyond our limitations, and his loving compassion embraced our pain and turned our hearts to see what he saw. And in this he opened for us ways we could never have imagined. He brought us news of the real joy beyond our tears, and that is what he leaves us with now.

'My friends, most of whom I have never met, we are all blessed to be included among those whose hearts were eased in some way by contact with our dear Sa'id bin Adam, and this blessing we have in common remains with us now. His translation to the world beyond does not mean an end to this blessing. He has entered an altogether bigger life, and so that joy comes now magnified, as we see in the obvious delight this day has brought. So, let us all give thanks for the life and soul of Sa'id bin Adam, that he may be blessed in return, forever.'

Daud's words were quickly transcribed, translated and broadcast to the farthest circumference of the gathering whence a chorus of amens, amins and other murmured mantras of agreement and accord arose like the hum of well-honeyed bees. The sun of Damascus sank into the sea somewhere beyond the heights of the Jebel Lubnan, and rose madder clouds streaked the skies from the shores of Yemen to the Straits of Hormuz in one glorious pink moment which faded reluctantly as the veil of night fell over the resting land.

The Rememoration Feast extended throughout the whole of the following week, and if we were to recount the stories that were told, the reminiscences related, forgotten anecdotes remembered, the chance encounters and unexpected meetings between long lost friends and relations, the new bonds of friendship, old vows renewed, the fallings in love and the further betrothals, the anticipated births and the contented deaths, the exchanges of gifts between strangers, the further feastings and the oaths of future hospitality, the dancings and the *zikrs*, the eucharists and hallelujahs, the mystical visions and the vows of fidelity, fond kisses of farewell and then their severance, ah! this earth would stop spinning before this tale reached its end.

THIRTY-THREE

A drum roll

OVE has the first word and the last. It is the one that arrives in all our greetings and embraces in our fond farewells. It hides in our longings and resides in every object of desire, sacred or profane. It is the master which enslaves each one of us. There is no escape but by love itself, when the puppets are cast off and love shows its hand in all. So let us resign ourselves freely to its way.

The conditions by which Takla was permitted to leave Seydnaya and marry Daud were simple, and had been agreed with Mother Superior at the Rememoration Feast for Sa'id. In the period between the betrothal and the wedding, Takla was to ensure that the roll of cook in the convent was filled by a suitable candidate possessed of the manner and taste which such a position demands. Within the following week there appeared at the convent gate a young novice who subsequently would maintain, right up until her very last breath at a great age, that she was merely the candidate for the position, not the cook herself. She was strong-willed, a young girl with aptitude and attitude, who had fled from a rather strict convent in Jerusalem. She came by way of Beirut, where, after a brief period of employ in one of the city's more fashionable houses of pleasure, strictly as a kitchen assistant, she had been rescued by a certain Circassian lady of our acquaintance. In Gülbahar's villa the girl had furthered her vocation as cook before being invited to Seydnaya on Daud's recommendation.

Takla took the candidate cook under her wing and processed her through a series of tasks, beginning with the tub of salt in the corner of the kitchen, a few grains on the tongue each day to awaken the taste buds, a kind of obeisance to the life-giving value in the ingredients about to be prepared. Then they went about the daily regimen of the kitchen: baking before breakfast, vegetable preparation, butchery, stocks, the midday meal of stew or pilaf, yoghurt and cheese making, preserves, soup for supper, etc. She worked hard and learnt quickly, writing up each day's lesson into a notebook. In every respect the new girl inherited the manner of the kitchen to both Takla and Mother Superior's satisfaction.

One other condition of Takla's release, more a request, but easily fulfilled, came from Takla's side: that, all things being equal, she might return from time to time to perform the Lenten retreat within the convent. Daud and Mother Superior were both in agreement to her request. From Daud's side, this unwritten prenuptial allowed that from time to time he might also, if so inspired, take to the hills for a period of internal reflection. In practice this often meant hanging about the coffee shops in Damascus, dropping a story here, a strange tale there, for as long as the mood was upon him. Sometimes he did indeed make journeys, and therein lies another tale. Daud then fulfilled the normal duties of the bridegroom to the bride's parents by providing a dowry sufficient to build new guest rooms for the convent.

The wedding of Takla and Daud took place on the feast of the Nativity of the Virgin, the eighth day of September, which that year coincided with Moulid al Nabi, the birthday of the Prophet Muhammed. So a nuptial blessing given by Mother Superior within the convent was followed by a small ceremony under the open sky performed by a wizened old sheykh, a friend of the Cairene, who happened to be passing from Balkh on pilgrimage to Mecca. Takla hardly slept the night before the wedding and rose early to visit the holy icon of the Virgin. It was quite a different experience from that time little more than a year ago when tears had drenched her heart. Now the dark room seemed to brighten in response to her uncontained joy. She then dressed in white, putting on the simple jewellery she had inherited from her mother, silver anklets and bracelets which tinkled as she walked. From her ears hung two pearls, a betrothal present from the Cairene. Her hair was uncovered, loose and braided with flowers. Then, perfumed with scent of lily of the valley, she veiled her face and came out to meet her beloved.

Daud had been got up by Touma in fine white Egyptian linen under-garments and a long-sleeved coat striped in black, red, yellow, blue and green silk with gold piping, bound around his waist with a red sash. Takla had given him a new blue woollen scarf with which to tie up his tumbled locks, as the old one that had served as his talisman during their seven years of separation was now little more than a rag. He fasted a full twenty four hours and then perfumed his beard with Medina musk and Maghrebi ambergris before entering Seydnaya to meet his bride.

The bridal couple and their friends collected in the main chapel where Mother Superior addressed the assembly. Her words were brief but as ever to the point:

'We are here to celebrate love. Remember, all love originates in the Divine Love. It is the same love that moves the whole cosmos. You cannot find love, love finds you. You cannot have love, love has you. You seek it because it seeks you. If you find love's stream, follow it back to its source, you will find the source of the whole cosmos, and become the place where love appears. Add nothing, take nothing away. Do not make it 'I love this or I love that.' If love finds an object, know that object to be no other than the reality of love itself......Add nothing to love – no feeling of yours, no emotion, no thought or opinion or desire from what you think you are can ever reach its height. Leave all that aside and let love be love for its own sake. If it has an object let it be Beauty, and let that Beauty expand so that all may be sunk to the utmost depth in the ocean of love's infinity and oneness.'

The party trooped out of the convent. Under the morning sun, in the middle of the meadow the old sheykh performed a brief ceremony of marriage. Then the Cairene stepped forward, leaning upon his stick and spoke to the gathering: 'My dear friends.' he turned and smiled at Takla and Daud, who were standing next to him, hand in hand, 'It is said by those who know, (and here he twirled his moustache and gave a knowing look, somewhere between an indulgent frown and 'I told you so') that when two people hold hands in real love, the whole of God's Mercy passes through those hands. Relationship means the first rung of Love in a ladder which soars to heights infinite. This story you must have heard, but for the benefit of those who haven't:

THE CAIRENE'S STORY

"A man knocked on the door of a Sheykh, famous for his wisdom, and asked to become his student. The Sheykh asked the man why he had come to learn from him.

'Because,' said the man, 'I have heard of you and many come to learn from you, and I see the results and I would also like to learn and profit.'

'But,' said the Sheykh, 'have you ever loved?'

'No,' said the man, 'Never.'

'Not anything in this world? Money, a woman, or something?'

'No,' said the man.

The Sheykh said, 'I am sorry but I can not teach you, go.'

The poor man bent his head and slowly headed towards the door. The Sheykh watched him go sadly; and he thought he would give him just another try: 'Is there nothing in this whole world towards whom you feel a special affection, a relationship of sorts?'

The man stopped at the door; he was shy and did not know how to start what he was going to say:

'There is,' he said, 'my donkey, with whom I work all the time, and we understand each other and I am fond of him.'

'Thank God,' cried the Sheykh, 'come back, and we shall start just there!'

Relationship is the first rung of the ladder of Love; work at your ladder well."

It was a real country wedding, celebrated more as a grand picnic than a formal feast. The fields around Seydnaya were filled with open-sided tents spread with brightly coloured rugs and cushions. This time, with both Shams' and Uncle Sa'id's tacit approval, the merrymakers did feast on the new season's kid goats, boned and stuffed with apricots, butter and spinach, spiced with scented mace, then sewn up and baked slowly in olive-wood fires in the long ovens of the convent, and served on huge platters with mounds of fluffy rice scented with rose-water and sprinkled with ground pistachios.

Touma gladly performed the duties of best man for Daud. The Cairene came in place of Takla's late father to give the young bride away. The

Cairene had, in the maturity of his years long since transmuted any personal feelings for the young lady chef into a more universal longing for love. As well as a cargo of the best of the best Egyptian comestibles, the Cairene also brought piles of sheets of finest Egyptian cotton for the bridal bed, and box upon box of linen kitchen cloths in such a quantity as would dry the dishes of the descendants of Daud and Takla until the seventh generation at least. His Bolu chef supervised the wedding feast, bringing with him a cartload of watermelons whose flesh was bright as coral and sweeter than the sugar of the Indies.

The deepest cellars of Seydnaya were plundered of their mellowest wines, their noblest araks and most ancient brandies. Casks encrusted in decades of dust and cobwebs were carried out well in advance of the wedding day and left to settle before being decanted for the table into flasks of the finest Syrian glass. Clear spring water from neighbouring Maaloula filled dozens of bronze ewers. The youngest nuns and novices pleaded so much to be Takla's bridesmaids, until Mother Superior told them off roundly, afterwards relenting and letting them all take turns in holding the bridal train.

As is the custom, the wedding feast continued through seven days and seven nights. As each dusk fell, the hillsides were illuminated with hundreds of tiny oil lamps so that even the earth joined in reflecting the starry heaven's delight. The guests danced in wide circles, and Refik and his musician friends played until dawn's sweet breath blew in from the direction of Yemen. By day the guests slept in the shady tents, resuming their feasting with the coming of evening. Then after a week the newly-wed couple and the child with his new-found parents departed with the revellers down the Damascus road. They detached from the main party before the descent into the city, and made their way to their new home on Mount Kassioun.

For the sake of those who should have known better but didn't, Yahya was formally adopted by the couple, so that among the hill folk of Mount Kassioun Daud henceforth became known as Abu Yahya, and Takla as 'Umm Yahya. As an adoption present Yahya was given a young billy goat with a deep reddy-brown coat, which he named Sa'id, the happy and contented one, 'accepted and accepting'. In spite of this name, the young billy seemed to have inherited something of the quality of his great-grand-father Shams, for until Sa'id the goat was hung with a heavy brass bell and began to realise his place within the herd, Yahya was forever having to collect him from some neighbour or other whose she-goats he had been pestering.

And for the sake of those who must know more than they need, and haven't the patience to wait and see what may be their own portion in this world and the next, and for the sake of leaving as few loose ends as possible so that the carpet of this tale may not unravel before its appointed time, and so that its pattern be seen to be a whole, limited and short lived though it may be, for all these reasons we shall conjecture just a little with regard to certain of the characters we have met with in the course of our journeyings, whom it may appear have been left by the wayside.

Daud and Takla without a doubt live happily ever after, even if from time to time a passing local squall or avalanche of world events unsettles momentarily the steady climate of their lives. Takla keeps in close contact with her adopted Mother Superior, and Daud stays in touch with the world through a certain Damascus coffee house in a street behind the Great Umayyad Mosque. Yahya may have his own story to tell, God willing, one day.

As for Gülbahar, well, you can't keep a good girl down. She took up with a wealthy Ottoman widower, a gentleman of Constantinople who had lost his first wife in a Bosphorus storm. This First Wife, a harridan of the harshest brand, was a high-born lady who never had a kind word for her devoted husband, a dutiful soul who toiled ceaselessly to please his spend-thrift spouse on his modest salary as the Sultan's representative in one of the more insignificant European capitals. The First Wife could only remark on the fact that the diamonds of the other wives were larger, that their retinues more numerous; that the chests of their husbands displayed more gold medals and silver stars than his modest row of campaign stripes, and their bellies embraced by flashier cordons and broader cummerbunds than his slim purple sash. So, when against all advice First Wife took ship across the Sea of Marmara in the face of a predicted Lodos wind, the Ottoman gentleman was not entirely surprised, nor was he unduly upset, to hear that the ferryboat bound for Yalova had foundered on the shore of Heybeli Island. Although everyone, captain, crew and passengers had managed to disembark without serious injury, this high-born lady who was a difficult First Wife chose to return aboard to collect her bags, at the moment when an even larger wave than the one which had grounded the vessel uplifted the wreckage from its rocky perch and returned its unwitting passenger to deeper water for a burial at sea. As a result of this change of fortune, the Ottoman gentleman now independently wealthy had retired to Beirut, where his interests in viniculture and oenology, nurtured during long years of ambassadorial dinners, lead him to the cellar door of Gülbahar, the full-bodied and luscious reputation of whose wines now threatened to overshadow that of the chatelaine herself. Well, one glass led to another, and it was not long before a wedding date was set. One early springtime, just after Takla had returned from her lenten retreat at Seydnaya, Daud made the short trip alone over the mountains to Beirut on the pretext of taking stock for sale at the port. This he did, but there was another, more serious duty he had come to perform, that of giving away Gülbahar. It had been all arranged. There were enough of Daud's clothes from the old days still in storage in Gülbahar's villa, so he was able to appear well turned out in threads of finest, if a little old fashioned, quality. As a wedding gift he brought some very old Persian root-stock, said to be directly descended from original Shiraz vines, and a pair of young kid goats. As the hills above Beirut rocked to the strains of the oud, kanun and dumbalek, Daud slipped away from the merriment and made his way back over the mountains.

Then there was the matter of Daud's family back in Arwad. His death had been officially recognised, due to the intervention of a certain well-placed Imperial agent. To this day there are stories told in the narrow island streets of the strange disappearance of Daud the Merchant, cautionary tales mostly, told to children in vain attempt to keep them from straying beyond the shores, but with little or no effect. The children of Arwad still ply the seas of the world, not just in their little Syrian-flagged general cargo ships, but crewing the great fleets of the Greeks in search of wealth and adventure. Only Kush and the Captain knew the true story, and they never told anyone; not even though Kush eventually became Hadida's closest business advisor and general factotum supervising all the overseas offices and their trading activities. Hadida married him off to one of her and Daud's daughters. Once the grandchildren began to arrive, she lost the taste for business and began to enjoy the fruits of her long years of endeavour. She went on luxury cruises to the capitals of Europe where she spent small fortunes on fabrics and dresses. But by then she had become a very rich woman, and to be lavish from time to time was a caprice she could well afford. In time Kush relocated the business to Damascus, as much to keep the mother-in-law at a safe distance as to renew his contact with Daud. Later, long after both Daud and Hadida had passed on, he transferred operations to Smyrna. By the time the Turkish War of Independence came, which destroyed that city and scattered its inhabitants far and wide, Kush, by then a very old man, had already moved most of the assets to Argentina. From here a branch of the line of Daud through Kush spread throughout South America where it continues to multiply to this day.

As for Touma, he remained in Damascus for many years, serving his Sultan in various ways which we have no need to enlarge upon here, other than to say he was doing what spies do best. Through wise and judicious dispensation he helped maintain a favourable arrangement in his master's realm, and he eventually retired to his yali, a splendid villa on the Asian shore of the Bosphorus. His loyalty remained unquestioned throughout, and perhaps it was fortunate that a chill March wind blowing off that blue ocean stream took Touma with a bout of influenza before the dark clouds of rebellion which were gathering in the name of democracy over the House of Osman removed his Sultan, and ultimately his empire, forever.

'And the Drum? What happened to the Damascus Drum?' you ask.

One night, years later, it just upped and rolled away, down the slopes of Kassioun, through the market at Salihiye where it paused for breath before the tomb of the Great Sheikh, before continuing down the narrow lanes and byways. It rolled and rolled, through the gates of the old city, past the tombs of Baibars and Saladin, the Great Mosque of the Umayyads with its shrine to John the Baptist, and out again through the Souk Hamidiyeh, eventually coming to the door of a shop selling second hand objects: old furniture, broken musical instruments, pieces of brass and ironwork, old pots, the sort of things that people leave out with their rubbish because they no longer have any use for them, and which are then collected by others who see their potential, repair them and sell them on for a fee. And here the Drum stopped. The shopkeeper saw it when he arrived to open up in the morning and thought it worth keeping. He hung it up on a wooden peg high on the back wall of the shop where it remained awhile collecting dust.

One day a young man came by the junk shop. He was a soldier, a country boy newly recruited in the army of the Sultan. He was on his way to defend the Ottoman lands in the Big War, and he wanted something to keep his mind off things when he was far from home. He greeted the shop-keeper who casually raised his head, barely acknowledging the young man's presence, and indicated with a swivelling movement of his eyes that the soldier should go in and look around. The moment he walked inside the darkened hall crammed with its dusty objects, the Drum detached itself from its wooden peg, bounced onto the top of a broken piano, rolled along the ivories for an octave or so with a jolly tinkle and presented itself with a deep walloping boom into the arms of the young soldier.

There was life in the old goat yet.

Daud sat on a rocky ledge on the slope below the tomb of Sa'id and Maryam. In the distance the dark greens, reds and browns of Damascus sifted through the early morning smoke of the breakfast fires. From the east the sun was breaking through; it was spring again, the air was crisp. The day would be fine. He hadn't a care in the world; in fact if at this moment the earth and the heavens and all in it vanished, it would not have mattered to him one jot. That it didn't was a bonus. It didn't add anything, but it was a bonus. With this thought, he rose and went back to the farm house, poured some tea and woke Takla.

EPILOGUE

The story teller's eye is the net
   catching meanings,
      setting them in order.
      Like the oud player's fingers
         upon the fretless board,
            his words draw sweet melodies
               from the unsung harmonies of existence.

            This life's mirage, its magic thread
            we blindly follow, and are lead
            along its winding story line
            back to once upon a time.

THE END